"Are you hungry?"

Theda hesitated, glancing at the food, longing in her eyes. Setting a firm hand to her back, the gentleman began to propel her gently toward the table. "You need not fear me, ma'am. As you have so wisely observed, I have consumed far too much brandy to be capable of amatory advances."

"Yes, that is what I feared. Not that you might attempt anything, perhaps, but—but in my situation, one is vulnerable to…to certain propositions."

Hidden Flame

ELIZABETH BAILEY

TORONTO • NEW YORK • LONDON
AMSTERDAM • PARIS • SYDNEY • HAMBURG
STOCKHOLM • ATHENS • TOKYO • MILAN • MADRID
PRAGUE • WARSAW • BUDAPEST • AUCKLAND

ISBN 0-373-30388-2

HIDDEN FLAME

First North American Publication 2001

This edition published by arrangement with Harlequin Books S.A.

Visit us at www.eHarlequin.com

Printed in U.S.A.

ELIZABETH BAILEY

grew up in Malawi, returning to England to plunge into the theater. After many happy years "tatting around the reps," she finally turned from "dabbling" to serious writing. She finds it more satisfying, for she is in control of everything: scripts, design, direction and the portrayal of every character! Elizabeth lives in London and teaches drama to high school students.

Chapter One

Thunder crackled over the dark, empty street. One of the horses whiffled a protest and shuffled a hoof, dragging slightly at the tether that held it and its fellow securely fastened to the single lamp-post, which imperfectly lit the inn yard, its small flame dancing as the glass about it shook in the uncertain weather. Behind the horses, the curricle, its hood up against the piercing March wind and the oncoming rain, shifted on the cobbles, and settled again.

The gentleman did not even turn his head. Outlined against the dim glow from outside, his tall silhouette filled the open doorway. A towering, greatcoated apparition, its face shadowed by a low-brimmed beaver. A dark figure, seemingly at one with the angry elements at his back.

Involuntarily the landlord of the Feathers shivered, peering uncertainly up at this late wayfarer, whose peremptory summons on the front door had recalled him to undo the bolts he had only just shot to.

The gentleman's pose seemed negligent enough. One gloved hand rested casually against the doorjamb, drawing the folds of his greatcoat wide. Which was why, Mr Pigdon told himself firmly, he looked so all-fired *big*. The landlord drew a breath.

"And what might you be wanting this time o' night?" he demanded belligerently.

"What the devil do you think I want, fellow?" came the irritable reply. "Do you take me for a highwayman?"

Mr Pigdon relaxed a little. Not only was the gentleman's intonation unmistakably genteel, but he was slurring his words very slightly. Furthermore, decided the experienced landlord, if that wasn't the fumes of brandy on his breath he didn't know his own business. A question, it was, whether he was propping up the door, or the door was propping him!

A streak of lightning forked across the sky behind, and the gentleman grew impatient. "Do you mean to keep me standing here all night, man?"

Mr Pigdon started, his attention drawn back from the threatening sky. He stood aside to let the gentleman pass. "Come you in, sir, come you in."

"I am obliged to you," the gentleman returned, a satirical inflexion in the light voice. "I will be still more so if you will have someone look to my horses."

"Aye, sir, that I will," the landlord agreed, thankfully shutting the front door as another burst of thunder erupted overhead.

"Immediately!"

"Aye, sir." Mr Pigdon picked up the candle which had been ready to light him to bed from a shelf in an alcove by the door, and bustled past the visitor down the hall. He threw open another door. "If you'd care to wait in the coffee-room, sir, I'll fetch the ostler."

The gentleman nodded briefly, and, as the landlord left, stepped into the dimness of a dark room lit only by a single candle on the mantel above the hearth, and the glowing embers of a dying fire below. He halted before it, looking about at the relentless blackness with an expression of distaste, pursing the fine lips that were visible below the hat. A sudden glare from outside lit up the windows briefly. There was a muted refrain of the crackle of doom, and he heard the rain start.

A miserable night! Appropriate. A night on which witches roamed, and the gods were angry. A night to bring any man to contemplate the dogged scourge of Lady Fortune's whip with a jaundiced eye. Lady Fortune? Lady *Ill*-fortune more like! Had she got him marked out for her vicious games for life?

The landlord came back into the room just then, interrupting his gloomy thoughts.

"Now, sir. The lad'll bed down your cattle. I take it you'll be needing the same yourself?"

"Certainly. Though I trust you may have something slightly better than a stall," suggested the gentleman wryly.

Mr Pigdon bristled. "True it is that we ain't in the habit of entertaining the likes of you, sir, most of the gentry as stops here in Newark preferring to bait down Saracen's Head with that there Mr Thompson, but—"

"My good fool, I am perfectly aware of that. But the plain fact is that I have had a devilish run of ill luck, and I do not care for Thompson's tariff. In a word, my pockets are damnably to let. Now, have you a bed, or have you not?"

Such a ready admission of his circumstances startled the landlord. Furthermore, if the gentleman had no money—

"Don't put yourself about!" recommended the visitor, stripping off his gloves. He added with uncanny perspicacity, "I have enough to cover my shot *here.*"

The slight, disparaging inflexion on the last word annoyed Mr Pigdon, but he gruffly assured the gentleman that he should have the best spare bedroom and all the comforts his poor house might afford.

"I trust that includes brandy? Bring me a bottle, if you please. And—" with another unfavourable glance around the room "—perhaps some more light?"

"Aye, sir. At once," said the landlord, hastily bending to put a couple of logs on the fire and poke it back to life.

When he rose, he discovered that the gentleman had removed his hat. The light from the candle on the mantel fell on a countenance so classically pleasing, topped by a quantity of gold, curling locks that brushed the high-caped collar of his greatcoat, that the landlord was startled. The changed look at once dissipated the sinister aspect that the gentleman had generated thus far.

He seemed to recognise the effect he was creating, for he suddenly smiled. It was a smile of great charm, causing even the toughness of Mr Pigdon to crack.

The landlord found himself returning the smile

with a grin of his own. "You wouldn't care for a bite to eat afore you takes to your bed?"

"Now that," the gentleman said in a more friendly tone, "is an excellent suggestion. Nothing troublesome, mind."

"It's no trouble, sir," the landlord told him cheerfully, and went out.

Left to himself, the gentleman let his smile fade.

"Let's hope the fool hurries with those candles," he muttered. The atmosphere in this dark room was oddly disquieting, giving him the distinct impression that he was not alone. Or was it the heavy rain slapping against the windows, the wind's eerie message as it whistled down the chimney and flickered at the flames that had begun to lick about the new-laid logs?

Shrugging off the thoughts with his greatcoat, he threw the latter over one of the two big tables and turned back to the fire.

"Cleaned out again, confound it!" he said aloud, kicking moodily at one of the logs, and sending a shower of sparks up the chimney. He had enough for his day-to-day needs, of course, but he would be hard-pressed to see himself through another month if he was to live in the style befitting a gentleman. Unless he were to pay his godmother a second visit in as many weeks? Or would that make her suspicious? He should have remained with her for the hunting, devil take it, instead of going to his friend Woolacombe! The man had always a pack of gamesters about him. Useless to have imagined he might resist temptation! Now what the devil was he to do?

The opening door recalled him to the present situation. A stout woman entered, bearing a candelabrum and a tray, and on her plump face, under the nightcap that concealed the rags curling her hair, was an expression of the gravest displeasure. The gentleman took due note of it in a single glance, decided that nothing was to be gained by ill temper, and, reassembling his smile, he turned it upon her full-force.

''Good evening. I am afraid I am giving you a great deal of trouble.''

Mrs Pigdon was in no very amiable humour. The late arrival had necessitated her getting out of bed and throwing on a voluminous dressing-robe in order to prepare suitable accommodation—on a night such as this, moreover, when all a body wanted was to curl up under the quilt and hide from the horrors outside. She was not impressed when her spouse informed her there was a member of the gentry below, for the only visitors of that sort to frequent her humble hostelry were those who had fallen on evil times. Like that hoity-toity voiced little madam earlier in the evening. She'd seen through *her* in a twinkling, she had! But she'd at least enough to pay her board. *This* party had the nerve to announce his shameful embarrassments to all the world!

But Mrs Pigdon was a sharp-eyed dame for all that. No sooner did she set eyes on the gentleman than she recognised his pecuniary position to be merely temporary. There was nothing shabby or worn about the close-fitting blue coat or the buckskin breeches; and the starched neckcloth—no longer as neat as it might have been—and the ruffles to his shirt-sleeves were of the finest linen.

Her first concern laid to rest, Mrs Pigdon examined the gentleman's comely countenance, and, like her husband, visibly thawed at the onslaught of the smile.

''No trouble, sir, I assure you,'' she answered, unconsciously echoing her spouse. She set the candelabrum and the tray down on one of the tables, removing his greatcoat and placing it carefully over the back of a chair so that she might lay out a cloth and utensils. ''We'll have a supper of sorts ready in a twinkling, sir.''

''You are very good,'' the gentleman said.

She bustled to the door and her voice took on a repressive note. She had not been pleased to hear that the gentleman was a little the worse for drink!

''Pigdon's bringing the other, sir.''

He merely nodded. Perfectly aware of the veiled disapproval, his kindlier feelings abated, to be replaced by a resurgence of ill humour. Devil take it! Was it for this common servitor to censure his habits? When the brandy arrived, he filled a glass and tossed it off, in a gesture of childish defiance. But when the landlord had left the room he reached into a pocket of his greatcoat and brought out a flat silver flask. This he carefully filled from the bottle and then replaced in the greatcoat.

Mrs Pigdon, returning with his meal, noted the disgracefully lowered level of the liquor in the brandy bottle and gave him a look that spoke volumes. It was productive of a sudden gleam in the gentleman's eyes, of unholy amusement.

''Don't trouble yourself,'' he said, gently sardonic. ''I have a hard head.''

The landlady was not amused. Her face pinched in disapproval, she laid out a dish of sliced cold beef, a platter of bread and butter, the remains of a pigeon pie and some cheeses. Also a jug of water and another of sobering porter, thoughtfully provided by the landlord. A parting sniff as she left the room gave the gentleman to understand that he had disappointed her.

Mr Beckenham felt a perverse satisfaction. To hell with the woman! Who was she to censure him? With a liberal hand, he poured himself another glass. But as he raised it to his lips the windows flashed bright again, and the heavens gave forth another stream of rumbling abuse.

"God, what an accursed night!" mumbled Mr Beckenham, and, sipping his liquor, he looked over the makeshift meal with revulsion. "To what am I reduced? Hell and damnation!"

As if in response to his cursing, the wild night struck back at him, flaring a double blow of brilliant whiteness that seemed to tear at him through the windows.

His head turned, eyes narrowing against the glare. As the room lit, an image crossed his vision—of a thin black figure seated in a corner, crouching witch-like in the gloom.

His heart lurched sickeningly. The devil! He was seeing things. Too much brandy!

But as the dark closed in again and his eyes began to adjust, the glimmering outline of a pale face encroached upon his senses.

The thunder rolled away as Mr Beckenham stared, leaving the place eerily silent, and his heart still. Was it a ghost? Or merely his imagination playing tricks? Cursing briefly, he closed his eyes, looking away.

As he opened them again, they flicked, almost out of his own control, to check. *It was still there.*

Mr Beckenham froze. His fingers about the stem of his glass tightened. There was a sharp crack, and the broken glass fell from his hand, tinkling on to the table and spilling its golden liquid on to the pristine white cloth.

"Hell and the devil!" swore the gentleman, starting forward.

There was a frightened gasp and the ghost rose, too, staring at him out of the two hollows that were its eyes.

"I—I beg your pardon," faltered the ghost. "I think I startled you."

"Dear God in heaven!" ejaculated Mr Beckenham on a tide of relief. "You're *real.*"

A flicker at the window and a faint cackling echo of thunder laughed at him. The gods were enjoying their own cruel joke! Mr Beckenham decided savagely. Well, he would have his revenge!

He seized the candelabrum, and, lifting it high, moved towards the pale face. It shrank back against the wall, edging towards the door. As he neared, he could see that it belonged to a slight female form encased in dark garments, its hair entirely concealed by a white cap. Small wonder she looked like a ghost! No. A witch! A black witch, casting spells from her hiding-place in the corner.

Abruptly the woman speeded up, making a dash

for the door. He strode forward to intercept her, grabbing one wrist as he reached her.

''Come here, witch! You don't escape me so easily.''

''Let me go!'' came in a harsh whisper from the pale face.

''By no means.''

Tugging her away from the door, Mr Beckenham pulled her close, holding the candelabrum high. In its light was revealed a thin face, with skin so pale that it was almost translucent, whose high cheekbones emphasised the hollows below and under her brows. From within these, a pair of deep grey eyes looked up at him. There was fear in them, but more than fear—defiance, a little, and challenge.

''Why were you hiding there?'' he demanded compellingly. ''Spying on me!''

She shrank a little, the eyes dilating. Her voice was pitched low, the fear overlaid with edgy defiance.

''I didn't mean to *spy*. I couldn't help it. I came down for the fire, for it was cold in my room. Then I heard the door, and you came in, and—and I did not dare to reveal myself because—''

''Because I am a man, and because I am drunk?'' he guessed.

''Yes,'' she agreed, and a little of the fear seemed to leave her.

''My good girl, I am not in the least drunk,'' he told her, his brows lifting haughtily. He saw her glance across at the table and followed her gaze to the brandy bottle. ''Oh, well. Perhaps a trifle foxed, but that is all.''

Then he recognised that her eyes had strayed to the food, glistening a little. The pink tip of a tongue touched her pale lips.

Mr Beckenham had hold of her wrist still, and all at once he felt how slim it was. His hand was closed loosely over it. Like a bracelet! he thought. God, but the girl was a stick! Sudden pity softened him towards her, and he forgot his urge for revenge.

''Are you hungry?'' he asked abruptly.

Her eyes flew back to his and she swallowed painfully. ''Oh, no, I—I was just—I did not mean...''

Mr Beckenham let go her wrist and stepped back with a little bow, gesturing to the table. ''Pray share my supper, ma'am.''

She shook her head. ''Oh, no, I could not. I should leave you now.''

''Should'', not ''shall'', he noted. She *was* hungry. He smiled, charmingly, and saw the grey eyes widen. But she did not smile in return.

''It would be a kindness on your part, ma'am,'' he said persuasively. ''These good people have been to an enormous amount of trouble on my behalf, and I am sure I shall be quite unable to do justice to their generous provision.'' Forgetting his earlier disgust at the food that had been set for him, he thought only that this girl would appreciate it, whatever its quality.

She hesitated, glancing again at the food, longing in her eyes, and back to him, uncertain. ''I don't think—it would be seemly.''

''Who is to know?'' he countered, and, setting a firm hand to her back, he began gently to propel her towards the table. ''You need not fear me, ma'am. As you have so sapiently observed, I have consumed far too much brandy to be capable of any amatory advances.''

''Yes, that *is* what I feared,'' she said, glancing up at him as they reached the table. ''Not that you might attempt anything, perhaps, but...but in my situation, one is vulnerable to—to certain *propositions.*''

He held the chair for her to sit. ''You mean, I dare say, that, having given you supper, I might expect payment in kind.''

There was no trace of a blush on her pallid cheek. Her attention was on the food. Her voice was vague as she responded. ''Yes, that is usually the way of it.''

She drew a breath as he offered her the platter of bread, and her fingers shook as she lifted a slice from among the pile. He sat down and watched her, fascinated, as she put the bread to her mouth, her eyes closing in a kind of ecstasy when she bit into it. It must be many hours since she had eaten.

The shock of her discovery and his malevolent thoughts of her were gone with the lessening of the storm. Only the sound of the rain, pattering more gently against the window, disturbed the quiet now. It was like coming to harbour after a rough passage—with an armful of comfort to hand. Only there could be no comfort from *this* bosom. His glance travelled over the girl's face and the visible parts of her upper body, and with another pang of compassion he saw that she was woefully thin.

Suddenly urgent to feed her, he looked about the table and discovered that there was only the one plate and set of utensils. He stood up. ''I had better ring for another cover to be laid.''

''Oh, no, *pray*,'' she begged, dropping the bread and rising also, and casting an apprehensive glance over her shoulder at the closed door. ''No, no, don't. It would not do to be discovered in so—intimate a situation.''

''What the devil do you care for the opinion of such persons as these?''

She looked away. Low-voiced, she answered, ''I *have* to care.''

He was silent, moved a little by the underlying pain he detected in her voice.

Her eyes came back to meet his, and a tentative smile glimmered on her lips. ''May we not share your things?''

Mr Beckenham found himself quite unable to withstand the plea. An idea occurred. ''I know! We will take the gamester's way, and follow Lord Sandwich.''

''I don't understand,'' she said, sinking back into her chair and gathering up the hastily discarded slice of bread.

''Watch.''

The gentleman laid several pieces of beef between two slices of bread, and, putting it on his own plate, placed it before the lady. She put down the slice she already had, and looked at the plate. Abruptly she broke into a delicious laugh, her thin face lighting up. Then she seized the offering in her hands and began to eat.

She tried at first to do so in a properly genteel way, nibbling daintily. But gradually, her appetite quick-ening, she ate faster and faster, stuffing the food ravenously into her mouth and bolting it down.

In a very short space of time, she had demolished two more such beef sandwiches supplied by Mr Beckenham, with the addition of a large slice of pie, the whole washed down with gulps of water in between, only so that she might clear her mouth for more food.

Mr Beckenham, at once amused and touched, watched her, eating little himself. He preferred to drink—ignoring the landlord's porter—from his silver flask, which he had substituted for the broken glass of brandy. It was only when at last the girl sat back with a sigh of satisfaction, apparently replete, that he ventured to address her, his tone unwontedly gentle.

"How long is it since you had a square meal?"

She closed her eyes briefly and shrugged. "I do not remember."

He gave a soft laugh. "You ate that as if it was to be your last meal on earth."

A gleam of humour appeared in her eye. "It may well be. Oh, not on earth, perhaps."

"I am relieved to hear it."

She smiled at him. "I have to thank you. That was—oh, like finding an oasis in the desert!" She glanced at the windows, where the rain had almost ceased. "Quite the wrong simile at such a time. But I feel exceedingly warm and cosy, as if the storm is over—for now."

His grin was rueful. "I fear it is merely a lull. Listen!"

The girl's eyes lost their sparkle as the faintest of rumbles came to her ears, and Mr Beckenham was sorry he had drawn her attention to it. He saw her shoulders shift, and she unconsciously raised a hand to undo the buttons of the bodice of the dark pelisse she still wore over an equally dark gown, the top of which was now revealed, made high to the throat.

He glanced up at her face again, and discovered that she was looking at him with some interest, and it struck him that until now starvation had held her attention to the exclusion of all else.

"What?" he demanded, disconcerted by the direct gaze, framed by the small white frill of her otherwise severe cap. "Why do you look at me so?"

"You do not appear to be foxed at all," she explained.

He laughed. "Is that all? The truth is, I have had only enough to permit me to drown my sorrows."

She nodded, as if she understood. "You mentioned something of the sort when you first came in. You are short of money?"

Taken aback by her frankness, he gave a self-conscious laugh. "Devil take it, ma'am, is that a question to ask a stranger?"

"Perhaps not in the ordinary way." She smiled, and a glow entered the deep grey eyes. "But when the stranger has done one a signal service—"

"None of that! You have done *me* a favour, I told you so."

"It is kind in you to make such a pretence, but I saw the compassion in your face, and I am grateful for it. If I may make a return by listening to your troubles, I am very willing to do so."

"My good girl," Mr Beckenham said in some embarrassment, "I can assure you my troubles are vastly inferior to your own. What in the world is a girl of your quality doing at such an inn? And alone?"

Her face closed in and she eyed him with a return of the defiance and challenge he had seen in her eyes at first. A glimmer of lightning lit the window again, and the thunder could be heard, distant and muted. The gods were displeased again! he thought facetiously and held up a hand, as if he read her thought.

"No, very well; it is none of my concern."

She looked down at the table, and then raised her eyes to meet his again, the challenge gone.

"That was ungracious of me, when you have been so kind. The fact is, sir, that I have been alone for several years now. And when I..." She hesitated, as if seeking the appropriate words.

Mr Beckenham did not interrupt. He was thinking how unconscious she seemed now to be of the awkwardness of their encounter. Or had her initial fears been merely a result of the disorder of mind induced by her very apparent hunger? One could never think straight when the body's ills took all one's attention.

She continued, breaking his train of thought. "When I spoke of your circumstances, it was only in the belief that I might understand your plight. For I am at such an inn because it is all I can afford—and *you* would not be here had you better means."

"True enough," he admitted.

She inclined her head. "I am on my way to take up a situation as companion and had to put up here to catch the cross stage tomorrow." She bowed her head a little, and began to falter. "It is—it is many months since my last situation, and...and I have had to eke out my remaining funds. That is why—'' raising her head to give him a grateful look ''—I had none to spare for a meal at this place.''

Mr Beckenham took a long pull at his flask, and then carefully topped it up from the bottle. He did not look at her as he spoke.

''Your frankness does you credit, ma'am. If I was not similarly open, it is merely because my embarrassments can only be laid at the door of my own folly, and not to the workings of chance.''

''Sir,'' said the lady, looking him straight in the eye as he paused in his task to glance at her, so that his hand stilled and his gaze remained on her serious face, ''I am no more the victim of circumstance than are you. I am as I am through the choices I have made, and I will not whine at fate.''

There was a silence. Complete silence, for the rain had ceased and for the moment the storm seemed to have moved away. Mr Beckenham continued to stare at her, an odd sense of unreality invading his mind. Such steadfast determination in her voice! And what pride she had, that transcended her meagre purse and the threadbare pelisse that so little kept out the winter cold that she still wore it inside the house, and had been obliged to come down from her room to seek a little warmth from the dying fire.

''May I know your name?'' he asked quietly, laying down his flask and the brandy bottle.

She shrank into herself, and then gave a tiny shrug. ''You may think of me as 'Theda'.'' Almost as an afterthought, her eyes clouding, she added, "No one has called me that for years."

Before he could answer, the door opened. They both looked round, and met the startled eyes of Mrs Pigdon, the landlady.

"Miss!" she gasped. "Why, miss, I thought you was long abed!"

"No," Theda said quietly, but Mr Beckenham could hear a quiver in the voice. "I came down to be warmed by the fire."

The landlady's eyes narrowed. "Oh, you did, did you?"

She glanced from one to the other, at the remains of the food on the table, and wrath entered her face. Arms akimbo, she made herself ready for battle.

Ranging on her side, a flare from the window lit up the coarse, reddening features, followed immediately by the uncouth clatter of the skies, echoing her strident voice.

"And what might be the meaning of all this, may I ask? I'll have you know this is a respectable house, and 'goings on' I will not put up with!"

Mr Beckenham was on his feet. "Now listen to me, my good woman—"

"Don't you 'good woman' me!" snorted the outraged dame. "I know what my eyes are telling me. And as for you, miss," she said, rounding on Theda, "you're no better than you should be, just as I suspected at the outset."

"Just one moment—" began the gentleman.

But Mrs Pigdon was not in a mood to listen. "Come down to be warm by the fire, indeed! Heard the gentleman's voice, more like, and come down to see what you might get out of him."

"I *beg* your pardon?" gasped Theda, rising from her chair. Even she had not bargained for such an insult as this!

"You may well!"

"How dare you speak to me so?" Theda demanded, her voice husky with distress.

"Dare? *Dare?* How dare *you*, miss, turn the Feathers into little better than a bawdy-house? Out you'll go, this minute!"

Theda blanched even paler, a wicked flash and an ominous rumble preventing her from hearing the curse that issued from Mr Beckenham's lips. All outrage fled before the hideous prospect of being thrown into the streets on such a night.

"You are quite mistaken," she said desperately, but she might as well have spared her breath.

"Mistaken, am I? We'll see that. I won't have it! Not in my house. I'm a respectable woman, and I won't have no 'goings on', not if you were ever so high and mighty, the pair of you. Which you ain't, not by a long chalk!" she averred, descending rapidly from outraged virtue to mere verbal abuse.

"You are being quite ridiculous, my good woman," began Mr Beckenham loftily, trying again to stem the flow.

But this time, Theda interrupted him. "Pray don't, sir. The blame is mine."

"To be sure it is!" concurred Mrs Pigdon aggressively. "And you'll pay for it, my girl. You can get your things, such as they are, and clear off out of my establishment.''

''*What?* Don't be a fool, woman!'' The gentleman flung out an accusing finger at the window, through which the flickering and crackling still lingered on. ''Send her into *that?* Besides, you can't turn the girl out at this hour.''

''Pray, sir,'' begged Theda, white to the lips and trembling. ''Say nothing more! I am quite ready to go.''

''Wait!'' called out the gentleman, as she moved swiftly towards the door.

But Theda heard only the landlady's vicious tone following her. ''Aye, and so you should be. Think shame to yourself! Calling yourself a gentlewoman and all!''

At the door, Theda almost bumped into the landlord, who was standing in amazement at the acrimonious scene within the room. As the girl disappeared through the door, Mr Beckenham seized Pigdon's arm and turned to confront his wife.

''You are come in a very good hour, sir! For mercy's sake, persuade your good woman here to allow the lady to stay. What she proposes is positively inhuman! Besides, the girl has done nothing wrong, and I cannot allow her to be treated this way.''

Together the landlady and her shocked spouse burst into voluble speech, which beat at Theda's ears as she fled up the stairs. Shame churned inside her, and the storm was forgotten. She was a fool not to have foreseen the outcome. Mrs Pigdon had shown herself to be anything but sympathetic when she arrived at the hostelry earlier that evening.

She'd had to walk from the more expensive inn up the road which was the official halt for the north-bound stagecoach. Her shabby appearance and the battered portmanteau had weighed heavily against the genteel tone of her voice. It was worse, in fact, than if she had been obviously of a more humble station, for a gentlewoman in her circumstances was instantly under suspicion of a fall from respectability. Which, lord help her, was indeed the truth! She was not, however, the common harpy for which the landlady had taken her! she reflected angrily, stepping hastily into the garret room which was all she had been able to afford. Cramming her worn, out-moded bonnet on her head, she stuffed the few belongings she had unpacked back into the portmanteau.

Taking it up, and with no very clear idea of what she meant to do—apart from escaping from the humiliations to which she had been subjected—Theda crept out of the room, down two sets of stairs, and slunk past the open door of the coffee-room, where the landlord's voice was joined to those of his wife and the gentleman.

Thankfully they were all too engrossed to notice her, and she gained the front door unmolested and slipped through it, closing it softly behind her.

The chill of the March night struck at once through her thin pelisse. It was no longer raining, but the sky was pitch-black with cloud, as she saw when the unremitting storm sent flittering light across it. It must be past twelve, for the gentleman, she knew, had arrived after the clock on the coffee-room mantel had struck eleven. The lamp-post that welcomed travellers to the inn had long lost its cursory flame, and she had neither candle nor lantern to light her way through the darkened streets.

In mounting dismay she peered into the gloom, the invidious nature of her position coming home to her with a vengeance.

Chapter Two

There was not a soul in sight as Theda began resolutely to trudge down the street, looking for a lane that might lead her off the main road, which, being only of packed dirt, was already a hasty-pudding of mud which churned under her mercifully booted feet. She tried to hold up her long skirts with her free hand, grateful for the moment to the intermittent lightning which showed up the worst of the puddles ahead.

The only idea she had was of discovering some sort of shelter for the night, for she must catch the stage to her destination early in the morning. The eerie stillness of a town asleep caught at the edges of her already stretched nerves, and she shivered with apprehension as well as from the biting wind.

Come now! she encouraged herself. There was no one about. And even if there were, what had she to fear from some sturdy citizen?

Then she found a lane and turned down it, thankfully feeling cobbles under her feet. She let go of her skirts, but immediately felt a prickle of fear at putting herself out of reach of the inn. For a craven moment she was tempted to go back and throw herself on the mercy of the landlady. But the woman's insults rankled, as did her earlier insolence—for her contemptuous glance had raked Theda's person when she had dared to ask at the Feathers for a room for the night.

Theda thought she had learned to subdue the spirit of rebellion that threw her into defiance on the receipt of such slights. But she had not. Storm or no storm, she could no more have returned to the inn than she had been able to return penitent to the bosom of her family six long years ago, when the same stigma would have been laid to her then as had been laid to her now.

The thought gave her courage, and she stepped out more boldly, coming into another road that ran parallel to the main one. Her eyes had become accustomed to the dark, and she could see, as she peered down it either way, that to the left this road opened out. A square, perhaps?

Another horrible crackle overhead pushed her into decision. Changing direction, she hurried towards the place, and found it to be a large open space, surrounded by little shops, their shutters closed now, but by the legends she could just see painted above their doors they were given over to trade. The whole area was saturated with water, which still trickled in little rivulets through the uneven cobble stones, and down the walls from the tiled roofs.

It must be the market square, Theda decided, glancing about and finding odd shapes that looked like empty barrows. And that thin stump of a thing, that must surely be the pump.

She checked about for a likely place of shelter. There was a small colonnade to one side before a large building. The Corn Exchange? She would investigate that. At least it would be out of the wind, and hopefully dry. Although the miserable cold was likely to keep her awake all night—if one could sleep at all in the open air, with a raging storm about one and the fear all the time that someone might find one camped out like a vagrant!

She was just crossing the square, and wondering where in her portmanteau she had placed her woollen shawl, when she became aware of footsteps that were not her own.

She froze momentarily. They were coming down one of the streets that led to the square. In her fright, she could not judge which one, and looked fearfully this way and that. One thing only was certain. *They were coming this way.*

Unreasoning panic blanked out her thoughts, and, grasping her portmanteau, she flew for the colonnade of the Corn Exchange. Just as she reached it, the light from a lantern spilled on to the square, and she saw a man enter the place behind it.

Holding her breath, Theda crept behind one of the wide pillars, carefully put down her portmanteau, and crouched down, trying to make herself visible only as an unidentifiable hump.

The footsteps halted, and she could see the beam of the lantern swing from side to side. Her heart was thumping so hard that she could feel the breath catch in her chest. Not even hearing the rolling crackle above, she was conscious only of the moving light, as the footsteps began again and it swung this way and that, searching something out.

Instinct told her that she was being hunted. Panic kept her from wondering why. She crouched there, her eyes, enormous in her white features, fixed on the light that came steadily closer.

A sudden explosion of brightness lit up the whole sky. Unable to help herself, she looked up, and knew at once that her movement was seen, as in the instant gloom that succeeded it the lesser light of the lantern swept an arc and found her face.

The beam stopped there, and Theda remained a moment, blinking in its glare, like an animal's prey, frozen with fright. Then, as the thunder roared, startling her out of immobility, she leapt up and ran, blindly, as for her life.

At once the footsteps started after her, and she heard a voice calling out. But the words were meaningless to her, and she ran on, her breath ragged. She was not watching the uneven cobbled ground beneath her racing feet, and an unexpectedly large stone tripped her progress, bringing her to a stumbling halt.

The running steps behind her closed, and a hand grasped her shoulder, swinging her round.

"You little fool!" scolded a voice—muted, but blessedly familiar. "What the devil do you mean by running from me?"

Theda stared up at Mr Beckenham's handsome features under the shadowing beaver hat, her mouth open on gasping breaths, her eyes dilating in fear.

"I—I don't *know*. I thought—I *couldn't* think!"

His face softened. "You poor girl! I'm sorry I frightened you."

She shook her head a little, and found that her hands were grasping at his coat. A warm, large one closed over them, reassuringly.

"Come, now, it is all over. There is nothing more to fear."

"It—it was f-foolish of me, I know," she managed, her teeth chattering.

"Your hands are like ice!" he said in concern, and placed an arm quickly about her, his thought only to warm her. "Have you no gloves?"

She nodded. "Y-yes, but in my anxiety to be gone I f-forgot them." Her voice trembled on a laugh. "Just, I suspect, as you did!"

His light laugh sounded above her. "Quite right. I did."

As she hunted for a worn pair of leather gloves in the pocket of her pelisse, she did not appear to notice that she had been pulled closely in to the gentleman for a few brief seconds. Recollecting herself suddenly, she jerked away sharply. But not before he had felt the painful thinness of her upper arm, the jutting of her hip against him.

"The devil!" he muttered, almost to himself. "The girl is skin and bone! Small wonder you are so cold. Here, hold this a moment." He gave the lantern into her now gloved hands, and proceeded to strip off his greatcoat.

"I have always b-been thin, you kn-know," Theda told him, but with a tremor still in her voice.

"You are positively skeletal, girl!" In a moment,

the huge greatcoat was placed about her shoulders, drowning her, and as he retrieved the lantern he began to scold. "You are an irresponsible little fool! The storm may break again at any moment and you will be drenched. You should know better than to walk out into strange streets alone."

"What else was I to do?" she protested with spirit, hugging his warm coat gratefully about herself. "Would you expect me to remain after what that woman said of me?"

"Better to endure her insults than to die of exposure."

A bleak look flitted over her face. "I don't know that. Sometimes it seems that death might be..." She faltered to a halt as her eyes met his again. As if she was ashamed of her momentary weakness, her chin came up. "In any event, she threw me out."

"To be sure she did," agreed Mr Beckenham impatiently. "But that was in her first rage. You had only to ride out the storm—*inside* preferably—" with a flash of humour as the heavens reminded him of their still present threat "—and the dust would soon have settled. And I had the situation well in hand."

"Oh, indeed? It seemed to me that you could not edge in a word!" retorted Theda.

"I did so after you left, and would have done so had you stayed." He grinned engagingly. "I am a specialist at handling irascible women."

A tiny choke of laughter escaped her. "So I perceive."

His eyes roved the pale features, a stirring in his breast that was not quite compassion. On impulse, he put out a hand, and touched the back of it to her cheek. "Still so frozen! You are like to die in any event, if you will not look after yourself better!"

"I am much more resilient than you suppose," Theda said, a faint smile on her lips.

"Well, I am not! I am growing cold." He took hold of her arm. "Let us go at once."

Theda held back, urgency in her voice. "You cannot ask me to go back there!"

"Yes, I can. If you had not so stupidly bade me keep quiet, I should have done the trick long since, and you would not have had to leave the place at all. It is all settled now, so you may be easy."

"No! No, I will not go back." But she sounded unsure now.

"Most certainly you will," stated the gentleman, urging her irresistibly forward. "I am not making this sacrifice for nothing."

She halted, staring up at him. "Sacrifice?"

"Yes, sacrifice. The good lady has agreed that you may return for the night only if I remove," he explained.

In the light of the lantern, her eyes were pools of deep distress. "Oh, you should not have done that! What will you do?"

He was touched by her concern, but he smiled. "I shall go on to the Saracen's Head."

"But you cannot afford it!"

"Don't fear for me. I know Thompson very well. He will chalk up my shot for another day."

Theda continued to look at him uncertainly for a moment. Then she sighed. "I have only to thank you.

Such chivalry is rarely met with by such as I, and although I know I should refuse it, for it will put you in debt, I confess I *cannot.*"

"What a pother you make!" he laughed. "It is nothing at all to me. I am forever in debt, you must know. One grows accustomed to it."

She said no more, but went to pick up her portmanteau from the Corn Exchange colonnade.

"That you will give to me," said Mr Beckenham firmly, taking it from her.

"But it is not heavy, and the inn is no great distance," she protested.

"You may carry the lantern, then," he conceded, and handed it over.

The sky above them lit again, and the next rumble produced the first spattering of rain.

"Quickly!" urged Mr Beckenham, stepping up his pace.

Theda had almost to run to keep up with his long strides, and had much ado both to keep hold of the lantern and prevent the mass of the gentleman's greatcoat from falling off her shoulders. She had no breath left to speak, and, beyond recommending her to beware of puddles, her companion wasted no words either.

Arrived at the inn, he hammered on the door. It was opened immediately by Pigdon, who had evidently been on the watch for them.

"Found her, then," he observed, moving back to allow them to enter.

Mr Beckenham looked down upon him from his superior height and handed to him the lady's portmanteau. "Take this. And mind you see to her comfort!" Without waiting for a reply, he turned to Theda, who was slipping off his greatcoat. He stayed her hands. "No, keep it."

Theda shook her head and his fingers fell away. She held it out. "I could not possibly do so."

He hesitated before taking it. "I have another."

"But not with you," she objected gently. "You have already done too much. My conscience would not suffer me to accept any more."

Reluctantly he received the greatcoat back.

Theda smiled at him out of her thin, pale face. "Besides, you look so well in it, and it is far too large for me."

Mr Beckenham laughed, and took the hand she held out to him. "Take good care of yourself... witch."

He said it only because he had forgotten the name she had told him, but the delicious little gurgle of laughter she gave coincided so precisely with another crackle of thunder that it seemed suddenly apt.

Then, disappearing up the stairs in the wake of the landlord's candle, like the ghost he had first thought her, she vanished out of his life.

Theda's eyes remained closed as the lumbering stagecoach rumbled its way from Newark, where she had caught it outside the Saracen's Head, to Ashby-de-la-Zouch, where it would remain for the night before proceeding to Stafford. But Theda was not asleep. Even if one could have slept, with the incessant lurching over the mired ruts that the storm had left behind, she was not tired.

On the contrary, she had slept remarkably well, in a large bed over the sheets of which the grudging Mrs Pigdon had passed a warming-pan before Theda slipped between them. She could not remember when she had last enjoyed such comfort. On a full stomach, too. Oh, the bliss of it! And she did not even know the name of the kind benefactor to whom she owed so much. It was not merely that he had paid her shot. He had paid it as if it were his own. For it was *his* room and *his* bed in which she had lain so snugly. Replete with his food, too.

He had not bought Mrs Pigdon's approval, but honour had been assuaged and she had done her duty as, she said, befitted a Christian.

"It's not what I hold with, nor yet what I'm accustomed to," the matron had said virtuously, as she'd brought a laden tray to the best spare bedchamber in the morning, "but I'm an honest woman, and I don't cheat nobody, be they never so undeserving! A breakfast he paid for, and a breakfast you shall have."

Theda had gazed with awe upon the dish of ham and eggs, the lavishly buttered bread and the pot of tea, bereft of words. Having discharged her duty, Mrs Pigdon had left the room, with a parting injunction to the unwanted guest to be sure and hurry.

"For the coach won't stay for you, and I don't want you begging back here, that I don't!"

Theda had hardly heard her, overwhelmed as she had been by the thoughtfulness of the unknown gentleman. She had set to with a will, but had been dismayed to discover that her appetite did not match it. She had only been daunted for a moment, however. She might be proud, but she had learned to be provident! Remembering her host's clever trick of the night before, she had made a sandwich of the remaining ham and wrapped it carefully in one of her pocket handkerchiefs, placing it securely in the pocket of her pelisse. At least she would not be hungry today!

For who could tell what might await her at journey's end? Her history was not such as had ever permitted her to procure any but the meanest of genteel occupations. No high-born dames, no wealthy patroness for Miss Theodosia Kyte! Her employers had been in general the aspiring mothers of young daughters of tradesmen—the honest working citizens whom her father would have disparagingly stigmatised as "cits"—hoping that a little of Theda's quality might rub off on their uncouth girls to help them to an advantageous marriage.

Miss Kyte considered herself fortunate to have finally been offered a post in a better class of household, for Sir John Merchiston's widow sounded a much more promising prospect than Mrs Mugglesby, to whom she had last been in service. Moreover, an older lady should need a companion for a much longer period than a girl on the catch for a husband.

Lord, how she longed for some such measure of security! Only to know each day that tomorrow one would still have a roof over one's head, a bed to lie in and food to put on the table. In six years she had never been able to cultivate that devil-may-care attitude that seemed to characterise the gentleman at the Feathers.

His face came into her mind as she thought of him. A comely countenance, with a degree of charm in that useful smile of his that should not be permitted to any one man. A fine figure, too—broad in the shoulder and muscled in the leg. And what was it about golden hair? Novelty, perhaps. It was not so long since that the fashionable had discarded their wigs and taken to cultivating natural heads. Yes, she had to concede that the gentleman's exterior qualities were uniformly pleasing.

Not that *she* was susceptible. Oh, no. She had long ago closed her heart against all invasion. Men—especially handsome men—were not *safe*.

She thrust her eyes open, as if she would banish the image from them. They fell upon the grey drizzle that followed the storm, and her spirits unaccountably sank. She discovered that she was hungry, and, having enquired the time of her neighbour in the coach, a thick-set farmer, decided it was safe to consume her sandwich. She would be in Mountsorrel, where she had been told to leave the coach, by three.

But the long haul through the muddy roads slowed the horses' progress almost to a walk, and it was not until after five in the evening that the vehicle finally came to a halt outside the George inn in Mountsorrel, a little place some distance before the larger town of Ashby-de-la-Zouch.

Weary to her bones, and once more cold to the marrow, Theda stepped down and requested the guard to unstrap her portmanteau from the back. She stood with it in her hand, looking about for some signs of a waiting servant. The George was busy with the stagecoach passengers, two of whom had gone in to bait, the others walking about to stretch their limbs while the ostlers led the exhausted cattle away and brought out a fresh team. But there seemed no one about who was not already occupied with his own legitimate business.

The air struck dank and chill, and the overcast sky pre-empted the onset of dusk. Apprehension began to filter into Theda's breast as she waited. Heaven send they had not given up on her! She shivered. The letter had definitely stated that she was to be met. But if they thought the coach was not coming...

Before she had quite given in to despair, however, from out of the doorway of the inn came a dour old man in ancient, shabby livery, with shiny elbows and tarnished braid. Back bent, he twisted this way and that, peering in a short-sighted way at the newcomers wandering around the yard.

This must be her guide! Theda decided, so relieved that she barely took in the poor quality of his attire, thinking only that the delay must have been made more acceptable to him by a lengthy sojourn in the tap-room. She hefted her portmanteau, and was about to cross to him when he spied her, and shuffled up, a trifle unsteady on his legs.

Squinting up at her out of a pair of rheumy eyes, he addressed her, his voice cracked and senile. "Be the name Kyte?"

Theda sighed thankfully. "Yes, I am Miss Kyte. Are you from the Merchiston house?"

The old man nodded briefly, chewing on something at the side of his mouth. Then he spat in the road, and delivered himself of a surly condemnation. "Late you be."

It was not an encouraging start.

There was little conversation exchanged on the journey to Merchiston Lodge, which was accomplished in a battered gig, drawn by a shuffling cob, long past its prime. The ancient servitor, who drove with a slack rein and a sublime disregard of the potholes, seemed to take it as a personal affront that Miss Kyte had kept him waiting for more than two hours. After animadverting bitterly on the demands made on his old bones, as he had heaved the lady's portmanteau into the boot, he had climbed laboriously into the gig without even offering to assist her to do the same.

Theda's lips had tightened, but she had made no complaint. She was used to insolent treatment from fellow servants—for she had long learned that a companion, be she never so genteel, was regarded as little more than that. Her tiredness fled before the immediate prospect of encountering her new employer. Despite the disrespectful non-welcome of her companion, she began to feel more hopeful as they left Mountsorrel. They were passing through pleasant country—hunting country, she knew, with open tracts of undulating land among the cultivated fields, offering a good many jumps and lengthy runs for the hardy spirits who rode to hounds. The prospects were pleasing even on this dismal day in the gathering gloom.

But a few miles on, the country began to seem wilder, with more clumps of trees, culminating in the distance in what looked like a considerable forest.

"What is that?" she asked, pointing.

The aged servitor glanced along her arm and responded shortly, "Switham Thicket."

"Thicket!" echoed Theda, astonished.

He seemed to understand her surprise. "Be none so big as looks. Lodge be just beyond. Village beyond that again."

"Switham village?"

But the old man had shot his bolt. He merely nodded, and Theda was left to contemplate the thicket as they approached, the stark silhouettes of its close-packed trees, still bare of leaves, jutting from the heavy underbrush like so many giant goblins. The road cut a swath through the centre of the belt of trees, and as the gig passed between them they seemed to menace, arms grotesquely waving, as if they resented this intrusion through their territory.

Theda shivered, and the old man beside her, flinging her a sidelong look out of his rheumy eyes, smiled sourly, as if he enjoyed the effect the place created on her. But he proved right about the size of Switham Thicket, for a bare quarter of a mile brought them to the outskirts of the other side, and almost immediately the horse was turned into a walled aperture of crumbling stone, its high, rusty iron gates wide open.

Even in the failing light, Theda could see that the drive was ill kept, and the surrounding gardens overgrown, and what must once have been a graceful line of trees bordering the rutted gravel lane now struck a flutter of apprehension in her breast. For the bald trunks with their empty branches thrusting into the blackening sky echoed the bleak and eerie threat of the thicket that ran parallel down its length, bordering the estate.

At the end of the drive, the house came into view, a low, rambling place of dark brick, crawling with ivy, with many leaded windows, some with broken panes, and gabled roofs. A long porch partially hid the squat front door, its arched cover all over tangled creepers, the grass and pavings all about it thick with weeds.

Theda's gaze ran over the shadowed building, dark but for a faint glimmer behind one or two of the myriad windows, dismay flooding her breast. To what kind of life had she come? Was this the genteel establishment she had hoped for? Even the least of her previous employers had a better-kept property than this!

The horse came to a stop before the porch, and the old servant got down and lugged her portmanteau out of the boot. Theda was more hesitant. She wished with all her heart that she could turn around and go back, depart from this unprepossessing, even *frightening* place before ever she discovered what awaited her within its mouldering walls. But there was no going back for the impoverished Miss Theodosia Kyte. Here lay her immediate future, and here she must stay.

Gathering her courage together, she descended

from the gig and waited for the old man to precede her across the porch. As he reached the door, however, it was opened by a sturdy-looking dame in an old-fashioned working gown of grey wool, covered with a comprehensive apron, and a mob-cap concealing most of her greying hair but for two neat bands at the front parted in the centre. She was holding up an oil-lamp and peering out.

"At last!" she said in relieved tones. "Miss Ara's fair spitting with impatience."

"Weren't my fault, Taggy," said the old man at once. "She be late."

The woman looked past him and caught sight of Theda. She came out on to the porch, lifting the lamp higher. "You must be Miss Kyte. I'm Agnes Diggory, the housekeeper, and this here's my man, Adam."

"How do you do?" Theda said, smiling a little and holding out a hand, insensibly warmed by the woman's greeting.

Mrs Diggory looked taken aback for a moment, but she took the hand and then ushered the lady inside, talking all the while.

"They stagecoaches ain't never to be trusted to keep time! I don't doubt you're in a rare hunger, miss. The mistress has had her dinner, but I've set aside a bite against your coming. I'll just take you in to Miss Ara, and when you're settled, like, I'll fetch it up to you."

"Thank you, you are very kind," Theda said gratefully, glad to find Mrs Diggory a much friendlier soul than her dour spouse.

The old man had disappeared outside again without

a word, having set Theda's portmanteau down in the wide hall. As she was led towards the back of it, there was time and light only for her to take in a number of doors on either side, a pervasive smell of must, dark wood panelling, and the central staircase leading to an upper gallery that ran left and right above.

"Diggory'll take your bag up, miss," the housekeeper told her, opening a door to the left. She poked her head in, raising her voice. "It's Miss Kyte, Mum." Then she gestured to Theda to enter.

In a small, ill-lit parlour, with the meanest of fires in the grate, was seated a middle-aged woman of daunting aspect. She was as thin as was Theda herself, with a scrawny look about the neck and chest, which were encased in a plum-coloured poplin gown that looked far from new, in spite of the now fashionable high waist, and a woollen shawl huddled about the shoulders. Her complexion was sallow, with lines of bitterness running down to a mouth pinched in discontent, and she looked at Theda out of a pair of lacklustre eyes, with patent contempt.

"So you're Miss Theodosia Kyte?" she said in a thin voice whose tone matched the air of acidity that hung about her.

Theda's heart sank. But she answered with composure. "Yes, ma'am. You are Lady Merchiston, I collect?"

"Do I look like a widow?" came the snappy response. "No, I am not Lady Merchiston. I am Araminta Merchiston, Lady Merchiston's daughter—for my sins! You are not come to be a companion to *me*."

Theda could barely repress a sigh of relief, although she wondered at the strange way the woman spoke. ''I beg your pardon. I thought, as Mrs Diggory showed me in here—''

''My mother keeps to her bed,'' Miss Merchiston informed her ''You will meet her directly. She's been fretting herself to flinders, in case you should've changed your mind.''

''No, indeed. I'm afraid the coach was delayed considerably by the state of the roads after last night's storm.''

''Don't waste your excuses on me! It's *her* you'll have to placate—if you can.'' She nodded at a chair opposite. ''For the moment you may sit down.''

''Thank you, but perhaps I might cleanse the journey's dust first?'' suggested Theda.

''Presently. Sit down.''

Theda did so. Strangely, she felt more resentful of this lady's peremptory commands than she ever had of those of the merchants' wives she had previously been obliged to swallow. What would Araminta Merchiston say if she knew just how far above her in station was this obviously despised new companion?

Araminta was appraising her in a considering way. ''You don't look up to much. Purse-pinched, are you? I dare say that is why you were induced to accept so low a wage.''

Theda felt herself stiffening. ''It would appear, then, that we have both struck a satisfactory bargain.''

Miss Merchiston's eyes narrowed to slits. ''Take care, Miss Kyte! I will not tolerate insolence.''

''You misunderstand me, ma'am,'' Theda said

sweetly. "I meant only to suggest that the advantages are mutual."

"That remains to be seen," said Araminta, relaxing again. "You have yet to prove yourself."

"I shall endeavour not to disappoint you, ma'am."

If there was a barb to this speech, it passed Miss Merchiston by. She snorted.

"It is nothing to do with me. Much I care! No one can say that it was I who insisted on having someone in. Squandering money, I call it. Except if your coming may release me from the necessity ever to speak to that old hag again! That would be money well spent."

Shocked, Theda could only stare at her.

"You need not look like that," snapped the other woman testily. "You will learn soon enough how matters stand in this rat-infested refuge from hell!"

Theda hardly knew how to answer such a speech. She had come to an unhappy house, that was clear. Pray heaven she might find the courage to endure the horrors that must lie in store! Pulling herself out of the dazed state into which the woman's embittered words had thrown her, she tried for a non-committal tone.

"Perhaps it would be best if you told me what duties I might be expected to perform."

"It is no use asking me. You will do what my mother demands of you, of course."

"I see. Then might it not be a good idea for you to introduce me to Lady Merchiston?"

"I dare say it would," agreed Araminta acidly, "but I shan't do it!"

Nonplussed, Theda said without thinking, "How very odd!"

"Pah! There is nothing odd in it. Why should I? I can't abide her, nor she me! Taggy will take you up."

The lines of bitterness seemed more pronounced than ever as she rose from her chair and crossed to the door. Theda, both amazed and troubled, got up to follow her. Miss Merchiston opened the door and called out in a piercing shriek for Mrs Diggory.

"Tag-gy! *Tag-gy!*"

Theda lifted her hands to cover her ears as the sound echoed about the cavernous hall, seeming to go right through her. Doubtless the bells in this house were broken—like everything else! Her spirits drooped, and she began to dread the coming meeting with Lady Merchiston. If the mother resembled the daughter, heaven help her!

Miss Merchiston had wandered out of the room, calling out again. As Theda came out into the dark hall, she heard someone bustling down the stairs, and recognised Mrs Diggory's voice.

"I'm coming, Miss Ara!" She added as she reached the bottom of the stairs where Miss Merchiston had arrived to meet her, "I've told the mistress as how Miss Kyte is come at last, and she said to bring her up straight."

"Then do so, Taggy, do so!"

"Not me, Miss Ara," said Agnes Diggory apologetically. "She wants *you* to bring her. Insistent, she was. You know her way."

In the light of the housekeeper's lamp, Theda saw Araminta Merchiston's face tighten into fury. Without a word, the woman began to ascend the stairs. Mrs Diggory nudged the new companion, her tone low.

"Better go after her, miss. I'll be following soon enough to make sure you get to your room and have that bite o' supper. Leave it to them two and you'd starve. Sleep in the barn, too, you could, for all of them!"

Theda threw her a grateful look, and hurried after Miss Merchiston, whose familiarity with the steep staircase enabled her to keep up a cracking pace. The upper gallery was lit only by two of the many triple candle-holders in wall-scounces, one at the top of the stairs, and one down the left corridor that led back to the front of the house. Miss Merchiston went to the last door, thumped twice on it with her clenched fist as if by such violence she announced her coming, and threw it wide so that it bounced off the wall with a crash.

There was a screech from within and an instant cacophony of barking and scolding broke out. Entering behind Miss Merchiston, Theda beheld a huge four-poster bed, its curtains fully open, the inhabitant of which was largely obscured by a black, woolly-haired mongrel standing astride her legs, apparently disputing Araminta's right of entry.

"Hector, be quiet!" came a croaked command from behind the dog, and a veined hand reached for his scruff and tugged him back. "Enough, I say, you foolish beast!"

The terrier allowed himself to be dragged down to lie on the blankets, and Theda was able to see her new mistress in the light afforded by a lamp on her bedside table and a set of two candelabra resting on a nearby chest of drawers. She had a glimpse of a lined face under straggling white locks, rising out of the bulges of an over-large nightgown, before the dog, Hector, catching sight of the stranger, set up another protest, rising as he did so.

"Hector! *Down,* do you hear me?"

"Dratted animal!" muttered Araminta over her mother's imprecations and Hector's excited barks, giving him a baleful glare. "He ought to be shot."

It happened that the dog was silenced just as her last remark emerged, and over his body, flattened now to the sheet where he lay panting, the old woman sitting up in the bed flashed her a look.

"I heard that!"

"You were meant to," snapped Araminta instantly.

"Liar!" snarled her mother. "You don't dare touch my dog, not while I'm alive."

"I never said I would."

"You said he ought to be shot. And you never meant it for *my* ears, that's sure. You wouldn't jeopardise your chances, no, you would not."

Araminta's face screwed into a mask of rage and she breathed deeply, as if she could barely contain herself. The old woman's mouth twisted into a smile of gleeful satisfaction, and she turned to Theda.

A pair of sharp black eyes looked her up and down out of the most wasted features Miss Kyte had ever seen. The wrinkled skin was stretched tightly over the bones, paper-thin, blue-shadowed over pink crêpe. The remnant strands of long white hair lay clumped and matted about the skull, and a stalk-like neck vanished into the white folds of her nightgown. Only the eyes, intelligent and keen, seemed to live.

"This is she, is it?" demanded Lady Merchiston in her croaking voice.

Theda dropped a curtsy. "I am Theodosia Kyte, ma'am."

The old woman turned back to her daughter, remarking belligerently, "Kept her talking downstairs so you might give her a mean account of me, eh?"

"Why should I?" responded Araminta, matching her tone. "You'll show her your true colours soon enough."

"No doubt she's already seen yours!" retorted her mother. "One look's enough to turn the girl's stomach. I'd wager she wishes she could turn tail and run already!" She flicked a glance at Theda. "Don't you, eh?"

"Well, she can't," said Araminta before Theda could reply. "Anyone can see she'd no choice about taking the post, worse luck for her."

Lady Merchiston's eyes snapped. "If you'd done your duty by me, as a daughter should, the post wouldn't have been there to take."

"Don't you begin that!" Araminta ordered shrilly.

Hector the dog growled under his breath, shifting a little and eyeing her. Lady Merchiston put out a hand and grasped his rough coat, soothing murmurs issuing from her as she gave her daughter a reproachful look.

Araminta ignored both the glare and the dog's menacing noises. "I've been willing and able all along to do what's needful,'' she went on. ''This was *your* idea, madam Mother.''

''That's as may be, but I shouldn't have to pay for what's mine by right.''

''Pah! Much you care for that. Well do I know you've gone to these lengths only to spite me. Using up as much of my inheritance as you can. Well, don't fret yourself. Diggory's on your side, as usual. He's done his best to ruin us these three hours at the alehouse in Mountsorrel, I'll be bound. And for *that* you may thank Miss Kyte.''

Theda, listening to this venomous interchange in open-mouthed shock and dismay, almost jumped at the sudden attack.

''It was not my fault!'' she protested involuntarily, and thus brought herself once again under the scrutiny of those keen eyes from the bed.

''What did you call yourself?''

''I am Theodosia Kyte, Lady Merchiston,'' Theda repeated patiently.

''You are, are you?'' All at once she fell back against her pillows, a grim smile playing about her mouth. The dog relaxed, too, settling more comfortably under her stroking fingers and closing his eyes. ''Very well, then, Theodosia, no need to look so downcast. Unlike me, you won't be in Purgatory for long.''

''Pah!'' snorted Araminta. ''Don't raise her hopes.''

''Pah to you!'' riposted her mother childishly. ''And don't you go nagging at Adam, you hear me?''

''Precious Adam? As if I would!'' returned her

daughter sarcastically. "Much I care for Adam! You can take him with you when you go, for all of me."

The old lady's cheeks flew two spots of angry colour. "*Wicked.* Take yourself off, Araminta Merchiston!"

"Gladly," said the other, making for the door.

"And send me Taggy!" called the old lady after her.

A slammed door was all the response she got. Hector's head jerked up, but was restrained by his mistress's hand.

"Steady, boy." Turning again to Theda, she grimaced. "Think you've strayed into a madhouse, I dare say."

Theda was so appalled that she could barely repress a shudder, never mind summon up a smile. She tried for a neutral tone.

"I may as well begin as I mean to go on, ma'am. Is there anything I can do for you?"

To her surprise, Lady Merchiston sighed wearily and the life went out of her eyes. Her voice sank tiredly, as if in the absence of her daughter's goading all energy had left her.

"I should not think so at all. She was right, you see. Pay no mind to what she says. Might have been my idea—well, it was, but I only said it in a fit of temper!—but *she* carried it out. That's her spite, you see. She knew I didn't really want you—or anyone."

An odd mixture of relief and apprehension made Theda's heartbeat flutter. "Does that mean that you intend to—to send me away?"

"Don't *want* to stay, do you?"

Theda bit her lip. She did not. But she was almost penniless. To leave here now would be nothing short of disaster. The black eyes had recovered some spark of life, a question in them, as the old woman lay looking at her.

Lord, what could she say? Well, the two of them had made no bones about what they thought of her. Why should she balk at plain-speaking?

"The truth is, Lady Merchiston, that I have no alternative. I came here at the instigation of your letter, believing myself to have secured a position. I don't wish to seem importunate, but if you do intend to sever the agreement I will be obliged to ask at least for the reimbursement of the expenses of my journey."

"Very correct, ain't you?" observed her ladyship. "You can stay—if you can stand it."

"But if you don't require my services—"

"I don't require a *companion,* Theodosia." A harsh laugh escaped the almost bloodless lips, and the eyes mocked. "What I need is an undertaker. I am a dying woman."

Chapter Three

Dr Spilsby laid down his patient's wrist and patted her hand. "Very much better, my lady, very much better."

"Don't lie, man!" croaked Lady Merchiston. "We both know I'll not live out the year. Or have you of a sudden found a cure for this wasting disease?"

"I don't pretend that you are to be cured, my lady," smiled the doctor, from under the Physical bob-wig that marked his profession. "But your pulse is not so tumultuous and your colour has improved."

"My spirits, too," agreed the old lady, throwing a wry glance at Theda, who was over by the windows.

"Certainly." Dr Spilsby rose. "I think I may safely say that you are in a deal sounder trim these last few weeks."

"That will be the onset of spring," said Theda lightly, coming forward to the bed and straightening the coverlet.

"The onset of Theodosia, more like!" uttered Lady Merchiston, quizzing her. "I declare to you, Spilsby, I was never so browbeaten! The girl is at me night and day. If she is not shovelling food down my throat, or forcing your noxious potions upon me, she is—"

"Opening the windows and changing the bedclothes," put in Theda calmly. "Both of which were much needed."

"So you say! Just as you will insist on my wearing this objectionable cap," complained her ladyship, flicking at the offending article with a bony finger. "And I hate chess!"

"That is because you always cheat when I am not looking, instead of applying yourself to win by intelligence."

"You see?" Lady Merchiston turned to the doctor's grinning face. "Why can't she leave me alone to die in peace?"

"Because I need the work, Lady Merchiston," Theda said, her eyes twinkling as she gently raised the old lady a little and placed an extra pillow at her back. "And you know very well that once you are gone Miss Araminta will throw me out of the house."

"I'll haunt the place if she does," threatened the old lady.

"I've no doubt you'll do so in any event," Theda remarked. "To look at you one would think you were practising for it already."

Lavinia Merchiston burst into cackling laughter, in which the doctor readily joined her.

"I begin to think that *you* are the tonic, Miss Kyte," he said jovially.

He was quite right. Theda had been struck by an unexpected pang of compassion for Lady Merchiston. She was a cantankersome woman, but she was literally at death's door. She looked much older than her sixty-odd years, wasted as she was. Yet her household, instead of doing what they might to ease her last days, were not merely neglectful, but downright cruel.

Theda had been horrified to discover, by daylight that next day, how filthy was the condition in which the poor lady was left. Not only was the bedchamber in which she was confined dusty and cold, but her bedlinen and clothing were soiled and damp, her person unwashed, her hair uncombed.

Theda had gone down to the housekeeper, tight-lipped and curt, to ask that these things be remedied forthwith.

"All very well, Miss Kyte," had said Agnes Diggory bluntly, "for you to come the fine lady over me, but I've only the one pair of hands! There's only myself and Adam, you know, barring Mrs Elswick as comes in to cook of an afternoon."

"What?" Theda gasped, shocked. "Do you tell me that you are the only two servants to manage this whole barrack of a house?"

"That's right, miss. Well, most of the rooms is shut up now, so Diggory does the cleaning and makes up the fires. He can't manage more besides the garden. I dare say you've noticed, miss, as he's a good many years my senior?"

"Yes, I had noticed," Theda agreed gently, without further comment.

"Well, he was a good fellow in his day," the housekeeper said philosophically. "A lifetime of this place, though, is enough to sour any man!"

Recognising the rough apology contained in this speech for the dour ill manners of her spouse, Theda smiled warmly. "Believe me, Mrs Diggory, I have already seen enough to convince me of that!"

A grim twist came on to Taggy's lips. "Then you can see how it is, miss. A body can't do more than it can do. What Adam doesn't see to falls to me. That means I've all the kitchen tasks and the washing to do, not to mention acting as lady's maid to both—and everything else besides!"

"But does not Miss Merchiston help at all?"

"*She?*" said Mrs Diggory witheringly. "She'd not lift a finger in this house, she wouldn't. Not if we was to up and go. She'd starve first!"

From what she had seen of Araminta, Theda was ready to believe it. She recalled the housekeeper's kindness to her the previous evening, when she had led her from her mistress's chamber and shown her the room that Miss Merchiston had assigned for her use. It was, as Theda had not been surprised to find, up in the attics in the servants' quarters.

Mrs Diggory had made some effort, and the little room was at least warm from a small fire in the grate, and there was a down coverlet on the narrow cot bed. But apart from a commode under the bed, and a rickety table with a cracked basin and ewer upon it, the only other furnishing the room afforded was a rail across one corner for her wardrobe, with a cotton curtain to conceal the clothes that would be hung upon it.

The housekeeper had looked about at her own handiwork with an apologetic air. "I had thought to put you next the mistress, but Miss Ara wouldn't hear of it, I'm sorry to say.''

''I will manage, thank you,'' Theda had told her, her senses by this time becoming dulled to the dreadful impressions that had battered her one after the other in this horrid house.

The food to which Agnes Diggory led her had been welcome, however, and she had chosen to consume it in the friendly housekeeper's little pantry next to the kitchen, rather than risk encountering Miss Merchiston once again tonight.

But next morning, she had woken determined to make the best of it. The house had seemed less threatening in the cold light of day, and it became obvious that a pretty establishment had been rendered hideous by neglect. The wood panelling was thick with grime, and everywhere there was a film of dust. Windows were kept closed, and their murky panes—added to the rampant ivy—kept out the light, leaving shadowed corners that would unnerve the stoutest heart.

Lady Merchiston's situation, Theda recognised, was symptomatic of the whole, and she could appreciate that the Diggorys could scarcely be expected to cope with a task that would baffle an army of servants.

''I beg your pardon, Mrs Diggory,'' she said contritely. ''I had not realised. If you will be good enough to furnish me with the necessary linen, I will take it upon myself to make Lady Merchiston a degree more comfortable.''

She had done a good deal more than that. It had taken a few days to persuade her ladyship to accept change, for she had for so long been used to living in squalor that she could not at first accustom herself to an altered way of life. As Theda cleaned and swept and polished, she subjected her to a series of scoffing remarks.

"You are wasting your time, girl! What matters it if the place is a pigsty? I am as good as dead, and Araminta will not thank you. She is more like to fly out at you."

"Then you may tell her that you ordered me to do it," Theda suggested. "She cannot gainsay you."

"Yes, but I didn't order it. I don't *care* about the dirt."

But Theda would not be deterred. At length she persuaded Lady Merchiston to allow herself to be tidied up. With infinite care and patience, Theda first cleaned the frail and malodorous body from head to toe, enduring in silence a barrage of abuse and complaint the while. Then she coaxed her employer into a fresh nightgown and placed a clean, although old-fashioned day-cap of cotton and lace upon the freshly washed and combed hair. When the old lady was helped into a newly made-up and just warmed bed, with clean sheets and blankets, and a coverlet of soft down unearthed from a trunk in the attics and hung outside to air, she sat back against the bank of lace-edged pillows and burst into a paroxysm of dry sobs.

"Ma'am, what is it?" Theda asked in quick concern. "Did I hurt you?"

Lady Merchiston shook her head weakly, her veined hand reaching out. Seating herself on the edge of the bed, Theda took it into hers and her fingers closed strongly about the bony ones she held. Finding her own pocket handkerchief, she gave it into the old lady's other hand. In a moment her ladyship's sobs had ceased and she dried her few tears.

"What ails you, Lady Merchiston?" asked Theda gently.

The black eyes snapped at her. "Did you never hear of killing by kindness? I dare say I shall expire without delay!"

For a moment Theda looked at her with hurt in her eyes, a little puzzled. Then she noted a curious twitching at the edge of Lady Merchiston's bloodless lips and an intensity of the creases at the corners of her eyes.

Why, the old lady was quizzing her! This was her way of thanks—the only way, perhaps, that she knew in the pitiful misery of her life.

Theda raised her brows. "I see you are determined to prove your assertion that I have been wasting my time. In any event, you will at least not now disgrace your coffin."

A crack of hoarse laughter was surprised out of her employer, and from that moment she began to improve in spirit. In the three weeks since, Theda had tried as far as possible to keep her so.

The one battle she lost was over the dog, Hector. He might be banished during cleaning, but he was still permitted to jump on to the bed. Compromising, Theda found a piece of old blanket to place on the coverlet so that his hairs might not spread everywhere. Occasionally, Hector gratified her by using it.

He had been ejected during the doctor's visit, and

she let the dog back in to the room as she escorted Spilsby downstairs to the front door. It was almost time for her mistress's luncheon, and she went towards the back of the hall to the breakfast parlour, one of the few rooms still in use, to see if Mrs Diggory had as yet laid out the tray. As she neared the door, she heard voices within, and hesitated.

"If you imagine she does not see through your wiles," came Araminta's shrill tone, "then you are a great fool, Benedict."

"Not as big a one as you, Araminta, believe me," responded a male voice contemptuously. "At least I have the sense to treat her with respect."

This was not Adam Diggory, whose surly growl Theda would have recognised. It was a light voice, and it stirred a chord in her memory.

"I would scorn to display such hypocrisy as you delight in," retorted Miss Merchiston. "It will avail you nothing, however. But don't let me stop you. Go on up, do, and play off your airs for her benefit. Much I care!"

"I shall certainly go up, but you will announce me, Araminta, like the dutiful daughter you are," he returned sardonically.

"Pah! I am no longer obliged to be dutiful, I thank God!" she snapped back. "There is a servant now to attend to all that."

The door opened as she spoke, and Theda stepped forward.

"You want me, Miss Merchiston?"

"No, I don't," Araminta said at once, walking into the hall. "But *he* does. Benedict, come out here!"

The gentleman stepped through the doorway, demanding testily, "What the devil is it?"

Then he caught sight of Theda and stopped dead, staring. Her eyes widened and she felt quite faint.

In the dim light of the hall, so reminiscent of that other time, she could not mistake. It was the gentleman of the Feathers inn, her kind benefactor.

Mr Beckenham blinked. In the woman's eyes he saw a like recognition and knew his senses did not deceive him. It *was* his ghost!

He opened his mouth to greet her, a smile lighting up his features, when he caught an unmistakable signal in her face. The grey eyes were frantic, and an infinitesimal shake of her white-capped head begged his silence.

Glancing at Araminta, he espied one of her venomous looks as she eyed the girl, lips pinched together. Dear God, what the devil had his poor ghost done to excite her vicious enmity?

"Aren't you going to present me, Araminta?" he asked blandly, and saw a flicker of relief in Theda's eyes before she discreetly lowered them.

Miss Merchiston flashed him a scornful glance. "Who do you think she is, a guest at a ball?"

"I think she is a *lady*," said Mr Beckenham in a hard voice, "and entitled at least to a modicum of courtesy."

Theda's head came up swiftly, and again her eyes flashed a warning signal, as Araminta turned on him.

"Pah! If she was so genteel, she wouldn't have come *here* for the pittance she's paid. Not that I care!

She's Miss Kyte, come to be *companion* to that evil hag upstairs, if you must know."

The gentleman inclined his head. "How do you do, Miss Kyte? Since I am certain that my dear cousin Araminta will neglect to inform you of it, allow me to introduce myself. I am Benedict Beckenham, Lady Merchiston's godson."

"Cousin? Pah!"

"*Distant* cousin," amended Mr Beckenham.

"How do you do, sir?" said Theda politely, sinking into a curtsy.

"La-di-da!" snapped Araminta angrily. "Go on, girl, take him up. No doubt he'll beguile you, too, with his famous charm. With what result remains to be seen—but don't think you'll get away with any of *that* sort of conduct in this house."

With which she stalked across the back of the hall to her little parlour opposite, and slammed herself into it.

"Phew!" uttered Mr Beckenham, grinning. "What a curst cat that woman is! How can you bear it?"

"Hush, pray!" whispered Theda. "She has the ears of a cat, too, and I shall suffer for it."

"I should think you would," agreed Mr Beckenham in a lowered tone. "Let us remove from this vicinity at once."

"You had better come up to Lady Merchiston," Theda said, leading the way to the stairs. "Thank you for not giving me away. If she had heard the circumstances of our former meeting, I am very sure she would prove as remorseless as Mrs Pigdon at the Feathers."

"Undoubtedly. It is as well you stopped me." He grinned down at her as they ascended the stairs together. "But what an extraordinary thing! That *this* is where you should have been headed. Had I had an inkling—"

"I am glad you had not," interrupted Theda. "If you had warned me *then* of the horrors in store, I should have thrown myself *under* the stage rather than have travelled inside it."

Mr Beckenham laughed. "As bad as that?"

"Worse!"

"The devil it is!" He looked her over as they reached the gallery, pausing at the top of the stairs. "At least you have gained a little flesh." He reached out a hand to cup her chin, scanning her still thin face with its near translucent skin. "But so pale still, poor ghost!"

Theda smiled, but pushed his hand away. "I am always so. And I had thought you had decided I was a witch."

His lips twisted wryly. "If so, you are come aptly to roost. In this establishment, the broomsticks are out in force!"

She gave that infectious gurgle of laughter, and his eyes warmed. Theda found herself looking into them and became aware of a tiny flutter of the heart. She stiffened, drawing back. None of that! She turned towards the corridor.

"I had better take you in to her ladyship, Mr Beckenham."

"Oh, not so formal," he begged, his hand staying her as he grasped her arm.

She met his eyes again and the full charm of his smile was turned upon her. Abruptly she recalled Araminta's words. "No doubt he'll beguile you, too." The picture flashed into her mind of the coffee-room at the Feathers inn at Newark. The smile had come out for the landlord, and disappeared when he had left the room. Again, separately, for Mrs Pigdon. Oh, yes, he had the power all right. But *she* was not to be beguiled. Not Theodosia Kyte. Reserve entered her voice.

"I think it would be best if we remained on formal terms."

"Why?" he asked unexpectedly. "When we are already friends?"

"Because..." Nonplussed for a moment, she hesitated. But the solution was obvious. "Because it would be inappropriate to my position here, and I have no need of further excuses to call down Miss Merchiston's reproaches upon my head."

He nodded, releasing her arm, but Theda thought there was a shade of disappointment in his face.

"Well, I've no wish to do that. I don't doubt your life is sufficiently trying already."

Theda continued along the gallery, towards Lady Merchiston's room, feeling ridiculously guilty, as if she had been ungracious. She did owe him something, after all. But he was dangerously attractive. She could not afford to allow her guard to slip.

There was no doubt of her employer's beguilement, she thought, as Lady Merchiston set eyes on the visitor coming into her room behind Miss Kyte.

"Benedict! My dear boy, what a lovely surprise!"

Hector, waking abruptly, looked up and set up a joyous barking, leaping to his feet and wagging a curly tail.

The gentleman's face lit as his smile came out and he went towards the bed with the intention of grasping the veined hands held out towards him. But he had first to respond to the overtures of the dog.

"Well, sir? No, don't lick my face! Down, Hector. Quiet, boy!"

This last was uttered so sharply that the dog at once lay down, uttering a whimper as he rested his head on his paws, dark eyes longingly fixed on the newcomer.

"No need to snap at him!" protested his godmother crossly.

The smile turned on and he took hold of her hands. "Your pardon, Aunt Lavvy, but he was stopping me getting to my favourite lady. How well you look!" he declared, saluting each of her hands in turn with his lips and then leaning down to kiss her cheek.

"I may look it, but my condition remains unchanged," the old lady told him frostily, but her bony fingers clung to his.

Mr Beckenham looked about the altered room, and seemed to take in the improvements in one swift glance. "On the contrary, your condition appears to me to be markedly different." He let go her hands, and made up for his earlier error by making a fuss of the dog, who was sitting on his own blanket, adding laughingly, "Even Hector is obliged to take notice of it, I see."

"That is all Theodosia," Lady Merchiston said in

a complaining tone, glancing at her companion. "She is a stickler for the tiniest mote of dust. You have no idea how she fidgets me with her never-ending spit and polish."

"Fudge!" said Theda. "It is you who fidgets *me*, Lady Lavinia, with all your carping and criticism."

Mr Beckenham left off patting the dog and looked quickly round at her, a frown creasing his brow. How could she dare to address her employer in such terms?

"Carping and criticism!" echoed the old lady. "Why, I am perfectly saintly about it, as well you know!"

Theda threw her a quizzing glance. "A trifle premature, ma'am, that adjective. But be sure I shall write to the Archbishop of Canterbury on your behalf when the time comes."

Lady Merchiston let out a cackling guffaw, and then noticed her godson's glance going from one to the other, his face a study. She leaned forward and tapped his hand where it lay on the coverlet, supporting his weight.

"Pay no mind to us, Benedict! Theodosia and I understand each other very well."

"So it would seem," he agreed, sending another frowning glance Theda's way.

She met it with a puzzled look in her eyes. Did he have some objection to such bantering? Could he not see how much good it was doing his godmother? As his eyes went back to the old lady, she saw the smile turn on again, and quick suspicion kindled in her breast.

Had Araminta been right in that brief exchange she

had overheard in the breakfast parlour? Was Benedict Beckenham out to "play off his airs" on Lady Merchiston for some purpose of his own? But for what? Surely there could be no gain to him from the old lady's death? It was not as if Merchiston Lodge and its inhabitants were possessed of any intrinsic value. Were they?

Giving herself a mental shake, she threw off the thoughts. It was no concern of hers, in any event. And if he was engaged on some scheme of his own, she had better leave him to pursue it without interference. She owed him that much at least.

"I shall leave you to enjoy your godson's company, ma'am," she said lightly, moving to the door.

"Seizing the chance of a respite, you mean," retorted Lady Merchiston.

"Naturally. Perhaps we may even persuade him to take my place at the chess-board."

"Certainly not," Mr Beckenham protested. "I am perfectly inept at the game and you always beat me to flinders, Aunt Lavvy, as expert as you are."

"There you are, Theodosia!" cackled his godmother. "He thinks I'm expert."

Theda was conscious of a feeling of sad disillusionment. There could be no doubt that the gentleman was out to flatter Lady Merchiston, for no one who had played with her could fail to notice that she cheated. What was more, the old lady *knew* what he was at, for the look she shot her companion had been brimful of mischief.

"In any event," went on her employer, black eyes

teasing, "you are not getting shot of your duties so readily. You may take Hector out for his run now."

"As you wish, ma'am," Theda said equably, and called to the dog from the open doorway. "Come along, boy! You're coming out with me."

Hector stood undecided for a moment, his eyes travelling from Theda's outstretched hand back to the gentleman who was obviously a favourite with him.

"Go on, Hector!" ordered Mr Beckenham, clicking his fingers and pointing to the door.

"Yes, go, you misbegotten hound!" added Lady Merchiston in the caressing tone she reserved only for her pet.

Thus adjured, Hector jumped off the bed with a short bark and trotted out of the room. Theda shut the door behind them both, but not before she heard Mr Beckenham begin to speak again.

"And now, dear Aunt Lavvy, I have you all to myself! Have you missed me?"

Disgust rose in Theda as she made her way along the gallery. At her lowest ebb, she would have scorned to stoop to such tactics. Her opinion of Benedict Beckenham dropped sharply. Why she should be surprised, however, she had no notion. She had witnessed the on-off charm for herself when he had thought himself alone in the Feathers' coffee-room. Well, it was none of her affair, she reminded herself again. What was it to her if he chose to conduct himself with duplicity? But she could not help reflecting that Araminta, with all her faults, was at least honest in her dealings with her mother.

As she reached the bottom of the stairs, Araminta

herself waylaid her, coming out of the shadows to place herself in the companion's way.

"You have left him with her, I collect? No doubt he is oozing and oiling his way into her favour. Much good may it do him!"

Hector had run ahead to hover by the front door, whining a little. But Theda hesitated, burningly curious suddenly. "Why should he do so?"

"Why? To get out of her more than his allowance, of course. He was run off his legs the last time and he had only just been paid for the quarter."

Theda's jaw dropped perceptibly. "An allowance! Lord, how can Lady Merchiston afford it?"

A thin smile creased the woman's pinched mouth. "Simpleton! You should not judge by appearances." Then she seemed to recollect to whom she was speaking and drew herself up. "Get on, girl—if, as I must suppose, you are taking that brute out for exercise."

Theda turned to go, but suddenly Araminta seized her arm in a claw-like grip and came close, almost spitting into Theda's face.

"Don't you leave him there too long, understand? Oh, he'll have his way, I don't doubt, worming it out of her. But he wants *more* than a few measly hundred—and I aim to see he does not get it!"

The grip left Theda's arm then, and Araminta hurried away down the hall, back to her eyrie. Hector whined his impatience, bringing Theda back to herself with a start. Lord above! What plague was there on this house?

She shivered as she went to the door, but all at once she recalled what she had been about to do when

Benedict Beckenham had made his astonishing appearance. She put a hand on Hector's woolly black head.

"Wait, Hector. Stay!"

It took only a few minutes to run to the kitchen and request Agnes Diggory to take Lady Merchiston's luncheon tray straight upstairs when it was ready, and then Theda passed out of the house into the early warmth of a sunny April day, Hector charging ahead.

Calling out to him, she turned to the right, making for the side of the house furthest from Switham Thicket, for she had not forgotten a previous occasion when he had dashed off into the belt of trees. She had never so much resented having been made to take over responsibility for the dog from old Adam, who had been used to walk him, than on that day. Chasing him, she had rapidly lost her bearings in the heavy forest terrain and only by accident had come out again behind the house into the vegetable garden. Although the stark trees were just beginning to be in leaf, and familiarity had lessened the menacing air of the place, Theda still found herself uncomfortable within it.

The house itself no longer held so much terror for her. She had found an opportunity to creep into the large saloon at the front downstairs, where in the gloom created by the velvet curtains drawn across the windows she had seen that the large and ugly old-fashioned Queen Anne furniture was shrouded in sheets. But in the massive ballroom across the way there were only a few chairs and a sideboard or two, and even on a dismal day the light had fallen on the intricate design of a wooden parquet floor and pretty chiaroscuro frescoes painted into the panels of gracefully arched walls.

In fact, Theda thought it a beautiful old building, and felt it to be a pity that it should have been allowed to go to rack. This she had thought until this moment to be due to a shortage of funds. Now, for the first time, here was Araminta hinting that this was not the case.

For the lord's sake, then, why did they not put in some repairs? And why be so penny-pinching in the matter of service, leaving poor Agnes and Adam Diggory overburdened with their load? It could not always have been thus. Was it perhaps since Sir John Merchiston's death that things had been allowed to slide to this pass?

With frequent admonishments to Hector—who not unnaturally found enormous pleasure in exploring the overgrown gardens—to keep close, she strolled to the back of the house where a huge stable block stood almost empty. In front of it was the kitchen garden, which was the only part of the grounds to be kept in order, for Adam Diggory, although he grumbled at the necessity, was obliged to tend it as it provided most of the vegetable produce for the household table.

There had at one time, Agnes had told her, been a full complement of horses and hounds, for Sir John had been a keen sportsman. Few men living in Leicester were not, Theda reflected, for in her former life she had learned early that this was the best hunting country in England.

It crossed her mind fleetingly that perhaps this was

the attraction for Benedict Beckenham. Did he want the house?

A footfall behind her made her turn, and she gasped to see the gentleman himself walking up to her. He was smiling, but the smile did not quite reach his eyes. Theda's heart began to beat rather fast, and she was conscious of a feeling of trepidation.

"So there you are!" he called in a friendly tone.

It sounded brittle, Theda thought. Unlike the way he had spoken to her earlier, or the previous time they had met. Was he wearing a mask?

"I have wasted a good many minutes hunting about the front."

"Does Lady Merchiston want me?" Theda asked quickly.

"No, I left her to her luncheon. It is I who want you."

He smiled again, but Theda could not respond to an overture she felt to be false. She eyed him with misgiving.

"Why do you look at me so?" he demanded, a frown descending on to his brow.

She shrugged and looked away, over to where Hector was investigating a hole in the base of the stable wall, not having noticed the new arrival.

Mr Beckenham seized her shoulders. "Look at me, confound you!"

She did, and the sudden flare of her eyes made him let her go. He stared at her in some perplexity.

"Have I incurred your displeasure, Miss Kyte?"

"No, how should you?" she said in a light tone at variance with the sudden trembling of her fingers.

"I don't know how," he said slowly, "but something has changed in your manner to me."

Theda bit her lip. "I might say the same."

"*Touché.*" He flung up a hand and a smile of genuine warmth lit his eyes. "Very well, let us be frank. My godmother has been singing your praises, you see, and—you will have to forgive my suspicious mind!—it set me wondering."

Theda's frown deepened. She felt a surge of anger. "You are suspicious of me? For what reason, pray? What is it that you 'wonder'?"

He was not noticeably discomfited by her tone. His eyes scanned her face, as if he sought there an answer to the problem perplexing his mind.

"I wonder *why* you have been so good to Aunt Lavvy. I can see for myself how much you have done, and how her spirits have improved. Yet when I first came, you tried to make me think your position here was untenable. It seems to me it cannot be as bad as you made out, if you are so well able to fascinate the old lady into thinking you indispensable to her comfort!"

Theda listened to this speech in rising indignation. Did he *dare* to impute such motives to her as he clearly had himself? What in the world had *she* to gain? In a low tone, husky with distress, she responded.

"Mr Beckenham, since I am in some sort indebted to you, I will, if you please, refrain from making you any answer, for I cannot take it upon myself to do so without speaking to you in a manner which must sound both insolent and ungrateful!"

She turned from him on the words and was aware that her tone had risen at the last. His voice followed her.

"Theodosia, wait!"

She kept on, and he was obliged to quicken his pace to catch up.

"Wait!" he repeated urgently, and, coming in front of her, grasped her arms, forcibly stopping her progress. Her smouldering eyes met the apology in his. "I have only to beg your pardon, Miss Kyte, and confess that I entirely misread the situation. Forgive me!"

Theda eyed him uncertainly, some of the fire dying out of her face. But she was still indignant, and she could not help the protest from leaving her lips.

"What could I have to gain, other than making the best of a bad bargain?"

"I know, I know," he said soothingly.

"If I have a motive," she pursued, her belligerence lessening, "it is no different from that which led you to aid me when first we met. The poor woman was left in the wretchedest discomfort. If I feel compassion for her, it is not to be wondered at." She found that tears were trickling from her eyes, and dashed them away with an impatient hand. "I have only done what lay within my power to better her lot. And if it is the manner in which I address her which concerns you, let me tell you that she derives great enjoyment from such acerbic exchanges. It brightens her mood."

"Yes," he agreed quietly. "I have frequently observed how she takes pleasure in goading Araminta into the worst of tempers."

"Yes, but those quarrels upset her, too. With me it is merely a game."

She sniffed and discovered that Mr Beckenham was offering her a pocket handkerchief. She shook her head, retrieving her own from the pocket in her petticoats.

"I don't seem to remember that the name you once gave me was 'Theodosia'," he remarked as she dried her eyes. "Though I'm afraid it slipped my memory almost immediately."

"No, it was Theda," she told him, replacing the handkerchief. A faint smile flickered over her lips. "It was the pet name for me that was favoured at home."

Mr Beckenham frowned down at her. "You have not been 'home' for some little time, I gather. I do now recall you saying no one had used the name in years."

"Six, to be exact," Theda said flatly.

"You must be older than you look."

"I am almost four-and-twenty."

"Dear God! Don't tell me you left your home at seventeen?"

Theda was silent. She looked at him with an air of apology. "I am afraid I cannot say any more. I should not have said so much. I know it must appear churlish when I am under such an obligation to you—"

"Oh, the devil!" he snapped suddenly. "Must you keep on throwing that up at me? For my part, there is *no* obligation. You owe me nothing."

"But I do."

"Oh, be quiet, girl! I don't want to hear another word on the subject."

She said no more, although she could not herself treat the matter so lightly. Turning, she began to retrace her path towards the house. He fell into step beside her, and presently spoke again, his tone more normal.

"I am glad, at any rate, that you do not find your position here as irksome as I had supposed."

Theda glanced up at him with an amused look. "You are easily brought to reverse your views, are you not, Mr Beckenham?"

"What do you mean?" he asked, slightly irritated.

"I came here to be employed as a companion," she told him. "Instead I find myself acting also in the capacity of lady's maid and sick-nurse, for neither of which occupations have I the least experience. Your godmother is *bedridden*, Mr Beckenham. Have you any idea what that entails?"

She saw by his face that he had not, and grimaced as she thought of the gruesome tasks she was obliged to perform, degrading both for herself and for her far from easy patient. She opened her mouth again and he quickly held up a hand.

"No, don't tell me! My imagination is of an order lively enough to appreciate the invidious nature of your position without a recital of the sordid details."

"I will spare you, then," Theda said, with an irrepressible gurgle of mirth. "I will remind you only that, added to all this, my employer is not likely to live very long, and I am therefore already at the necessity of seeking another post. Not, I may say, that almost *any* other post would not be preferable to this one!"

"I am sure it would," he agreed, with a sympathetic twist of the lips.

"Well, then, I don't need to elaborate on the miserable atmosphere of this place, where everyone is at outs, and I must be always on my guard. For when one is dealing with such volatile temperaments, the slightest thing may result in my instant dismissal. Which, Mr Beckenham, I shudder to think on!"

"I wish you will address me by name!" he said in some annoyance. "We are alone just for the moment."

"No. If I do it in private, I may easily fall into the way of doing so in public. You must realise that Miss Merchiston loses no opportunity that offers of scolding me."

"Of course she does," scoffingly answered Mr Beckenham. "Quite apart from the fact that she is regularly ill-tempered, she must be vilely jealous of you."

"Jealous? But why?"

"My good girl, don't be a fool! You have made such a hit with Aunt Lavvy that it was inevitable she should be."

Theda stopped still suddenly and faced him. "Why does she hate her mother so much? I have never seen such bitterness!"

He threw up his eyes. "Need you ask? She was thwarted in her youth in her choice of husband. I don't recall it very well, for it happened before I came, and I was too young to be much interested, in any event."

"You grew up here, then?"

"In this unloving family, yes. It deteriorated very much on Uncle John's death, but by then I had long left to live elsewhere. Once Aunt Lavvy became bed-ridden, Araminta had everything very much as she chose."

Theda looked curiously at him. He had spoken in a flat, matter-of-fact way, as if all this meant nothing to him.

"Could you not have intervened?" she ventured.

He shrugged. "I have no influence with Araminta. Besides, unless I chose to remain here, how could I see that things went on well? I have no claims upon the place, nor on Aunt Lavvy, you know."

"But are you not related?" Theda asked, puzzled. "And your aunt *is* your godmother."

"She is not my aunt. I call her so only as a courtesy." He looked at her. "As you do with your 'Lady Lavinia'. She is not entitled to that, you know."

"I know. It was agreed between us as the most suitable form of address."

He smiled. "You mean *you* decided it."

"Well, yes," she admitted, on a slight laugh. "After I had been criticised for employing 'Lady Merchiston' and 'your ladyship', I finally found that compromise which she accepted. But you call cousins with Araminta, do you not?"

"Remote cousins only. Her father and my mother were distantly related—second or third cousins, I dare say. So, you see, I really have no rights here. *Most* of what Aunt Lavvy does for me, she does from choice—over and above my allowance, that is, which is held in trust.'' His voice hardened. ''And she may easily choose *not* to continue to do it. Make no mistake! Araminta's selfishness and her spiteful, peevish nature are inherited.''

Chapter Four

Startled, Theda could only gaze at him. There was something in his voice that made her believe he was not speaking from malice himself. There was hurt behind the harsh words. What had Lavinia, Lady Merchiston done to make him speak so?

Could she have treated him to similar displays of ill will as she showed her daughter? But why? Surely Benedict had done nothing to attract her malice. Well, whatever else, this household was certainly intriguing!

As one, they turned to continue on around the side of the house, Hector racing along before them.

"A pity, perhaps, that Araminta was not permitted to marry," Theda remarked. "There is no doubt that they rub against each other. Why was he so ineligible?"

"Quatt? He was an apothecary in the village."

"Oh," said Theda blankly.

"Quite. One could scarcely blame her parents for disliking the connection."

"What happened to him?"

Mr Beckenham grinned suddenly. "The popular story is that he was so heartbroken he ran off to join a religious order, and has since been ordained."

Theda had to laugh. "How romantic! And poor Araminta. It is no pleasant thing to be crossed in love."

He looked interested and would have spoken further. But as they came around the corner to the front of the house, they heard a familiar reedy voice hail them and, turning, found themselves confronted by Miss Merchiston herself, her pale eyes going from one to the other with the air of one who had known how it would be.

"You're wanted, Miss Kyte," she said testily, "and I don't see why I should have to run around after you. Why can't you keep within earshot?" She gave Mr Beckenham a nasty glare. "Or had you other matters on your mind?"

"It happens, Araminta, that Miss Kyte was in the act of answering the summons," her cousin lied calmly, "for I had myself come to find her at Aunt Lavvy's request."

"What took you so long, then?" demanded Araminta snappily, looking daggers at Theda.

"I beg your pardon, Miss Merchiston," Theda began in the subservient tone of un underling, for there was no point in drawing Araminta's fire.

"I kept her," Mr Beckenham interrupted in a hard voice. "We were talking of your mother's health."

"Pah! Much you care," Araminta said rudely. "You want her dead even more than I!"

"Oh, it's clear enough what *you* want," he responded angrily.

Theda slipped quietly into the house, leaving them to their quarrel. Hector, who had been gambolling about the porch, slunk in behind her, depressed by the angry voices. Theda found Lady Merchiston in buoyant mood, very full of ''Benedict''.

''Such a loving boy to *his* mother, he was. So unlike that evil, back-biting bitch. I wish he had been my son.''

But he does not wish so, Theda thought silently. Except it might give him security. Loving, indeed! What he had said of her had hardly been the words of love. The old lady was in raptures over him, however. But she was shrewder than Theda had supposed, as she was brought to realise next day.

Mr Beckenham remained only the one night at Merchiston Lodge, sleeping in the room next to Araminta's, which had been made ready for him. He spent most of his time with his godmother, which left Theda free to do some long-neglected tasks for herself, for her meagre wardrobe of old—and some cast-off—clothing required frequent mending, and, there being so little service, she must wash her linen herself. Theda did not see much of the gentleman, for he ate with Araminta in the breakfast parlour, while Theda always had her meals in Mrs Diggory's little pantry.

But the next morning, when Theda was on her way to her employer's room, she heard Mr Beckenham's voice within it, and hesitated.

''Be sure I shall remember it, dearest Aunt.''

''Don't bother!'' came the almost snappy response. ''There's no use in storing it up. You can't repay a dying woman. Just take care you don't gamble it all away in one sitting."

"I won't, never fear."

"So you say. But I know you, boy. Can't keep away from the tables, can you?"

There was a tiny pause. Then Mr Beckenham said mildly, "I'm not really a hardened gamester, you know, Godmama. If I had the wherewithal to live in comfort, I wouldn't fritter it away. I do it only to augment my income."

"Not very successful, then, are you?" came the acid response. "Oh, get along with you! I've no patience. I'll find a way to make you run in harness, see if I don't!"

"Goodbye, ma'am. Keep well."

There was a cackle from the old lady. "Ain't me you want to kiss. Think I'm blind?"

"Of course I want to kiss you...there. Be good, old fellow!"

There was a whiffle from Hector, and next instant the gentleman's footsteps came swiftly to the door and Theda moved quickly away.

Mr Beckenham came out of the room, an expression of deep discontent on his features. He saw Theda and stopped short. Wrath entered his eyes and he hastily shut the door.

"Eavesdropping, Miss Kyte?" he demanded in an undervoice.

"I was waiting to come in," Theda protested.

He grabbed her arm, hustling her down the gallery as he spoke. "Then you should either have knocked or gone away. I trust you were sufficiently entertained!"

"Let me go!" she said in a fierce whisper. "If Araminta were to see us...!"

He pulled her down the small corridor that led to the steps to the attics. "She will not see us here. Now, then, what do you mean by it?"

"I meant *nothing,*" Theda told him urgently. "What does it matter what I heard? I know you are dependent on your godmother."

"And now you know how she despises me!"

"Fudge! She dotes on you."

"Oh, yes? Besotted, is she? If she were, confound it, she'd treat me less shabbily!"

Theda's eyes narrowed. "I thought you told me she owes you nothing."

"She does not," he said, adding savagely, "but she might *care* for me a little!"

There was a brief silence. The corridor was dim and Theda could not see his face clearly. She felt unexpectedly touched by the pain she detected beneath the hot words.

"One cannot *buy* affection," she said softly, "any more than one can bargain with fate."

His head turned, and although she could only just see the shadow of his eyes she knew he was looking at her. All of a sudden she was aware of an intensity in the atmosphere, as if the air between them itself became charged.

"Why can one not, Theda?" he murmured. "Is fate so strong? Is affection so scarce?"

Theda felt his fingers on her cheek. Her skin

seemed to burn at their touch. Into her brain came the certainty that he was going to kiss her, and she was powerless to stop him.

"Benedict, don't...please," she whispered.

But that fatal use of his name finished it. She heard the sharp intake of his breath, and then his lips found hers in the darkness and the fire was lit.

They stood together, barely touching. But the searing contact mouth to mouth set them both trembling. Almost at the same instant, they sprang apart, ragged in breath, staring, each at each, dim faces in the gloom.

Benedict's hoarse whisper shattered the strange enchantment of it. "Dear God in heaven, you *are* a witch!"

Then he was striding away from her, his boots echoing on the wooden boards as he made for the stairs.

For a moment Theda stood motionless, watching Benedict go. Then she turned and flew on winged feet up the narrow stair to take refuge in her garret room.

Was she mad? Was *he?* What devil had possessed them both?

She pressed a hand to her bosom to try to still the wild fluttering of her heart. Her breath was short, her lips burning hot from the touch of his. One trembling finger traced them, as if in disbelief she sought the source of that blistering torch that had fired her through and through.

So light a caress to do so much! Never had Theda experienced such a sensation. Yet she had been kissed—and more! Even at seventeen, which up to now had been the high point of her existence, the passions raised had not one tithe of the sizzling fire that had been generated by Benedict. There had been others—furtive fumblings, *not* by her design or wish, in corridors such as that. Certain men—husbands not excepted—seemed drawn like a magnet to a female in her circumstances. They must always *try*. But not one of them had made her feel as if a candle had been set to kindling within her.

A thought crept unbidden to her mind, causing a rush of liquid heat to course through her. Benedict had felt it, too! That was why he had called her a witch. Lord in heaven, what had come between them all at once? And why *now?* There had been nothing at all before. No, not even when his fingers touched her, as they had already, several times, just prior to the kiss. It had been his lips—*her* lips for him—that had sparked the sudden flame.

Her hands came up to press against her cheeks and she closed her eyes. This was *unendurable.* How could she remain here, see him again, and not die of shame at the memory? And if he *touched* her, what then? Would she erupt as she had just now?

An even worse thought came sweeping in, blotting out the first. What must he now think? Would he not read it that he might with impunity pursue her to her ruin?

Could it be worse than her present situation? whispered a treacherous small voice.

She rose abruptly from the bed. Yes. A good deal worse. She had not sunk so low as to join the ranks of *that* sisterhood! She might have renounced her family, but she had still her share of pride—in her lineage, in the family name. She would *not* disgrace it more than she had already. Certainly not for a wasteful spendthrift, who preyed upon a gullible old woman! *No,* Benedict Beckenham. You will *not* beguile me.

Full of determination, she went down to her employer, only to have her fierce resolution instantly undermined.

"Why did you not tell me how you were placed?" demanded Lady Merchiston the moment she walked through the door.

"I beg your pardon, ma'am?" Theda said, quite at a loss.

"Benedict told me you are housed in the attics, like a common servant."

Theda's jaw dropped perceptibly, and she was conscious of a sliver of tender warmth slipping into her heart. "How did he know?"

"Taggy told him. Why he asked her about it I couldn't tell you. Araminta's work, I collect?"

"Miss Araminta regards me as a servant, ma'am," Theda said, faintly smiling, and reaching a hand out to stroke Hector's woolly head where he lay on his blanket, as if to find some outlet for the feelings of gentleness running through her.

"Well, I won't have it!" snapped the old lady. "Perfectly good dressing-room next door. My maid used to have it. You'll move in there today."

"If it is anything like this room used to be, Lady Lavinia," Theda said wryly, "I fear that would be impossible."

"Don't quibble, girl! Set it to rights as you see fit,

and use it. *My* orders, and so you may tell Araminta if she makes any objection. Until I'm safe in my grave—where I long to be, let me tell you!—I am still mistress here."

"Naturally, Lady Lavinia." She moved away a little, patting her petticoats and looking at the dog. "Come along, Hector. Time for your walk."

Hector jumped off the bed eagerly, and gambolled around her. But she threw an impish look at her employer. "I may say I am surprised to hear you express a desire to be in your grave quite yet. I am certain you have still things to settle."

The keen eyes narrowed suspiciously, and something very like a glare marred the erstwhile good humour of Lady Merchiston's taut-stretched features.

"What are you at? Been poking and prying into what don't concern you, eh?"

Theda bit her lip. That was rash! She shrugged slightly. "I beg your pardon, ma'am. I—I cannot help but have become aware of the—the dissension at present raging between your…dependents."

"Oh, you have, have you?" repeated the old lady dangerously. "I'll thank you to mind your business, and keep your nose out of mine!"

Folding her lips closely together, Theda dropped a curtsy and prepared to leave the room. After an uncertain glance at his mistress, Hector slunk after her. A cracked shout arrested them both.

"Come back, Theodosia!"

The dog scratched at the door, but Theda turned and looked at her. The crêpey skin of her old cheeks was flying two spots of colour. The black eyes were alight with some emotion that Theda could not fathom.

"Come here to me!" she ordered gruffly.

With some reluctance, Theda warily approached the bed. The bony fingers reached out and grasped her petticoats.

"Sit! Sit down."

Hector, apparently under some confusion of ideas, raced to the bed and leapt up on it. His mistress automatically stayed him, grasping the scruff of his neck, her eyes, their excitement mounting, fixed on Theda as she did as she was bid. She lowered her voice confidentially.

"Now, then. Which of them shall I favour, eh? Who shall benefit?"

Theda's startled eyes met hers. "Lord, ma'am how should I know? It is not for me to say."

"I know that, I know that," muttered the old lady testily. "But you could *advise* me, at least."

"Lady Lavinia," Theda said firmly, "even were I to give you my advice, which must necessarily be based on very little knowledge, I cannot for a moment imagine that you would take it."

A crack of laughter left Lady Merchiston's lips. "Think I'm more likely to run counter, do you?"

"Yes," Theda said frankly.

"More than probable. Still, I want you to tell me what you think."

Theda sighed in an exasperated way. "Very well, then. For what it is worth, ma'am, I would recommend an equal division of whatever it is you have to leave."

Her ladyship nodded, eyes glowing in triumph. "Thought you'd say that." She reached out and seized hold of Theda's hand, gripping it strongly. "You're a good girl, Theodosia. How'd you come to this pass, my child?"

Theda looked away, although her fingers returned the pressure. "Excuse me on that head, if you please, Lady Lavinia. I would not tell you, even were you to dismiss me for it."

The bony fingers increased their pressure, crushing hers painfully with surprising strength. Theda gasped, glancing down at her hurting hand and back up to find a malevolent twist in the old lady's wasted features.

"*Insolent,*" she hissed furiously. "I should have you whipped!"

Theda's deep grey eyes grew dark with distress as she gazed into the vicious blackness of Lady Merchiston's own. Benedict's face flashed across her mind as she recalled his words. Yes, she thought wildly, this is surely the source of Araminta's inherited spite.

Then in an instant the look was gone, the painful grip relaxed, and Lady Merchiston was cackling with mirth.

"Very wise, Theodosia. You keep your own counsel, and I'll keep mine. But if either of them imagines they can force my hand, they much mistake the matter! Now go. Hector needs his exercise."

She waved a dismissive hand and Theda rose from the bed with alacrity. She was only too anxious to get out of this room now that her employer had "shown her true colours'' as Araminta had promised she would. Hector, as eager as she for the only brief release he was allowed from confinement in the bedchamber, trotted at her heels, obedient to her call.

But Lady Merchiston called out after her, very much in her usual manner, as if nothing untoward had transpired. ''Fix up that room. I want you within call. Who knows when I may need you? I am weaker by the day!''

No one would credit it! thought Theda with an inward shudder as she went away. Later, as, with Agnes Diggory's aid, she set about putting the dressing-room to rights, a new determination began to burgeon in her breast. She would begin at once to look for another post. Let her be beforehand with the world, if she could! The thought of returning to another sparse lodging in a back-street of London, to the endless trudging back and forth to the Register Office, to the days of scant food and less warmth, filled her with dread. She had already begun, surreptitiously so as not to excite Araminta's suspicions, to scan the advertisement columns of the *Morning Post.* It was time now to begin to write letters.

Not that she dared to hope for a reference from this place! Therein lay her difficulty. If only she knew someone, even of small influence, who might put her in the way of finding something more congenial—and in a genteel home. The thought of returning to the merchant world, even after this unhappy experience, was less than welcome.

May came, and with it the return to the neighbourhood of the surrounding gentry at the close of the

London season.

Mrs Rosalia Alderley, of Switham House, was the great lady of the village. She had been, before her second marriage a few years ago to Mr Alderley, Baroness to Lord Switham, who owned all the land round about, with the exception of Merchiston Lodge and other hunting boxes in the vicinity belonging to various members of the *haut ton.* Her son, Lord Switham, was still a boy, but the two Misses Switham were of marriageable age, and their mother had cleverly secured a good match for the elder in her very first season. She was, consequently, full of wedding plans when she came, as was her wont—for she considered it an inescapable part of her parish duties—to visit Lavinia Merchiston.

"Not that I am looking forward to parting with Serena, of course," she said mournfully. "In some ways I feel you are so lucky, Lavinia, to have kept Araminta by you all these years."

"Don't sham it so, Rose!" snapped the old lady. "You know perfectly well that the girl has been anything but a comfort to me."

Mrs Alderley sighed. "Such a pity she took to that unfortunate boy Saul Quatt, instead of that good-looking young officer that was quartered here that year."

"I wouldn't have let her marry him if she had!" declared Lady Merchiston. "A half-pay lieutenant, with no family connections, and nothing to recommend him but his pretty face? As well have handed her to Benedict!"

"Oh, come, Lavinia!" protested the visitor. "Benedict's *birth* is the best of any in the district."

"Much good may *that* do him, with the stigma of a scandalous divorce attached!"

"Well, that is not his blame."

"No, but he has to wear it nevertheless."

Mrs Alderley hesitated. She had a soft spot for Benedict, and his mother had been her friend. If a word from her might help him, she was not the woman to withhold it.

"You *could* make it easier for him to bear, Lavinia," she suggested tentatively.

The dark eyes fired up in an instant. "Yes, I could. *He* thinks I will."

"You've let him think it," Mrs Alderley said repressively. "If you did not mean it so—"

"I've Araminta to think of, haven't I?" interrupted the old lady. She cackled, throwing a mischievous glance at her visitor. "Maybe I'll make it a condition that they *do* marry each other, the two of them. What a jest that would be!"

"Oh, *no!*" uttered Rose, horrified. "Good God, she is his senior by more than ten years for one thing. For another—"

"They loathe each other. Yes, I know. But what a fitting punishment for both!"

"*Lavinia,*" gasped Mrs Alderley. "That is a *wicked* thing to say."

"Ain't it, though?" agreed Lady Merchiston cheerfully.

Rose sighed, casting up her eyes. "I never know whether to take you at your word, Lavinia. You say the most shocking things. Benedict has done you no harm. And as for poor Araminta, what did she ever do but fall in love with the wrong man?''

The veined hands on the coverlet clenched suddenly. ''She *defied* me. As for Benedict...'' She broke off, turning her eyes back on Mrs Alderley. ''Well, never mind that. I tell you, Rose, there are times I wish Araminta *had* married Quatt, and welcome.''

An odd look came into Rose's face, and she glanced away, shifting uncomfortably in her chair.

Lady Merchiston's eyes narrowed. ''What is it, Rose? You look like a child caught with her fingers in the jam cupboard.''

Rose looked back at her, the picture of guilt.

''Out with it, woman! What's to do?''

''Well, if you must know,'' Rose burst out, ''it concerns Quatt.''

''Eh?''

Mrs Alderley drew a breath. ''You recollect the gossip that was rife at the time—that he had run away to a monastery?''

''Well, what of it?'' demanded Lady Merchiston, her eyes eager.

''It seems to be true. At least, he may have begun in a monastery, but in the event he took orders and was for years a junior pastor somewhere in Worcestershire. *Now,* however, he is returning home.''

''What?''

''Yes. To take up a vacant living in Mountsorrel.''

Lady Merchiston's eyes seemed in danger of popping out of her gaunt head. ''He is to be a *vicar?* Saul Quatt?''

"Yes," insisted Mrs Alderley. "That living is not in Switham's gift, you see, so there was nothing I could do about it." She hesitated, and then added, "There is worse, Lavinia."

"Go on!" ordered the other grimly.

"It seems he—he is a *widower.*"

For a moment Lady Merchiston stared. Then she burst into a paroxysm of croaking laughter, spluttering wildly, her emaciated limbs rolling about under the covers. Shrieks of mirth issued from her wide-open mouth, and flecks of foam appeared upon her lips.

Alarmed, Mrs Rosalia Alderley rose from her chair beside the bed, and fidgeted back and forth, not knowing what to do. Fortunately, the door burst open and Theda ran into the room, accompanied by Hector.

"What is amiss?" she said quickly, coming to the bed. Hector was before her, leaping up and barking at his mistress. "Lady Lavinia! What in the world...?"

Dragging at the dog, she got him off the bed, and looked up at the visitor, whom she did not know. "What happened?"

"She began to laugh at something I told her, and..." Rose looked helplessly down to where the old lady still flailed against her pillows, catching her breath on each series of cackles as they left her throat.

Sitting on the bed, Theda took her by the shoulders and dragged her to sit up. "Lady Lavinia! Pray stop this! *Stop,* I say!"

The black eyes rolled at her, and the wild laughter came to a hiccuping halt. Theda held her while she fought for breath, taking in great gasps of air. At last, her breathing still rasping a little, she was lowered gently against her pillows. Theda brought a glass of water from the bedside table to her lips and obliged her to drink. Then Lady Merchiston closed her eyes wearily.

"I'm all right," she uttered weakly. "I will do very well." She half gestured with her fingers. "Leave me now. Both of you. See to Rose, child."

Theda looked her over, and saw with satisfaction that she was sinking into slumber. Hector, who had been whining all the while, now crept back on to the bed and pushed his nose under the veined hand resting on the coverlet. It ran once over his head and stayed there.

Quietly, Theda led the shaken visitor from the room.

"I never dreamed she would take it like that," whispered Mrs Alderley in a shocked tone.

"Take what, ma'am?" asked Theda, leading her away down the gallery.

"The news about Quatt." She saw the puzzlement in the other's face, and suddenly recollected that she had no notion to whom she was speaking. "I beg your pardon, but who *are* you?"

"I am Theodosia Kyte, ma'am," Theda replied. "I am Lady Merchiston's companion."

"*Companion?* Good God, when did you come?"

"In March."

"Ah, that accounts for my knowing nothing about you. I have been in London since February." She smiled. "I am Mrs Alderley, you know."

"Oh, yes, I believe Mrs Diggory mentioned you," Theda said politely. "I'm sorry I was not here when you arrived. I was walking Hector—Lady Merchiston's dog, you know."

They were by this time descending the stairs, and Mrs Alderley looked about. Rather apprehensively, Theda thought. In a moment, Rose confirmed this in an anxious whisper.

"Araminta is not about, is she? I think it would be better if she does not meet me on this occasion."

"She did not show you up, then?"

"No, Taggy did that. I only hope she did not see my carriage!"

Theda smiled. "Well, I did not, and I must actually have been in the gardens. We could walk round to the stables, if you do not object to it—I can vouch for it that the grass is not wet—and then perhaps Miss Araminta will not hear as the horses will not come to the front door."

"Excellent," applauded Mrs Alderley, and amused Theda very much by tiptoeing across the hall to the front door, casting guilty glances over her shoulder as she went. Once outside, she breathed a sigh of relief, and strolled with Theda around the left of the house, next to Switham Thicket, so that Araminta would not see them from the window of her parlour.

"I have to thank you, Miss—er..."

"Kyte," Theda supplied again. "There is no need of thanks."

She looked at Mrs Alderley as she spoke, and realised that lady was covertly observing her. She was a handsome matron, with a good figure, and a strong face topped by still glossy brown hair, untouched by grey. Theda judged her to be in the late thirties, perhaps. She was very fashionably dressed, in a morning gown of the latest sprigged muslin, the waist high, with a blue spencer over it against the spring chills. Theda felt shabby by contrast, and was hit by a passing pang of envy. If she had not so foolishly thrown away her life, perhaps she, too, might have worn such a gown!

"Forgive me, Miss Kyte," said the other lady softly, "but you look quite downcast."

Theda straightened her shoulders and quickly looked away. "Not at all, I assure you."

"Will you think me extremely uncivil if I say that I don't believe you?"

Theda's eyes turned to her, a question in them. Mrs Alderley smiled warmly.

"It is obvious to me that you were not born to the position you now occupy." She threw up a hand, laughing as Theda's lips tightened. "Have no fear! I am not going to be vulgarly inquisitive. I was rather going to ask how you come to have accepted a post which must necessarily be curtailed before too long."

Theda shrugged. "I did not know the circumstances."

"You mean Araminta kept them from you," shrewdly guessed the lady.

"Oh, no, it was Lady Merchiston herself who wrote to me."

"Nonsense! You may be very certain Araminta arranged everything herself, probably in her mother's name. It was an idle threat on Lavinia's part to hire a companion at all. I knew that the first time she mentioned it. That is why I was so surprised to see you here."

In silence, Theda digested this for a moment. It was just what Lady Merchiston had said that very first night, but she had been so appalled that she had not taken it in. Araminta had wanted to escape what she regarded as an irksome duty. Yet, the original idea having come from her mother, she had been able to heap all the blame on her, even to accusing her of using up her inheritance, and continually complaining of the "pittance" that she must *herself* have laid down in the terms of the letter she had written, purporting to come from Lady Merchiston. All to goad her mother, to punish her.

"I see that you recognise the truth of what I say," remarked Mrs Alderley perspicaciously.

Theda's frown was turned upon her. "Are you very well acquainted with the family, ma'am?"

"Intimately. Oh, I only pay dutiful visits now," Rose went on, "but I was at one time very frequently here. I was on very good terms with Isabel Beckenham, you know, poor thing."

Blinking at her, Theda barely grasped the last little comment. "*Isabel* Beckenham?"

"Benedict's mother." Mrs Alderley sighed. "She died, poor soul. And I shall always believe that it was the scandal that killed her. That and...*other* things."

Theda's head was whirling. Scandal? Benedict's *mother?*

They had come within sight of the stables by this time, and Mrs Alderley's coachman, seeing his mistress approaching, made haste to open the door, calling to the groom who had accompanied them to re-harness the horses which had been released from the bit.

Rose Alderley held out her hand. ''Goodbye, Miss Kyte. I hope we shall meet again.''

''I hope so, too!'' uttered Theda fervently, and then realised how this must sound. The woman would think she was avid for more of the background of Benedict Beckenham, which indeed she was, but it was scarcely polite to show it! ''I mean, I am sure we may, when you next come to see her ladyship.''

Mrs Alderley smiled, but made no comment. She got into the coach, the steps were folded up, and in a moment the horses were trotting around the house towards the main drive.

Theda stood looking after them for a moment, aware of her own burning curiosity. What a house of surprises and secrets was Merchiston Lodge!

Less than a week later, an opportunity to assuage her desire for knowledge presented itself. Not, she told herself, that she was at all interested in Benedict Beckenham, except in so far as he fitted into this household. But she could not help a resurgence of the queries raised in her mind at the hint of scandal in connection with his mother as she found herself in Mrs Alderley's coach, being driven to Switham House.

''Rose wants you,'' Lady Merchiston had told her succinctly. ''She needs help with the preparations for this wedding, so I said I'd lend you.''

At first, Theda did not know whether she was more

angry with Lady Merchiston for loaning her out like this, or with Mrs Rosalia Alderley for making such an impertinent request. What was she, a communal slave to be passed around at their pleasure? On the other hand, it was at least a change. She rarely came out of Merchiston Lodge, except to go to the village, and it was quite a pleasure, she discovered, to be driving *away* from it. As her fury drained, she felt a surge of uplift. She had not realised how low were her spirits!

When she came to Switham House, a much larger and better-kept establishment than Merchiston Lodge, she found Rosalia Alderley to have quite another motive.

"Oh, my dear, I don't need help at all," she declared, ushering Theda inside a spacious saloon, its windows, open to the fresh air, letting in a good deal of light. "But I had to have some excuse, you see. I could not simply invite you to visit me, situated as you are."

Theda gazed at her dumbly, horribly conscious of her drab, close-fitting gown of dark stuff, which was a hand-me-down from a previous employer. Its waist was in quite the wrong place about her midriff, instead of under the semi-exposed bosom where Rose Alderley's muslin petticoats began their graceful fall to the ground. Theda had followed in the *Gallery of Fashion*—which all her young charges had avidly studied—the steady rise of waists over the last three or four years, but never before had she felt quite so outdated. Her own bosom was strictly confined by the stays beneath her bodice, which was tightly hooked from her waist almost to her throat, with a neck-ruff concealing even the pale expanse between her collar bones. She must look worse than a dowd. She looked, she decided, just what she was—a servant.

"Don't look so dismayed," begged Mrs Alderley, taking Theda's hand and obliging her to sit on an elegant Sheraton sofa. "I just could not bear to see someone so young, and so obviously above those two cats, caught helplessly in that *bleak* place!"

Theda shifted puzzled shoulders. "Do you mean you—you have invited me here for...for *myself?*"

"Yes, my dear," smiled her hostess. "I mean exactly that."

Abruptly Theda rose. "But I cannot! Oh, ma'am, don't think me ungrateful, but you don't understand. It would be quite unseemly for me to meet anyone—to *socialise.* I am not any longer of your world!"

"Sit down again, pray," pleaded her hostess, reaching for her hand and pulling her back to the sofa. "No one will come in. My daughters are away visiting their grandmama, for I could not have them by, making a nuisance of themselves, during all these preparations. My son is at school, and my husband in his library. You are quite safe."

Theda relaxed a little, still biting her lip, however, her anxiety unquenched. "I beg your pardon if I seemed ungracious. I am uncomfortable in all this elegance. I confess I feel more at home at Merchiston Lodge!"

Mrs Alderley patted her hand. "I understand perfectly. You have grown unused to such comforts, I dare say." Vehemently, she added, "But that does not make it right! Good God, a companion is not a servant! I know any number of indigent dames who have found such employment, and they are treated quite as a member of the family.''

''I have never been so fortunate.'' Theda said in a low tone.

Mrs Alderley leaned towards her, saying gently, ''I guessed as much. That is why I sent for you, to be truthful. I might be able to help you.''

Theda's eyes lit with sudden hope and she turned eagerly towards her. ''Oh, *will* you? How kind you are! That is the very thing I had been wishing for—someone to recommend me. For I cannot hope for a reference from Lady Merchiston, and I am afraid that...''

She faltered to a stop, not wishing to appear callous.

''You are right to be afraid,'' Rose Alderley said bracingly. ''Poor Lavinia is certainly past hope, and whether she ends by giving the property to Araminta or Benedict you cannot possibly remain there.''

''No, indeed!'' Theda concurred feelingly.

''Then it is agreed. I shall look about my acquaintance. *Something* will come up. We have perhaps a little time. Dr Spilsby thinks she will last a few weeks yet.''

''I could wish it would be sooner! Oh, not that Lady Merchiston should go quickly, of course I don't mean that. But I would give much to get away from that house!''

Mrs Alderley nodded. ''It is an unhappy place. For

my part, I think Benedict would do better if she does *not* saddle him with it.''

Theda examined the striped wallpaper in the room with apparent interest. In a light tone, she suggested, ''He does appear to be wholly dependent on his godmother.''

''For the moment, yes.''

''What will he do, then, if she leaves him nothing?''

Mrs Alderley laughed. ''Go on as always, living by his wits and cards. Many men do so in society, you know. Or he may marry money. He is handsome enough to take in any silly young girl!''

Theda felt an odd tightness across her chest, and found herself disinclined, after all, to pursue the subject of Benedict. At her request, Rosalia took her on a tour of the house and grounds. When she was leaving, there was real gratitude in her farewell.

''You have given me a breath of fresh air, Mrs Alderley!''

''Call me Rose,'' smilingly requested the lady. ''And I won't forget my promise, Theodosia, don't fear.''

''You are very kind—Rose.'' She returned the smile warmly. ''My close friends call me Theda.''

It was in buoyant mood that she was driven back to Merchiston Lodge, and she entered her employer's bedchamber with a smile on her lips.

''There you are!'' ejaculated the old lady.

She was looking exhilarated herself, sitting up in bed with a welter of papers before her, her pen laboriously scratching over a sheet of parchment. Hector, for once restricted to the floor, gave a yelp of greeting and came to frolic about Theda's feet.

"You are come in excellent time, Theodosia!"

"Why, what is the matter, Lady Lavinia? You look to be in high gig."

"I am," cackled Lady Merchiston gleefully. "I've settled my affairs to my satisfaction at last."

"That is excellent. Have you had a luncheon?"

"Never mind luncheon! What do you say to this? I've sent for Saul Quatt."

Theda blinked at her. "I don't understand."

"You'll understand soon enough. *Quatt,* girl! He's Araminta's old lover. Don't tell me you've not heard of him! You must know everything by now. Rose tells me he's back and peacocking about as a vicar."

"Dear Lord!" uttered Theda startled. She remembered the name now. But she was even more astonished at her ladyship's next words.

"So I've decided to give him Araminta, after all. That'll take *her* off my hands."

"But—but..." Theda put a hand to her cheek, trying for some coherence.

"But what?"

"Well, supposing they don't choose any longer to marry one another? He may even be married already."

"No, he ain't. Had it from Rose he's a widower. And what if they don't want each other? He'll have her fast enough when he knows the sum of her portion."

"And she?" Theda could not help asking.

"She'll do as she's told, or lose the lot!"

Theda gazed at her speechlessly. Was she insane, that she imagined she could force people to bend to her will in this arbitrary fashion?

"No need to look like that, miss. I've got plans for you, too."

"*What* plans?" Theda demanded, involuntarily showing her instant indignation.

In a tone that brooked no argument, the old lady announced, "You'll marry Benedict, and make something of him!"

Chapter Five

"What?" Theda gasped.

"He can't expect to catch anything better," went on Lady Merchiston, "not with his history. I've decided you'll do."

"*You've* decided!" echoed Theda in a faint voice. "Have you taken leave of your senses?"

"Don't address me in that tone!" snapped her ladyship, eyes firing up. "You'll do as you're ordered, I tell you! And so will Benedict, if he knows what's good for him."

"And with what bribe is *he* to be persuaded?" flashed Theda. "This run-down rubbish heap of a house?"

"Hold your tongue!" commanded Lady Merchiston.

"Do you imagine you can compel my silence so easily after such an announcement?" demanded Theda furiously. "Dear lord in heaven! Am I in bondage, that you think to parcel me off as you see fit? Who do you think you are, Lady Merchiston? Even Royalty would not attempt such a thing! I will have no part in your paltry schemes, ma'am, and I utterly *forbid* you to mention my name again in connection with them."

Lady Merchiston was listening to the diatribe with her mouth at half-cock, but at this last she revived sharply, her skeletal head coming out of her gown as on a stalk.

"*You* forbid *me?* How *dare* you speak to me in so insolent a fashion?" she growled, almost choking with rage. "You have the temerity to refuse me, do you? You dare to *defy* me? Well, then, you may go without. And go *now.* Leave this house on the instant! Never return! You are dismissed, do you hear, you ungrateful slut. Dismissed without a character, what is more. Get out! *Out,* I say!"

Theda stood appalled, all her defiance collapsing as she realised the consequences she had brought down upon herself. Turning from the ugly sight of the old woman's contorted features, she fled the room, running incontinently down the gallery to the stairs, unaware that Hector, barking excitedly, ran out after her.

Below in the hall came running all the inmates of the house to gaze up at her, their faces stunned. Hector raced down the stairs and scurried about both Diggorys, who ignored him, their attention fully on the happenings that had taken place above.

"What is it?" asked Araminta in an unprecedentedly hushed tone. "What has occurred?"

"Your mother is out of her senses!" uttered Theda. She came running down the stairs. "She has dismissed me, Miss Araminta. Help me, I pray you! Speak to her!"

''Why should I?'' snapped the other woman.

''Because I tried to help you!'' Theda told her desperately. ''She has some scheme in mind to marry you off to this man Quatt.''

Unexpectedly, Araminta's pale eyes lit up. ''But that is famous!''

''And if you don't, you will lose your portion,'' Theda pursued. ''She has already taken the house from you.''

The thin, sallow features tightened and the eyes flared. ''So she wants to be rid of me! Well, she won't do it so easily, I promise you.''

''Miss Merchiston, she *has* got rid of me!''

''You!'' repeated Araminta scornfully. ''What do I care about you?''

''Have some pity!'' begged Theda, almost in tears. ''She means me to go without a character. And I have no money! What am I to do? Where can I go?''

''I don't care *what* you do, or where you go!'' snapped Araminta. ''Get out and stay out! For my part, I'm going to tell that old hag what I think of her!''

Then she was racing up the stairs. Theda watched her go, her mind blank with panic. She became aware that Mrs Diggory was at her side.

''Don't pay no mind, miss! Wait for it all to die down, do. I'm certain sure you'll be able to stay.''

Suddenly Theda could bear no more. ''But I don't *want* to stay!'' she cried, and, turning, she ran for the door, flinging it open and running through the arch of the long porch into the still sunny day.

Tears coursed down her cheeks and she ran blindly

down the wild jungle of the grounds parallel to the thicket. Furious barking about her flying feet penetrated the despair in her breast, and she looked down.

"Hector! Hector, what are you doing here?" she gasped, slowing to a halt.

But the dog, excited by the preceding events, jumped around her, barking frantically. Then, apparently deciding that this was a special day, he turned and made for the thicket.

"Hector, *no!*" she shrieked automatically.

But he ignored her, rushing away to disappear among the trees. Without hesitation, she set off in pursuit, unable to think beyond the fact that he would be lost, not even considering that if she was dismissed he was no longer her responsibility.

Through the undergrowth he led her, barking at every turn to encourage her progress. Headlong she ran, heedless of the branches that caught at her, tearing at her dark stuff gown, ripping away the white cap that covered her hair.

Of a sudden Hector set up an extraordinarily excited yapping. She could not see him but he was obviously close, and must have found something unusual to seize his interest. Theda pushed through the trees and found she was coming out into the road that ran through Switham Thicket.

A curricle was in sight, its bowling progress slowing as the driver recognised the dog that was bounding straight into its path.

"Hector, stop!" he called out, bringing his horses to a plunging standstill. "You bad dog! What are you doing there?"

Benedict. For a moment Theda stood transfixed, as everything that had passed, all Lady Merchiston's avowed plans for her and this man, came crashing in on her brain. Uttering a strangled sob, she turned back into the thicket.

She heard him call out and by the barks behind her knew that Hector followed. On she went, unable any longer to run, her chest heaving with effort, salt tears hot on her cheeks, the only thought in her mind that she must get away.

In her ears came the sound of staggering pursuit, added to the hysterical yapping of the over-excited terrier. She did not know that she gasped her sobs aloud. But as his hand grasped her arm, she recognised defeat, and, halting, she swung around.

Benedict cried out, "*Theda,*" and then fell silent, his eyes roving her, wonder in their depths.

For as she turned towards him, a great fall of bright copper hair, loosened by the wild chase, came cascading about her shoulders and fell to her waist, enveloping her in a rippling sheet of flame.

Theda opened her mouth to blister him out of the torment that consumed her...and paused, arrested by the look in his face.

She met the burning passion of his eyes, and time ceased. As one in a dream, unmoving, clogged with weighted air, she saw him shift. Above her, the sun cast dappling shadows through the waving branches, so that his handsome features seemed to flicker in her sight.

She saw his fingers come to her, dip into the fiery curtain of her hair. Slowly, so slowly, he brought up handfuls of the bright tresses, and they slid like silk through his fingers.

His face came down to her, passed by her own, and buried itself in the copper cloak. She heard a husky whisper in her ear.

"*Witch*...burning in your own flames...*take me with you.*"

Then his arms crushed her against him, and his mouth traced a path of heat across her cheek to find her lips. He struck. And time boiled back into being as the touch of his lips sent a shaft of fire down to sear her inside.

Her passion leapt to meet his, and she clung to him, her mouth dragging on his in a meeting so inflamed that she almost lost consciousness as dizziness swept through her brain. Then his face was in the hair at her throat as he sought the hollows, dragging aside the locks with urgent fingers.

"Theda...*Theda,*" he breathed hoarsely. "My witch—my ghost—*mine.* You're mine, do you hear?"

He was bearing her down, and her limbs began to give way beneath him. Then, at the edges of her consciousness, outside the explosive heat of the passage of his lips about her neck, of his fingers reaching into some recess of her costume to make her bare flesh tingle, she heard the faint echo of Hector's bark. With it came the sense of the words Benedict's tongue had scorched into her skin: "you're mine".

A whirling kaleidoscope of Lady Merchiston's shrieking face, Araminta's callous mouth and Agnes Diggory's sympathetic eyes hurtled through her mind, changing the flaming heat of passion to searing fury.

With strength born of the alarming change, Theda thrust the heaviness of Benedict's body from her and staggered out of reach.

"Leave me alone!" she screamed at the startled anger in his face. "How dare you touch me? How dare you lay claim to me, as if I am yours for the taking?"

"What the devil...?" he began furiously.

"*You* are the devil!" she railed, almost beside herself. "You and that hateful monster, that scheming wretch up there in that bed. There is a *witch,* if you want one. Go! Go and see what she has planned!"

"What are you talking about?" he demanded. "What is the matter with you?"

"*You* are the matter, if Lady Merchiston has her way. As for me, I am dismissed, since I don't choose to be parcelled off at her pleasure!"

"What?"

"She has turned me off, I tell you." Desperation lent an edge to her voice as the fury slithered away. "And Araminta will not help me. I don't know what to do."

Suddenly all her bravado collapsed. She stood shaking, setting the flaming tresses about her quivering so that they rippled in the shafts of light broken by the barrier of trees.

"Oh, Benedict," she uttered brokenly, "what shall I *do*?"

Seeing the mist that deepened the dark grey of her eyes, the pale translucent cheeks, both so beautiful now in their glowing copper setting, it was all Benedict could do not to snatch her back into the heat of his embrace, and force his way to that intimate deep caress, the thought of which now fired him with passionate yearning. But the distress in her face held him back. He could no more have overborne her resistance in her present state than he could kick a lame dog. Steadying himself with a deep breath, he mustered control.

"Calm yourself, Theda," he said gently, not daring to reach out and touch her, in case his own forced calm should desert him. "What has occurred?"

Drawing on her own ragged breath, Theda tried to still her shivering limbs. She did not look at him.

"I will leave Lady Lavinia to tell you her plans for herself—if she still holds by them. I think you will care for them even less than I."

"You intrigue me greatly," he said, puzzled. "But come. Let me drive you home."

"Home!" she repeated on a bleak note. "Would that you might!"

Benedict made no reply to this, but, calling to the dog, who was hovering near by, he started to lead the way out of the thicket to the road. As Theda followed, she began automatically to braid her long hair in a loose plait, searching among the tangle at her scalp for any pins that might have been left after the tresses had come loose from their moorings. She had lost her cap, and so could not again conceal the glory of her hidden beauty, but she twisted the plait in a knot behind her head and clipped it there as best she could with the two pins she had found, so that it resembled the thick queue of a man's old-fashioned wig.

In Benedict's glance, as he handed her up into his

curricle, she recognised regret, and knew that he had fallen victim—like other men before him—to the curse she carried with her always. That he was fully alive to its heady effect became evident in a moment.

Having lifted Hector into the vehicle, where he sat on the floorboards, panting with his tongue lolling out, and wagging a satisfied tail, Benedict swung himself up and grinned down at her as he took the reins into his hand.

"I now understand why you persist in wearing that very unflattering headgear. I can conceive of very few matrons who would entrust their menfolk to such temptation."

Theda lifted a hand to smooth down the edges of the fiery frame about her face. "Yes, it—it is in my interests to keep it hidden, I admit."

"In mine too," he murmured, "if I am to keep my hands off you!"

"Don't!" Theda begged. "You—you must not refine too much upon—upon what transpired between us. Forget it, if you please."

"Forget it! Are you *mad,* Theda? How can I possibly forget it? I don't even want to."

"You *must,*" she said in a stifled tone. "There can be no possibility of—of—"

"Hell and the devil!" he ejaculated angrily. "What do you take me for? Do you think I would use you like any common slut?"

Theda could not look at him, but she said in a subdued tone, "It is what your godmother called me. And—and many men in this situation would not *care* how they used me."

"Well, I care! I forgot myself for a moment back in the woods, it is true," he admitted in a goaded voice, "but the circumstances were exceptional. I was shocked out of my usual circumspection."

"Your *what?*" Theda asked in a stunned tone, casting him an irresistibly amused look.

"Don't laugh at me, Theda!" he warned, catching her glance.

"I beg your pardon." She eyed his profile in silence for a moment. Then she said, in a voice of intense interest, "Do you always delude yourself so?"

He tried to bite back a laugh, but the grin would not be entirely suppressed. "Confound you, Theda! Very well, then, you shall have it plain. Keep that head of yours well hidden, or I shall not be answerable for the consequences!"

"I thank you for the warning, sir," Theda said demurely, "and will hope to be forgiven for so wantonly playing the temptress."

"What you're tempting me to at this moment, my good girl, has very little to do with passion!" declared Benedict roundly.

Theda gurgled. "Very well, I shall desist, and thank you instead. For you have raised my spirits immeasurably."

"I am happy to have afforded you amusement, ma'am," he said ironically, and turned in at the gates of the Lodge.

"Wait!" begged Theda suddenly. "Stop before we reach the house, if you please, and set me down."

"Why?"

"So that I may enter alone, of course. Things are bad enough without laying more fuel to the fire."

"Don't put yourself about," Benedict said unconcernedly, driving on, but slowing his horses. "I will see Aunt Lavinia. If I cannot persuade her to keep you on, I promise I shall arrange matters for you in some other way."

"*What* way?" Theda asked sceptically.

"We won't concern ourselves over that until we know the outcome of my interview with my godmother," he said firmly. "Rest assured that I will not abandon you."

Theda gave him a grateful smile, but rueful withal. "I am causing you a deal of trouble one way and another."

"Yes, you are," he agreed unexpectedly, turning a grin upon her, "and I have a strong notion that there is worse to come!"

As she laughed, his eyes travelled briefly over her features, a smile in them, and then brushed lightly over the frame of copper that had struck him with so devastating an effect.

"I should have guessed," he said, and there was a caress in his voice. "With that pearly skin of yours, dear ghost, that flame was inevitable!"

A warm glow invaded Theda's heart, and the grey of her eyes deepened, giving them a luminosity that lit her features. Benedict drew a hissing breath, and pulled up his horses, his eyes never leaving hers.

But Theda's face changed at once, and she pulled back. "No, Benedict!"

His lips tightened, and he cursed under his breath,

jerking the reins again. With the return of constraint she put a hand to her fluttering bosom and discovered that several hooks on her bodice had come loose—No, had been torn loose by Benedict's hand! She tried surreptitiously to refasten them, to conceal the bare expanse of flesh with the ruff that lay open, and looked away when the movement made him glance round at her. She knew he saw what she tried to do, and her embarrassment increased.

The atmosphere between them was so tense that no further words were exchanged until he stopped the curricle at the edge of the house.

"Go in," he said curtly. "I will drive to the stables and then go to Aunt Lavvy. Hector may come with me."

Theda slipped unobtrusively into the house, which seemed unnaturally quiet after the hurricane that had driven her out of it. She wondered what had been the outcome of Araminta's promised confrontation with her mother, whether this Saul Quatt had answered the summons and been drawn into the inevitable altercation.

Without being seen, she managed to gain the safety of the dressing-room she now occupied, next door to Lady Merchiston's bedchamber. It was in fact a large room divided in two, one half being given over to the mistress's wardrobe and dressing stool, with the pier-glass in the corner, the other providing a small chamber with room only for a cot bed. Adam Diggory had grumblingly moved in a clothes-press and a table for Miss Kyte's personal use.

Not knowing what else to do, Theda first found a

fresh cap and tucked away her dangerous locks, and then began to lay out her clothes, retrieving her portmanteau from under the bed. She was afraid to make much noise, for fear of being overheard by her employer next door, for she did not want to see her until after Benedict's promised visit.

Presently she heard footsteps coming along the gallery, and sat on the bed, waiting, her heart hammering a little.

What if she did have to go? Where would Benedict take her? Would he help her at all, after that last little exchange when her stiffness had angered him so? Suddenly she remembered Rose Alderley. Had it only been this morning that she had visited Switham House and received that kind lady's offer of help? It felt a lifetime ago! Dared she go to Mrs Alderley? It was one thing to ask for a reference, quite another to throw herself, bag and baggage, on the lady's mercy!

She could hear voices in the next room. What was Benedict saying? What *would* he say when—if!—Lady Merchiston informed him of her plan to make him marry her companion?

Presently another set of footsteps came tapping by, and Theda recognised Araminta's hasty step. The sound of a door shutting was instantly followed by raised voices. Theda's heart sank. In a moment, the door slammed and heavier footsteps passed, retreating down the stairs.

Benedict! Then he had *failed.*

But next instant came the patter of lighter feet and a fist banged on her door. "Come out, Miss Kyte!"

Rising from the bed, Theda opened the door, apprehension in her eyes as she confronted Miss Merchiston's glare.

"Yes?"

"Go to my mother at once!" ordered Araminta sternly. Then she grasped Theda's wrist and came close, lowering her voice to a murmur. "And afterwards, I want you in my parlour. Understand?"

Theda nodded, too heartsick to answer. Araminta released her and sped away, leaving Theda to draw a breath, square her shoulders, and make for Lady Merchiston's door.

The old lady was lying back against her bank of pillows in an attitude of exhaustion, her eyes closed. Her skin was paler than ever, her breathing shallow. On the coverlet her fingers twitched a little, but otherwise she did not move. There was no sign of her dog.

Shutting the door softly behind her, Theda tiptoed to the bed and stood looking down at the still figure in some alarm. Was she dying? Had the excitement been too much for her? All Theda's earlier resentment faded with the onset of pity. How pathetic a creature she was, poor Lady Lavinia! So close to her own end, and still trying to run other people's lives. What would any of it avail her when once she was gone?

Lady Merchiston's eyelids fluttered, but did not fully open. She gestured vaguely with a finger, and a weary muttering issued from the pallid lips.

"You're there, are you? Good...Stay...Sit and stay."

Theda sat on the bed and took the fingers gently into her hand. They clasped hers weakly and a smile flitted over the wasted features. For a few minutes they both remained thus, motionless. Then the old lady pressed Theda's hand and opened her eyes.

"My cordial," she uttered.

Theda got up and went to the cabinet to pour a dose of one of the mixtures prescribed by Dr Spilsby. After it was drunk, Lady Merchiston seemed to recover a little of her lost vitality. She sat up straighter, and patted the bed for Theda to sit.

"I am glad you had not run away," she said in an unwontedly meek voice.

"I had, Lady Lavinia," Theda said quietly, "but Benedict brought me back."

"You should have known I did not mean it," complained the old lady in a fretful tone. "What would I do without you? Who would care for me half as well, eh? Ought to know my bark's worse than my bite."

A gleam entered Theda's eye. "Your *bite,* ma'am, draws blood!"

Lady Merchiston's lips curved with amusement. "Does it so? Well, well." She shot a speculative glance at her companion. "Had a worthy champion, though, didn't you?"

Theda gave her a straight look. "Because your godson is kind, ma'am, that does not mean—"

"That you'll take him to husband," finished the old lady. "Never fear. I have abandoned that scheme." She eyed Theda narrowly. "Now where is the sigh of relief, eh?"

A light laugh escaped Theda. "You misunderstand me, Lady Lavinia. I have no objection to Benedict as a suitor. At least, I am sure he has enough to recommend him, should—should any female be inclined to consider him in that light."

"But not *this* female?" interpolated her employer.

"*No*—at least, I mean...I had not *thought* of such a thing. Besides, *I* am not eligible! But that is not it."

"Oh? Then what is 'it'?"

"Lady Lavinia," Theda began, drawing a steadying breath. "I left my home—I *ruined* my life, except that I did not know *then* that I was doing so!—only because my par...I mean, only because *others* attempted to compel me to do as they thought fit in the matter of matrimony." She smiled a little. "Unlike Araminta, I was not content to bow to their decree. So you see, although I have tried since—needs must!—to subdue that dangerous spirit of rebellion, I have so little succeeded that—that..."

"That when I 'dared' to so compel you, you flew out at me like the spirited filly you are under that demure exterior," stated her ladyship with a quizzing look.

"Yes, that is how it was," Theda admitted.

Lady Merchiston snorted. "Well, if you'd been *my* daughter, you'd have felt the rod!"

Theda looked away. "Believe me, ma'am, the punishment I brought on myself was far more salutary than any thrashing could have been."

There was a silence. Theda was aware of the keen eyes on her, but she did not turn to confront them. She had said enough. Too much! And what had been inadvertently revealed in that last remark made by Lady Lavinia? Poor Araminta, how she must have suffered! Still, she must be grateful to Benedict, who *had* been her "champion", and glad that the old understanding had been re-established between herself and Lady Merchiston. She would be more on her guard in future, however, now that she knew the unpredictable nature of the old lady's malevolence.

But just at that moment, she felt a tug at her scalp, and turned her head to find that the bony fingers had seized a stray strand of copper hair, pulling it from under her cap. Theda had shoved it on so hastily that she must have carelessly left a little hair visible.

"So *this* is your secret!" the old lady said in a tone of quiet satisfaction, a smile on her face. "What a girl of surprises you are, Theodosia Kyte!"

"I am come to the right house, then," Theda retorted.

The keen old eyes sparkled unexpectedly. "Oh, I'm not finished yet, girl, not by a long chalk! There are more to come, don't doubt it."

"Heaven help us all!"

"And heaven help you," riposted Lady Merchiston swiftly, giving the lock of hair she held a sharp jerk, "if you let Araminta know of this!" She cackled. "Make the most of it, Theodosia." She let the strand slide through her fingers to its full length and lay playing it between them. "It will fade soon enough. Seen it before. Runs in my husband's family, too, you know. Araminta almost had it as a child, but it went fair—and then mouse, poor wretch!"

Taking hold of her lock, Theda pulled gently. "If you please, Lady Lavinia."

The old lady let it go, and watched Theda hastily tuck it out of sight. "Yes, keep it close. If Araminta sees it, her jealousy will be increased tenfold. She'd have killed Isabel if she could!"

Theda stared, her mind rioting. So she *knew* of Araminta's jealousy! And what did she mean about Isabel? Why should Araminta have been jealous of Benedict's mother?

Seeing that her employer's eyes were once again drooping heavily, she got up from the bed. "Would you like anything, ma'am, or shall I leave you to rest?"

The fingers moved vaguely. "Go, child. Bring Hector to me when next you come up. Benedict left him with Adam...and he don't pet him."

Her voice was sinking, and Theda quietly left the room. She was about to return to her own chamber to put her clothes away again when an urgent hiss came at her from down the gallery.

"Psst!"

Turning, she beheld Araminta at the head of the stairs, and remembered that Miss Merchiston had instructed her to go down to her parlour when she had left her mother. The woman beckoned imperiously, and, sighing, Theda turned down the gallery and followed her downstairs. There had been enough emotion this day. Pray heaven Araminta was not going to vent her spleen again!

As she entered the little parlour behind her, Theda was brought up short by the sight of a stranger standing before the fireplace. He was an odd little man, peering anxiously up at her out of hunched shoulders through a pair of gold-rimmed spectacles, on his head an outdated tie-wig.

"Miss Kyte," said Araminta, a most unusual smirk on her face, and with a note of pride in her voice, "allow me to present the Reverend Mr Saul Quatt."

Theda was just able to prevent her mouth falling open, but her eyes widened, and her voice trembled on the veriest hint of laughter as she held out her hand.

"H-how do you do?"

So this was Araminta's old lover! And after—what?—fifteen, twenty years, there was that in her altered manner that showed she could still regard him with affection. But what of the gentleman himself?

"I am happy to make your acquaintance," he was saying in a very precise tone, executing a small bow.

"I have brought you here, Miss Kyte," resumed Miss Merchiston in what was for her a pleasant tone, "that you may tell Mr Quatt of what passed between yourself and my dear mother."

Flicking an unconsciously amazed glance at her, Theda met in her eyes a warning. Play my game, it said, or suffer the consequences. But surely she could not wish her to reveal the matter to this poor dab of a parson?

He was looking acutely uncomfortable already, and entered upon a feeble protest. "No, no, I beg of you, Miss Merchiston...*Araminta,*" he amended as the pale eyes turned upon him in gentle reproach, "there is no need. If your good lady mother is indisposed, I would not for the world—"

"Nonsense, Saul!" said Araminta, smiling in what she evidently felt to be a winning fashion. "She summoned you here, and it is only right that you should know the reason, albeit she is too unwell to see you herself. Go on, Miss Kyte.''

Saul Quatt turned his apprehensive gaze upon the companion, his frown shifting the spectacles upon his nose. ''I thought perhaps her ladyship, being, as I have heard, in such ill health, had need of my services as a man of God,'' he ventured hopefully.

''No, sir,'' Theda said, her sympathy roused. Poor man! He little knew what fate had in store. And he did not look to be equal to the formidable task of escaping the net that had been spread for him.

''Go *on,* Miss Kyte!'' prompted Araminta, moving in close enough to deliver a vicious prod to Theda's ribs while she bestowed a melting look upon the hapless Reverend gentleman.

''The truth is, Mr Quatt,'' Theda said in an even tone, ''that, in view of your altered circumstances, her ladyship is prepared to reconsider her decision regarding your erstwhile proposals to Miss Merchiston.''

Under the glass of his spectacles, his eyes goggled. ''My—my *proposals?* But—but—''

''You see, Saul, how opportune has been your return!'' beamed Araminta, coming up to him and taking his flaccid hand between both her own.

''I—yes—um—I...I don't know what to say!'' stuttered the stunned suitor.

''Of course nothing can be formally arranged just at this present,'' went on Miss Merchiston, and Theda almost laughed out to see the burgeoning hope in the poor man's face, ''for with dear Mama in this sad condition, I could not reconcile it with my conscience to leave her in the care of other hands. But it won't be long now before all our fondest hopes will be realised."

Looking at Saul Quatt, Theda could not help feeling that his fondest hope was likely to be that he might be struck by a thunderbolt! He looked anything but gratified, and she could only marvel at Araminta's inability to see how unwelcome was the good fortune that had come to him.

Adjuring Theda, in the prettiest way, to wait for her here, Miss Merchiston then escorted Mr Quatt to the front door, presumably bidding him a fond farewell in the sickeningly sugary tone she had chosen to adopt towards him.

It had vanished, however, when the woman returned to the parlour, the familiar peevish look once more marring her features. "I'll have him if it kills me!"

"Does Lady Merchiston know he was here?" Theda asked, adding, "I only wish to be adequately prepared if she should question me."

"Don't tell her!" snapped Araminta instantly. "I waylaid him on his arrival. I will not have her think me acquiescent in her schemes. Let her go to her grave imagining me defiant to the last. Besides, if I marry Saul now, she will think I am provided for and leave the house away from me."

"I thought Benedict was to have the house," Theda uttered without thinking.

"He may yet—*if* he can win back into favour."

Theda was seized by a pang of conscience. "You mean he is out of favour...because of me?"

"*You?* Pah! I knew that scheme would not hold. Benedict marry for other than money? I wish I may see it!"

The words hit Theda like a douche of cold water. Of course. Why should Benedict even have *considered* the proposal? He might desire her—he *did* desire her—but he would not *marry* her only for that! Oh, no. Just like that *other,* nameless—for she would not utter his name, even in mind—betrayer…

Brushing off the thoughts, she looked at Araminta. "Has Benedict—Mr Beckenham, I should say—gone away from here, then?"

"I should imagine so, after the manner in which he stormed off. Merely because I reminded him how unlikely he was to catch an heiress."

There was contempt in Theda's glance. "I suppose you told him, just as your mother did, that he might as well take me?"

The shaft glanced off the armour of Araminta's self-satisfaction. "I said you were sunk low enough to match his sordid background, yes."

Inwardly Theda flinched, but she replied coolly, "Since I am unfamiliar with his background, Miss Merchiston, I am unable to comment."

"Who wants you to?" demanded Araminta rudely. "Go back to your duties and mind your business!"

Curtsying, Theda left the little parlour with alacrity, and went to the kitchen to find Adam Diggory and retrieve Hector from him. The dog was under the kitchen table, gobbling scraps of meat given to him by Mrs Elswick, busy at the stove.

"So you are being spoilt, are you, sir?" Theda asked of him, mock-stern.

A wagging tail was her only answer, for the woolly black head remained buried in the interesting bowl. But her voice, penetrating to the little pantry next door, brought Agnes Diggory out.

"Oh, Miss Kyte! Can you spare a moment?"

"Yes, of course, Mrs Diggory," Theda said, coming into the little room and closing the door on the housekeeper's conspiratorial signal.

"Is all well?" Agnes asked in a whisper.

Theda shrugged, her smile awry. "As well as anything can be in this house."

Mrs Diggory nodded. "True, miss. Still, you're back to your post, and that's the main thing." She put a hand in her apron pocket and brought out a sealed billet. "Mr Benedict asked me to give you this, miss, quiet like."

"Thank you," Theda said, aware as she took it that her fingers quivered. She slipped it into her pocket, smiled at Agnes, and went back into the kitchen to collect Hector. The dog safely delivered to his still sleeping mistress, who did not stir when he sneaked on to her bed, Theda sought the privacy of her own chamber and broke the seal of Benedict's note.

Did you shrink from marriage with me, indeed, dear ghost? I assured Aunt Lavvy that it was so, and that I could never coerce an *unwilling* female. I don't know what maggot has got into her head, but I will not dance to her piping, any more than you. Yet I am so much under the spell of *your* witchery I might have viewed parson's mousetrap with a kindly eye were you the bait—and not the false promises with which I am to be lured. *Don't trust her.* And pay no heed to Araminta's spite. Confound you, Theda, you have set me afire and I *burn!*

On the day of the wedding of Mrs Alderley's daughter in early June, Merchiston Lodge was unusually quiet. Araminta had been driven to the celebrations in the gig by Adam Diggory, scorning Benedict's escort, and Mrs Diggory had been permitted to accompany them so that she might visit her mother, who lived on the Switham estates. Benedict himself, who had stayed the previous night, had driven himself over there in his phaeton, glad to be relieved of his cousin's irksome company. There was therefore left at the Lodge only Mrs Elswick in the kitchen and Theda attendant on her ladyship.

There was an air of excitement about Lady Merchiston for which her companion was quite unable to account. She was unusually alert, for her health had deteriorated in the brief time since the upset of Theda's near-dismissal. Dr Spilsby had confided to Theda his belief that the end could not now be far distant.

But today the eyes were vibrant with an anticipatory light and Lady Merchiston sat up against her pillows, her glance alternately flicking to the window and following her companion as she moved about the room, tidying up. Hector, aware of the change, sat up on the bed, following the direction of his mistress's altering gaze with his head cocking, in an air of puzzlement, from side to side.

When Theda would have left the room with a pile of soiled linen, the cracked voice stayed her. "Wait!"

Theda turned at the door. "Ma'am?"

"Leave that and come here a moment."

Laying down her burden, Theda obediently approached the bed and sat as her ladyship patted the covers. "What is it, Lady Lavinia?"

The sharp black eyes held the grey. "What's between you and Benedict?"

Theda drew back, a frown in her eyes. "What do you mean?"

A claw shot out and seized her wrist. "Don't trifle with me, girl! I know you were kicking up a dust last night, the pair of you. And it ain't the first time! What's to do?"

"You are mistaken, Lady Lavinia," Theda said firmly.

The old lady's eyes flashed. "No, I ain't! My body may be past mending, but I've still all my wits. Answer!"

Theda paused, wondering who could have been her ladyship's informant. Mrs Diggory, perhaps? Her mind flew back to the moment last evening when Benedict had come at her out of the shadows of the hall as she had come downstairs with Lady Merchiston's empty supper tray.

"I must talk to you!" he had uttered in an urgent undervoice.

Theda had been conscious of guilt. She had deliberately kept out of his way until now, leaving the task of showing him upstairs to his godmother's room to Mrs Diggory. After the words he had written to her, it was churlish of her to avoid him, but she dreaded any interview because of what she must say.

He had been looking down into her face, lit by the candle he carried, but some sound had turned his eyes to the back of the hall. A moment later he had been dragging her, tray and all, through one of the doors into the vast ballroom.

Chapter Six

"Benedict, for heaven's sake!" Theda whispered crossly.

He paid not the slightest attention. Shutting the door, he put his candle down on the nearest chair and drew her across to the glow that streamed in from the setting sun.

"What in the world are you doing?" Theda demanded.

"Be quiet!" he ordered, and before she knew what he was about he had snatched at her white cap and pulled it off.

Burdened with the tray, she could do nothing but back away, protesting, "Are you mad?"

"I've been going mad," he returned in a hoarse voice, "thinking of this!"

Then one hand was holding her still, while the fingers of the other were busy in the folds of her hair. Theda, her heart beginning to race, acted without conscious decision. Shoving the tray into his chest, she cried out, "Take this!"

"The devil!" he uttered, and as her hands left its

edge he let her go and seized the tray before it could fall.

Theda stepped back and caught at the back of her hair just as it came tumbling down over her shoulders. Her fingers tried uselessly to stem the flow of flaming tresses, and Benedict, mesmerised, stood with the tray stupidly clasped in his hands, staring at the mass of struggling copper, bright and flickering like fire in the glow from outside.

"Lord above, Benedict!" Theda scolded. "You must have taken leave of your senses indeed!"

"I have," he agreed, grinning suddenly.

"Where is my cap?" she asked distractedly, as she fought with her hair.

He put down the tray on the floor, and brought out her cap from the pocket in his coat into which he had stuffed it, saying, however, "Let go your hair or I don't return it."

Theda had perforce to let go, for she could not contain the hair now it had sprung in so disorderly a way from its moorings. As it fell about her, she saw Benedict take a step towards her and moved quickly away.

"Don't touch me!"

His eye gleamed. "Are you afraid I may burn my fingers?"

"No, your boats!" she retorted.

He stared. "What the devil are you talking about?"

"I am referring to that foolish note you wrote me," Theda said, winding her hair into a plait as she spoke, her voice deliberately cool over the tremors inside her.

"Foolish?" Benedict repeated. "I meant every word."

"Fudge! You know very well you will never marry to your own disadvantage."

"Why to my disadvantage?" he demanded, his voice thick with passion. "You heat my blood so greatly, I could readily give up all my hopes just to have you to myself."

"You are talking like a green youth. It would serve you out if I chose to use the letter in an action against you for breach of promise!"

For a moment he looked taken aback. Then a short laugh escaped him. "I know you better than that, Theda. But I swear to God, if it was not so prejudicial to my future, I'd marry you tomorrow."

Theda's grey eyes grew dark and her voice shook. "Only for the opportunity to slake your desire? I am flattered!"

"And *yours.*" He seized her shoulders, but her hands came up to hold his wrists and prevent him from pulling her close. He was obedient to the pressure—for he could easily have overborne her with his superior strength—but his voice was guttural. "You want me, too. You know you do. You never boggle at plain-speaking, so why do so now? This passion between us is not one-sided."

Theda wrenched his hands from her shoulders, but she did not release his wrists, her grip on them tightening. "I will say this. A woman in my situation may be vulnerable. Loneliness and a personable male are tempting seducers."

His face changed. "Then why hold temptation so strongly?"

She let go his wrists as if they were scalding hot, stepping smartly away. "Give me my cap!"

He held it out. "Yes, you had better tuck it out of the 'seducer's' sight!"

Theda was busy with her hair, but at that she glanced at him and saw the hurt in his eyes. She took the cap and made herself once more respectable in silence. Then she took up the discarded tray and looked back at him where he stood now, leaning against the wall between the French windows, his silver flask of brandy open as he sipped defiantly, watching her with a black scowl on his face.

"Benedict," she said in a kindlier tone, "even were it possible, I would not—*could* not—marry you."

"Oh?" His voice was hard. "Am I that bad?"

A rueful smile flitted over her face. "No, there is nothing at all wrong with you. It is myself who is 'that bad'."

Turning from him, she made quickly for the door. He called out her name, but she did not pause. In another moment she was outside the room, her heart hollow, and the tears pricking at her eyes.

Now, as she came back to the present, Lady Merchiston's own eyes were on her in a compelling look, demanding an answer. "What's between you two?"

Theda drew a breath. "Benedict is dazzled by my hair, ma'am."

"I'll warrant he is!" the old lady cackled unexpectedly. "So he's seen it, has he? Well, well. His first experience of woman, that hair. And of love—of the most enduring kind. Even at the end, there were echoes of it still.''

Theda knew an instant of blinding, devastating hatred of the red-headed woman who had once been Benedict's love. Then the feeling was gone as Lady Merchiston claimed her attention with another acute observation.

''Not so averse to the boy as you had led me to believe, eh?''

''I like him very well, ma'am,'' Theda said quickly, ''but I couldn't marry him even if I wanted to—which I *don't*.''

''Why not?''

This time Theda met the demand in her eyes without flinching away. ''Forgive me, Lady Lavinia. I would tell you if I could, I promise you, but my story involves others and—and I simply cannot in honour divulge it.''

For a moment or two Lady Merchiston continued to regard her steadily, as if she tried to read Theda's story in her face. Then she reached out a hand to clasp one of hers.

''Child, I will not press you,'' she said, unwontedly gentle, ''but only tell me this. Were you in your proper station, you would, I think, take precedence even over me?''

Theda bit her lip. Then she sighed and nodded. ''Yes, ma'am. But an outcast takes *no* precedence, as you well know.''

''Ah, but you need not have been an outcast,'' shrewdly guessed the old lady.

"It is true that I could have braved the scandal, brazened it out," Theda admitted, "but either fear or pride, perhaps—"

"A mixture of both," interpolated Lady Merchiston.

"Probably. In any event, I chose this route and I must ever take the consequences."

"Ah, yes, consequences." With sudden energy, her ladyship sat up a little straighter, raising her frail body in the bed.

"If that is horses I hear on the drive, here come a purveyor of consequences." She chuckled as Theda looked a question. "My lawyer."

"Your lawyer? But did you invite him, ma'am?"

"You are thinking there was no letter passed through your hands," said Lady Merchiston gleefully. "But it did. You recall me writing to my bankers in Ashby-de-la-Zouch?"

"A day or so ago, yes."

"Well, I enclosed my note to Aycliffe within that, so that no one would know of his coming. You are to keep it a secret, Theodosia. Swear it now!"

"Very well, ma'am, I will say nothing if you wish it," agreed Theda, but she was nevertheless consumed with curiosity.

The old lady saw it in her face. "Aha! You want to know why he's coming. Can't you guess?"

"Your will, ma'am?"

"That's it. I've decided on my dispositions at last." She leaned towards Theda suddenly. "And you're not to worry over your own case. I'm taking care of you."

"Of *me?*" uttered Theda, astonished.

"Don't you think I owe you something after employing you under false pretences? Oh, I've been aware of your fears, child."

"Lady Lavinia, I beg of you, don't make me any gifts! Or if you must, let me have it *beforehand.* It would be quite dreadful for me to benefit by your death."

"So you say! Don't talk rubbish, girl! It will keep you here a little so that you may have time to make your plans."

"Finding another post is all the plan I have, ma'am."

"Very well, whatever it may be. I would not rest easy knowing Araminta would see you off without so much as a penny piece the moment I breathe my last."

"Lady Lavinia, it is very kind of you, but—"

"Don't fidget me with prattle and thanks, Theodosia! I *owe* it to you. And you know it! Now go down and send Aycliffe up to me. Take Hector and don't come back, either of you, until he has gone. Now *go!*"

Theda gave it up, calling to Hector as she left the room. If her ladyship's mind was made up, there was nothing she could say to change it. There was no time to think over this latest development, for by the time she got to the hall downstairs the doorbell was already jangling.

Mr Aycliffe was a man in late middle age, whose sober garments and air of portentous solemnity at once proclaimed his calling.

"You must be Miss Kyte," he ventured, holding out a hand.

Theda was surprised. "You've heard of me?"

"Everyone has, you know," he said with an apologetic smile. "Mountsorrel is a small place and we generally hear of all the doings round about."

Theda frowned. "But no one comes here! Or, wait...Mrs Elswick?"

The visitor's brows rose. "Possibly, but she lives in Switham."

"Adam!" Theda exclaimed. "Doubtless he visits the alehouse when he goes in for supplies."

"Extraordinary fellow, old Diggory," remarked the lawyer, without confirming or denying Theda's suspicion. "Devoted to her ladyship, as he was to Sir John, you know."

All at once Theda was struck by the obvious solution to her own vexed question. It had not been Mrs Diggory who had told Lady Lavinia about herself and Benedict. Adam it was who made up the fires of a morning, when his mistress, who slept only fitfully at night, was already awake, Adam who crept noiselessly about the place, unnoticed, who must have seen them together last night outside the ballroom. Devoted indeed! She summoned a smile and nodded at Mr Aycliffe.

"Naturally you will have heard of me. Even had you not been so well acquainted with the family, I dare say. We live so isolated an existence here that to me it seems quite odd. It was foolish of me to forget how news spreads in a village."

"Unwise, I agree, ma'am."

"To forget? You are very right. It is something I particularly ought to remember."

His brows rose, but he said nothing, merely appraising her out of a pair of shrewd eyes.

"You are expected, Mr Aycliffe. Will you go on up?" Theda suggested. She smiled, adding, "I am barred during your visit, so pray excuse me."

He bowed and went off up the stairs. Theda took Hector to the kitchen and left him with Mrs Elswick to do what he might in the way of cajolery, for she had several morsels of interest to his ever ready stomach, and Theda was obviously not going to take him outside.

In fact the weather had not smiled on Miss Switham's wedding day, and the overcast sky did not invite a walk. Instead, Theda slipped into the ballroom to think about Lady Merchiston's determination to make her a bequest.

She could not but be gratified and relieved at the possibility of a small sum to see her through the likely lean period before she could get another post. But her mind did not dwell long on what she privately felt to be a remote contingency—Lady Merchiston was so changeable! Instead she found herself, in this room full of memories, thinking of Benedict Beckenham.

Unconsciously she put up a hand to that fatal head of hair, and her fingers, coming into contact with the enveloping white cap, brought her a sobering thought. She had hurt him. But she *had* to. It was a matter of self-preservation.

Her mind ran on the wedding celebrations as she moved to the window where a stray shaft of sunlight, escaping through the thick cloud, threw a beam across the parquet floor. Her feet began to move in the *fleuret* of a minuet. There would be dancing. For an instant, in her imagination, the ballroom was peopled with guests, and Benedict was partnering her, his gold hair gleaming in the light, his eyes on hers...dancing with the bride.

The sun went in and the ballroom was again shrouded in gloom—empty, but for Miss Theodosia Kyte, dreaming a foolish dream!

But as she gazed from the French windows on the tangle of weeds outside, and the now dense greenery of Switham Thicket, a plea formed in her mind as she thought of Lady Merchiston upstairs, in conference with her man of business.

Don't disappoint him, pray.

''I'm glad she waited for the wedding to be over,'' whispered Mrs Alderley in Theda's ear, as she joined her by the French windows that had been opened to the terrace outside.

The ballroom had been thrown wide to accommodate the funeral guests, and Mrs Diggory was busy serving refreshments to the gentlemen who had just a short time since returned from the graveside of the deceased Lady Merchiston.

For Theda had been woken one night, a few days after Mr Aycliffe's visit, by Hector whining next door. She had risen from her bed, slipped on her dressing-robe, and lighting her bedside candle with the tinderbox on the table, she had taken it in her hand and gone into Lady Merchiston's chamber. Hector had been huddled by the door, and he had snuffed at once at her feet, whimpering. Theda had drawn the curtain about the four-poster open, and the light from her candle had fallen on the old lady's face.

Her eyes had been open in a fixed and vacant stare, and the waxen tinge to her skin had told its own tale. Theda had reached down to clasp her trembling fingers lightly about the cold wrist lying on the coverlet, but she had known already that there was no pulse to be discerned.

Oddly, Theda had found herself distressed by this long-expected demise. She had known it must come, and soon, particularly after the day of the wedding. For once the lawyer had concluded his business, having called upon both his own groom and Mrs Elswick to witness the document he had drawn up, and had been seen off the premises, Theda had gone back upstairs to find her employer in a state of near-collapse.

''All done now,'' she had murmured, the once vibrant eyes quite as lifeless as the rest of her emaciated form. ''Nothing left to hang on for. Be gone soon.''

Now she had indeed gone, and her household, strangely bereft, seemed lost and forlorn all at once. Hector had clung close to Theda, and was even now shut up in her tiny bedchamber, where he had taken to sleeping. Mrs Diggory was herself but little touched, Theda believed, but she had been upset by her husband's woeful demeanour. For of them all, Adam Diggory had been the most deeply stricken by grief.

Even Araminta had been sullen and silent ever since her mother's death, and Theda had been relieved to see Mrs Alderley, who had driven over, elegant as ever in rustling black silk, to offer her condolences at a time when she knew all the men would be attending the service.

"For I wanted the opportunity to talk to you privately," she told Theda quietly, "although I could not see Araminta allowing it."

She had managed, nevertheless, to seize a few moments with the erstwhile companion when the gentlemen returned, for Araminta had at once gone over to greet Mr Saul Quatt, who had, at her request, presided over the service in the local church—much to the chagrin of its incumbent, whose ruffled feathers Mrs Alderley had been obliged to smooth when she heard of the plan from him.

Miss Merchiston, who had refused to wear mourning up until today, was now correctly attired in black crêpe, but Theda had been obliged to content herself with her dark stuff gown and black ribbons to her cap. Benedict, who had arrived yesterday, was looking extremely handsome in full mourning, even to a black cravat.

Theda had been unable to exchange more than a few words with him, for she had been—on Araminta's orders—busily engaged in packing up all Lady Merchiston's things into trunks to be stored in the attics, and cleaning out her bedchamber.

"I hardly knew whether I would find you still here," Benedict had said, catching her on the gallery as she went towards the attic stairs, burdened with a small wooden box containing the contents of Lady Merchiston's medicine cupboard, Hector at her heels.

"Araminta wanted me to clear up first," Theda answered, trying to still the flutter that had attacked her pulses at the touch of his hand on her arm.

He acknowledged the dog's overtures, but he eyed her with a good deal of concern. "Have you anywhere to go?"

Theda shook her head. "No, but it is not the first time I have been in such a situation. I will come about."

Benedict frowned. "The devil! I wish it were possible for you to come away with me."

"Well, it is not!" Theda said, startled.

"I know that." His hand caressed her arm. "If there was somewhere you might stay in the meanwhile, I may shortly be in a position to help you."

"To *what,* Benedict?" she demanded sharply. "A discreet establishment that you may visit from time to time?"

His eyes flashed and his fingers tightened in a vicious grip. "You have a curst low opinion of me, by God! Why should you think I meant that?"

"Why should you suppose me any less proud than more fortunate females?" Theda countered. "You know very well that a lady cannot accept pecuniary assistance from a gentleman without being thought to have taken up a *carte blanche.*"

"You didn't quibble at the Feathers," he snapped.

"I *did,* but you made it impossible for me to refuse."

There was a silence while he eyed her smoulderingly in the light from the candles in the wall-sconces. The dog Hector, seated on his haunches beside them, glanced from one to the other in mute puzzlement. Theda sighed and gave Benedict a kinder smile.

"I am sorry. I know you mean well, and I *am* ever grateful for what you did—"

"Oh, be quiet! Do you think I want gratitude? Theda, I thought we were *friends.*"

"Well, and so we are."

He grinned suddenly and touched her cheek lightly with his fingers. "But no more than friends, eh?"

"You know that is impossible."

"So you say!"

Theda laughed. "You sound exactly like Lady Lavinia. That was one of her expressions."

A frown came into Benedict's eyes. "I never thought it would be so, but I miss her like the devil!"

"I, too. Odd, isn't it? I knew her so short a time."

"What difference does that make? You've known *me* but a short time."

For some reason the words rang in Theda's head. Had he *meant* to give them that special significance? That charge between them sparked all at once. She heard his breath hiss, and quickly drew back.

"I must take this box upstairs."

"Running away, Theda?"

"Yes," she said staunchly, and clicked her fingers to Hector, who, bored, had wandered down the gallery.

He laughed, but there was urgency in his tone nevertheless. "Stay a moment longer! What *are* you going to do? I hate to think of you blundering about, alone and unprotected."

She gave him a warm smile. "Don't fear for me,

Benedict. For one thing, Rose has kindly offered to help me find a place."

"Yes, I know," he said unexpectedly. "She told me. If she had offered you hospitality, I would be the better pleased."

"Lord, why should she? I will have wages to tide me over initially."

"A pittance!" scoffed Benedict.

"Yes, I know, but..." She hesitated, biting her lip. Should she tell him?

But next instant, he came closer and his fingers cradled her face, the box in her hands keeping them apart. His voice was low and very tender.

"Dear ghost, I don't want you to float out of my life, to disappear without trace. Do you see?"

Yes, she did! She saw that she *must* do exactly that—run away from him as he had suggested, but as far away as she could go! But she could not say so. She summoned a light laugh. "You are being quite absurd, you know."

He let her go. "Am I?" he said grimly, stepping back. "Then do without me!"

"Don't be angry!" she begged quickly. "I—I ought not to be telling you this, but Lady Lavinia told me she would...leave me something."

Benedict's eyes snapped to attention, and his body went rigid. "You mean she made a new will?"

Lord, now what was she to say? She had promised to keep silent. But Benedict's eyes were on her, as compelling a question in them as had been in those of his godmother.

"Theda, answer me!"

"She made a will, yes."

"Dear *God!* What was in it? What did it say?"

"I don't *know,* Benedict. I did not see it, nor was I told. Only she said she had brought me here under false pretences and she chose to make amends this way."

"What the devil do I care about her confounded amends?" he said harshly. "What has she done by *me?* That is my sole interest in it!"

Hector, distressed, gave a whimper and hid himself in the skirts of his chosen protectress. Theda hardly noticed him, for hurt and disappointment flooded over her in a wave. How quickly had his attention turned from his vaunted concern over herself to his own interests!

"Does Araminta know?" he was asking urgently.

"No one knows," Theda said, her voice shaking.

"Except you!"

There was something in his tone that brought her eyes up to his in a look of vibrant anger.

"Excuse me, Benedict," she said with forced calm. "I have work to do. Come, Hector."

This time he did not try to stop her and she made her way to the attics in a seething temper, depositing the box of Lady Merchiston's effects without even thinking what she was doing. How dared he insinuate that she lied? For he had done so, if only by the manner of his speech. Now she saw the true worth of all his protestations. *Friends?* On *his* terms, she supposed. Benedict Beckenham, *you* are the liar, not I, for you caress with a false tongue for purposes of your own!

He had not sought another interview with her, and, as the ladies naturally did not attend at the graveside, the first she had seen of him since then was when the party returned from the funeral. Sighting Benedict, Theda immediately found it difficult to concentrate on what Mrs Alderley was saying.

"I have not forgotten my promise to help you find a place, although I have not done so yet."

"You have scarcely had an opportunity, ma'am," Theda answered with automatic politeness, "what with the wedding and the bereavement in this house."

"Yes, but the matter is now become of some urgency, and I feel very guilty—"

That took Theda's full attention. "Don't say so, ma'am! Besides, it is not quite so urgent as I thought. At least, I hope that—"

She was interrupted. The lawyer, Mr Aycliffe, had come up. "Miss Kyte, how do you do? I am about to retire to the breakfast parlour with Mr Beckenham and Miss Merchiston. Will you find the Diggorys, if you please, and join us?"

"Certainly, sir," Theda replied, and turned as he went off to find in Mrs Alderley's face a look of blank astonishment.

"Good God! She has left you something?"

Theda grimaced. "She said she would. It is what I was about to tell you. A little to tide me over, I gather."

"Well, I wouldn't have believed it of Lavinia. What an extraordinary woman she was, to be sure!"

It seemed to Theda that neither Rose nor Benedict appeared pleased that she was to benefit thus. Perhaps, after all, it was only Lady Merchiston who'd truly had her interests at heart, even if only latterly. Certainly Araminta was unlikely to be gratified.

In this she was perfectly correct. She entered the breakfast parlour, in company with Agnes and Adam Diggory, the latter red-eyed and bowed down with sorrow, to find Miss Merchiston seated on one side of the big table, opposite Benedict, while Mr Aycliffe occupied the head.

Araminta took one astonished look and jumped to her feet, pointing. "What is *she* doing in here?"

Benedict's head snapped round and last night's frown again descended on his brow.

"Miss Kyte is here at my request," said Mr Aycliffe in a repressive tone.

"You mean she's in the will?" demanded Araminta shrilly.

Benedict threw her a contemptuous glance. "That would seem to be a fair inference."

"Please sit down, everyone," intervened the lawyer.

The Diggorys each pulled out a chair and perched on it, obviously uncomfortable. But Theda stayed where she was by the door, meeting Araminta's malevolent stare with a fast-beating heart. Did she *have* to face this?

"Miss Kyte?" said Mr Aycliffe.

She bit her lip. "I—I would prefer to be excused."

"I am afraid that is not possible," returned the lawyer.

Benedict rose and came down the table. He pulled out the chair at the bottom and bowed. "You may as well sit down.'' Glancing at Araminta as Theda began to move towards it, he added, ''If she's in the will, she's in it. Dagger looks will not change that.''

As he moved back to his place, Araminta transferred her glare to his face. But she said nothing.

Benedict nodded to Mr Aycliffe. ''We are all agog, man. Do carry on.''

The lawyer rustled his papers and cleared his throat. ''This is the last will and testament of Lavinia Dorothy, Lady Merchiston of Merchiston Lodge, Switham, Leicestershire.''

The will began in the usual way, with small bequests to several relatives of whom Theda had never heard, and a lump sum and pension for the Diggorys—at mention of which old Adam had again recourse to his handkerchief. Theda had thought her own small portion would come next, but the lawyer cleared his throat again, and read on.

''To my daughter, Araminta Dorothy Merchiston...''

Miss Merchiston's eyes glanced at Benedict, who merely raised his brows, and then passed to the paper in the lawyer's hand and there remained.

''In addition to the agreed sum of her own portion, all my jewellery, all the silver and plate, and any items of furnishing she wishes to remove from Merchiston Lodge, which property itself she may not have.''

Benedict's eyes met hers in triumph as she turned a fierce look of venom upon him.

''If my daughter Araminta requires a home,'' went on Aycliffe, ''let her marry Saul Quatt, whom I am perfectly aware she has planned to entrap in any event.''

A shriek of rage and chagrin escaped Miss Merchiston's lips, and she leapt to her feet. ''The old hag! How dared she double-cross me?''

Theda could not but feel sorry for her, but Benedict's eyes were on the lawyer, who had paused.

''If you please, Miss Merchiston,'' he said quietly, ''I am not finished.''

''Very well, very well, continue!'' snapped Araminta, quivering with temper, and shooting killing looks at her cousin on the other side of the table.

''In addition,'' resumed Aycliffe, ''and in consideration of certain advice, I leave to my daughter a further sum of ten thousand pounds.''

Theda blinked. Ten *thousand*! Lord above, she had not imagined there to be much above ten hundred to be left!

''Advice?'' Araminta uttered, her fury ludicrously arrested by a look of blank astonishment. ''What advice?''

With uncanny certainty, Theda knew that Lady Merchiston referred to her own words. She must have decided that the house, which would go to Benedict, was worth that much above the other items she had left to Araminta.

''To my godson, Robert Benedict Beckenham, the sum of twenty thousand pounds with which to gamble his way into a debtor's prison...''

There was a concerted gasp of shock around the table, and Benedict himself stiffened, his frown deepening so that it cut heavy lines across his forehead and between his brows, marring his looks.

"Where I hope he will reflect on the unwisdom of employing his charm and duplicity on a woman as sharp as I."

No one spoke as Mr Aycliffe paused. Even Araminta was too awed for words. Theda could almost hear her late employer cackling. Then Benedict, in a voice of ice, asked the question in everyone's mind.

"Is that it?"

The lawyer shook his head, and Theda saw the sudden hope flicker in Benedict's eyes. Araminta's glance left his face and returned to Aycliffe.

"Well? Does he get the house or not?"

Clearing his throat yet again, his nervousness now apparent to all, Aycliffe resumed, his tone over-loud in the suddenly still room.

"The residue of my estate, including Merchiston Lodge and its contents other than those already specified, together with the grounds in which it is set, I bequeath to the one person who has made my last days worth living, Miss Theodosia Kyte."

Chapter Seven

Paralysis held Theda blank of mind and body, as still and silent as everyone else in the breakfast parlour.

Then a piercing crowing shattered on their ears, and they all leapt in their seats as Araminta Merchiston broke into hysterical, shrieking laughter.

"Oh, oh, oh!" she gasped between paroxysms of mirth. "A jest...a marvellous, cruel jest. So much for you, B-Benedict! *That* will teach you to play off your airs! Oh, oh!"

Benedict was on his feet, overturning his chair in one violent gesture, a face of livid fury turned on Theda.

"You lying, traitorous, scheming *witch!*" he snarled.

Theda's eyes met the scorching flame in his as she rose shakily to her feet to face him.

"You think *I* did this?" she whispered hoarsely, not even conscious that Agnes Diggory rushed to Araminta's side where she lay back in her chair, hiccuping on her choking laughter.

But Benedict's tongue lashed out again. "Don't

come the play-acting with me, you vicious, conniving *she-devil*. Innocent as sin, by God! May the whole accursed edifice rot about your evil little heart of stone, and *bury you!*''

Then he strode from the room, passing her chair without even glancing at her, and slamming the door with such force that the chandelier rattled above the table.

''Come, Miss Ara, come!'' Agnes Diggory was saying, dragging at Araminta's shoulders where she sat, her laughter quenched, tears streaming down her face.

''Diggory, help me!'' the housekeeper called out, jerking her husband out of the stupor into which he appeared to have fallen. He hurried to her aid and between them they managed to half-carry Miss Merchiston from the room.

Theda, meanwhile, had sunk back into her chair, a stricken look in her eyes as she stared unseeingly at Aycliffe.

There was a long silence. The lawyer seemed to be studying his papers, waiting, it seemed to Theda as her brain began to function a little, for her to take the lead. She was shaking so much that she could barely speak. But she said his name.

''Mr Aycliffe?''

He glanced up, a grave look in his face. ''Yes, Miss Kyte?''

''Is there...?'' She swallowed on a dry throat, licked burning lips, and tried again. ''Is there any way I can escape this inheritance?''

He frowned. ''Do you wish to?''

"Yes. Oh, Lord above, *yes!*"

There was another pause. Then the lawyer sighed, rose from his chair, and came down the table to take another next to hers. "Miss Kyte, you are either a very good actress, or an innocent victim of an old lady's wiles. Which is it?"

Theda grimaced. "Why do you ask when, like Benedict, you will take your own view?"

"Mr Beckenham is naturally upset, and therefore prejudiced. I am neither."

"Upset?" Theda repeated with a faint smile. "That is your word for it?"

Mr Aycliffe did not answer this. Instead, resting his elbows on his papers, he laced his fingers together and regarded her over them. "You see, Miss Kyte, things do not look very good for you."

"How do you mean?" Theda asked quickly, frowning over the distress in her face.

"Look at the picture, ma'am. This will was made on the day of the wedding at Switham. No one but yourself was in the house when I came, barring the cook, who is not of the household. The letter that brought me was sent by your hand through the bankers in Ashby-de-la-Zouch. You are the person, moreover, who found Lady Merchiston dead."

"What are you saying?" Theda demanded, indignation warring with the hurt she was experiencing from the dreadful blow that had been dealt her, the vicious attack to which she had been subjected.

"I am enumerating the items that could stand against you should the will be contested," said Mr Aycliffe patiently.

"Contested?" Theda was suddenly eager. "They *could* do so. Both of them!"

"They could. I doubt they would either of them succeed. But in a court of law much could be made of these things."

"There is no need for a court of law. I neither desire this house, nor do I wish to deprive the rightful heirs of what is their own."

For the first time, Mr Aycliffe smiled. "Miss Kyte, there are no *rightful* heirs. Lady Merchiston was under no obligation to bestow her property except as she saw fit."

"Oh, legal quibbling!" Theda uttered irritably. "You know as well as I that both Benedict and Araminta have every moral right to enjoy whatever she had, while I have none at all."

"But *you* are the beneficiary."

"I don't *want* to be the beneficiary!"

"I am afraid it is too late for that," Mr Aycliffe said with a faint smile. "You cannot escape it. Once probate has been granted, which should not take many weeks, this house, and everything in it that is not chosen by Miss Merchiston—"

"Which may well be nothing!" interpolated Theda with a flash of humour.

"Everything, I say, in addition to the rest of her fortune, will be yours."

Theda's eyes widened. "Fortune? Lady Merchiston?"

"Fortune is what I said."

"Oh, come, now, Mr Aycliffe," Theda begged, a laugh of pure exasperation escaping her lips. "After she has already left thirty thousand and more elsewhere? Don't forget, I have lived here three months, and although I know the family to be close-fisted there *cannot* have been much more than that."

"Miss Kyte, it is often the most penny-pinching who have the most at their disposal," the lawyer told her, his eyes twinkling.

Theda shook her head in disbelief, but said, "Very well, sir. You may as well tell me the worst." A glimmer of amusement twisted her mouth. "Since I am like to be murdered for it, I had better know the tune!"

"The tune, ma'am," said Mr Aycliffe lightly, "is in the region of one hundred and fifty thousand pounds—safely invested in the funds."

His face danced in Theda's sight and she sank back in her chair. "Lord help me!" she whispered. "Benedict will *never* forgive me."

Mrs Rosalia Alderley looked about the library at the gleaming, polished wood, the dust-free shelves and the shining leather bindings on the many volumes stacked upon them, and brought her gaze back to Theda's face.

"You have lost no time in setting things to rights, I see," she said in a carefully neutral tone.

It did not deceive Theda. "You don't approve?"

Colour tinged the other woman's cheeks. "No, no, I meant no criticism."

"The *devil* you did not!" Theda burst out. "You will forgive my intemperate language—culled from

Mr Beckenham, I fear!—but let there be no pretence between us, if you please."

Rose put out a hand, saying quickly, "Forgive me! I am sure *you* are not to blame for the iniquitous nature of this wretched will."

"Are you, ma'am?" Theda said sceptically. "Then you are alone in that opinion."

"Nonsense! Aycliffe himself assured me that he is convinced there was no complicity on your part."

"Mr Aycliffe had better post an advertisement to that effect, then, before I am burned at the stake!"

"Don't be so foolish!" said Mrs Alderley quite crossly, rising from her chair.

"My dear Rose, pray sit down again," begged Theda, softening. "I am excessively grateful to you for *not* deserting me in this hideous pass. But there have been local whisperings, so Adam tells us. To tell the truth, I had not expected to see you again."

"I *was* put out," confessed Rose, sinking back into her seat. "But it was not your fault, after all. It is just that being shown into the library, which has been shut up these many years, perhaps brought it home to me how very sad it was for..."

She faltered to a stop, Benedict's name hovering on her lips as she looked uncertainly into Theda's face. Miss Kyte chose not to take up the challenge.

"In fact this is the only room I have touched," she said. "It was a dilemma, you see. Apart from Araminta's parlour—"

"That poky little room! You cannot sit in there!"

"Exactly so. And the saloon is too full. It was only when Taggy found the key to *this* room, and I discovered it to be so beautiful, that we set to and cleaned it between us.''

The library, which had not been in use since Sir John Merchiston's death some seven years earlier, was a very pleasant room, positioned opposite the ballroom, between Araminta's parlour and the big saloon, with panelled walls, quantities of shelving, an ivory inlay desk, leather chairs before the fireplace, and a good deal of light, even on this overcast day, coming in from a glazed door leading out into a pretty walled garden.

''It *is* a nice room,'' Rose agreed.

''The whole house is delightful,'' Theda said decidedly. ''Or it would be if it was rendered habitable once more.''

''Is that what you intend to do? You are going to *stay* here?''

For the first time Theda's veneer of composure cracked a little. ''I would give much to be able to do so...to have a *home*. At least Araminta has achieved that, in spite of being cut out.''

For Araminta Merchiston had become Mrs Saul Quatt within a week of her mother's funeral. It was freely said in the village that the blow to the reverend gentleman had been considerably softened by the terms of his late mother-in-law's will. In a word, Mr Quatt had scooped up Araminta's promised ten thousand with alacrity.

''You may be thankful Quatt took her,'' observed Mrs Alderley. ''Otherwise you would have had her quartered on you forever.''

Theda shuddered. ''Enough to make me run from

here incontinently, as I promise you I had a mind to do!"

"Why did you not?" asked Rose in a more gentle tone than she had yet used.

"Because it would not have solved anything. The house would go more to rack than ever and serve no purpose but to make everyone concerned more miserable than they are already."

"I *knew* you would want to set all to rights," Rose said softly, smiling warmly at her. "You may easily do so, you know."

"How?" Theda demanded, eyeing her visitor with acute suspicion.

"Dear Theda, you must surely be able to see that for yourself. It is so obvious!"

"Indeed? We will have it in plain words nevertheless. How does a woman with a large inheritance commonly bestow it on a man? That is what you mean, is it not? I should marry Benedict."

"Good God, no!" ejaculated Mrs Alderley, startled. "I had not even thought of it."

Theda frowned. "You had not *thought* of it?"

"I swear not! It is Benedict who concerns me, yes, but—but *that* is not the solution I had in mind."

There was no mistaking her sincerity, nor the obvious distaste with which she regarded the very idea of such a union.

"What, then, *did* you have in mind?" Theda asked, torn between a rather misplaced indignation, considering her own views on the subject, and curiosity.

"Well, I thought that you would take something within reason for yourself. Enough, I dare say, to—

to..." She had started with confidence, but under Theda's unnerving eye she began to falter. "Well, to buy yourself a little house, perhaps. Something modest. Something *suitable,* as this really is *not.* And then, for the rest—"

"Yes? For the rest?"

Rose swallowed and came out with it in rather a rush. "Make it over to Benedict by deed of gift."

Theda blinked. "Deed of gift? Lord! Don't you know him better than that? It would stick in his craw!"

Mrs Alderley looked quite crestfallen all of a sudden. "Oh, dear, how right you are! I never thought of that."

"Besides," Theda added, her eyes flashing, "after the way he spoke to me, I am not of a mind to hand him *gifts.*"

"He was *upset,*" Rose said pleadingly, for she had heard from Aycliffe just what Benedict had said in his black fury.

"So everyone keeps telling me," Theda snapped. "As if I have no right to take it amiss."

"He must have hurt you very badly," Rose said in a conciliatory tone, for it was no part of her scheme to antagonise Theda.

"I was not...'hurt'," Theda lied. "It is only the injustice of it which—to which I take exception."

"But Theda, how was he to know?"

"He *should* have known," Theda said through her teeth.

"The—the heat of the moment," pleaded Rose.

"Fudge!"

There was a tense silence. Theda smouldered, trying to contain her anger. That first night, after the shock had begun to abate, the vision of Benedict's snarling features, the sound of molten rage in his voice, had come back to her again and again as she lay in her narrow cot bed, and she had wept. By this time, however, she'd had three weeks in which to move from bitter, aching despair, to bitter, aching fury. For she had been so sure that, once he had turned the matter over in a cooler frame of mind, he would recognise and acknowledge her innocence. He would return to her, to beg her pardon for so basely misjudging her, and they would find again the former ease of friendship, the lack of which now gaped in her life like an open wound.

But Benedict had not come back. He had sent no word. He was as hot against her as ever, and would probably remain so.

"In any event," Theda said, speaking her thought aloud, "he told me himself he had no claim on Lady Merchiston. She owed him nothing."

"That," said Rose Alderley flatly, "is a matter of opinion."

Theda turned her head and noted the set look in the other's face. Yes, Rose knew it all! With deliberation, she said, "It is a pity I cannot judge for myself."

Rose looked struck. Slowly she spoke. "Well, why should you not? After all, Lavinia is dead now, and you are no longer in her employ."

Theda waited. How much would Rose reveal? She had ever been curious about Benedict's background, and now more so than ever, when everything hinged on his moral claim to Merchiston Lodge.

Mrs Alderley sat lost in thought for a few moments. Then she nodded with decision and rose from her chair. "Let us walk outside. It is no longer raining, and I do not care to talk where anyone might hear."

They went out through a gate in the walled garden, and encountered Hector almost at once. He was now largely permitted to roam the grounds in freedom, and he came gambolling up to greet Theda with a bark, and then went off exploring again, just keeping the ladies in sight, and returning now and again for a pat or an encouraging word.

"There is at least one who has adapted himself to circumstance," observed Theda.

"Surprising," commented Rose. "I should think he was the only creature for whom Lavinia truly cared."

They began to pace along the drive, for the grass was still damp from the recent rain.

"I think you are mistaken," Theda said in an even tone. "I think she cared for Benedict."

"She had a strange way of showing it, then."

"Because she left the property to me? Yet she always came to his rescue when he was in difficulties."

"That?" scornfully responded Mrs Alderley. "A bagatelle! Sir John died seven years ago, but in all that time Lavinia has not increased Benedict's allowance, as she might well have done, nor made any provision for his accommodation, other than saying that he might live at Merchiston Lodge if he chose."

"Which he obviously did not choose. But why

should she have done those things?'' Theda demanded.

''Because Sir John wished it,'' Rose told her angrily.

''Not that he trusted her. His own wife, mark you! Apart from the measly sums she doled out from time to time, the allowance was Benedict's by right, for it was left in trust for him by her husband. He would have done better to have given everything to the boy outright, but it is my belief he did not want Benedict to lose touch with his godmother.''

''You mean if he had not to come to her for money, he would not have come at all?'' Theda guessed. ''I can readily believe it.''

''Yes, and I am sure it is because Sir John *meant* him to have the house. Benedict told me he said as much to him.''

''What about his own daughter?'' Theda asked.

''Oh, he was as bad as Lavinia on that count. He said she had ruined her chances by obstinacy and might count herself lucky to live on Benedict's charity.''

''But what a charming family!''

''You may well say so! And it was into *this* that Benedict was dragged, through no fault of his own, poor boy!''

Theda looked round at her. ''What precisely happened, ma'am? So far I have had only hints.''

Rose shook her head, distress in her face. ''It was all so *dreadful*. Isabel fell from grace, which is *nothing* new in our circles, let me tell you. Except that she became with child, and Robert—her husband, you must know, who was a brute with a terrible temper!—refused to acknowledge it as his own. The truth was, of course, that he was in love with someone else and chose to use poor Isabel as a scapegoat.''

''He left her?'' asked Theda, disturbed by an immediate rush of fellow feeling for the unfortunate woman.

''Worse!'' groaned Rose. ''He took his suit through the full panoply of law—Doctors' Commons, then a court of common law, and finally the House of Lords.''

''Divorce?'' Theda uttered in a shocked tone.

Mrs Alderley was hunting for her pocket handkerchief. ''Yes. You may im-imagine the shocking s-scandal!'' She blew her nose and wiped the tears from her eyes. ''And Isabel utterly cast off, immured in the Dower House the while.''

''Oh, how *cruel,*'' Theda said. ''But how did she come here?''

''She was in such despair, poor girl,'' explained Rose, having recourse to her handkerchief again. ''Pregnant, too, and without a sight of her only son. At last she wrote to Sir John Merchiston, who was a remote cousin, but whom she had known when she came as a débutante to visit here with her family for the hunting.''

Sir John, it appeared, had retained a sufficiently fond memory of his cousin, and was, besides, so moved by her plight that he went himself and fetched her back to Switham. There followed a long wrangle over Benedict's future, which Sir John Merchiston eventually won by virtue of the fact that Robert Beckenham's new wife was delivered of a boy. Benedict, at less than ten years of age, was himself delivered into the care of the mother he had not seen for almost two years.

"There was no inheritance in the case, you see, for Robert Beckenham was only a third son and chose to live at home in idleness rather than follow a profession."

It was evident to Theda that Benedict's father could find no favour in Mrs Alderley's eyes, but she could herself perceive some echo of his father's faults in Benedict—of temper, she recalled with a tightening of the lips, and Lady Lavinia had certainly considered him idle and spendthrift.

"What happened to the baby?" she asked.

"Isabel miscarried, which was why she became so mad for Benedict's coming here."

"But when she died? Was there no thought of sending him back to his father?" Theda asked.

"He would not have gone!" Rose declared. "In any event, he was near fifteen by then, and looked on Sir John very much as a father. Indeed, it was reciprocal. *Unfortunately,*" she added, with a quick look round as if she thought to check whether anyone might hear, "Sir John's partiality for Benedict extended also to his mother."

Oddly, Theda felt no surprise. "Thereby accounting for the jealousies of Lady Lavinia and Araminta both."

"Yes, for Sir John was so unwise as to hold up Isabel's beauty—and she was so *very* beautiful, the image, apart from the hair, of Benedict—against poor

Araminta. Comparing them, you know, and making his preference all too obvious. I heard him at it several times, pretending to joke his daughter, but in fact making her the butt of his mockery. And all this always *before* Isabel's face."

"Small wonder the girl ended by hating her!" Theda commented. "And Lady Merchiston? Did she know of her husband's faithlessness?"

"Oh, he was not *unfaithful*. At least, I never understood so from Isabel. But of course she knew. Wives always do, don't they? She behaved in a shocking way towards her. She was spiteful and unkind, both to Isabel and to her son—until his mother was dead, when she changed dramatically towards Benedict at least. What made it ten times worse, you see, was that Lavinia had strongly resisted Isabel's coming in the first place. It tainted them all with the scandal."

"It would, of course," Theda agreed, able even in the pain he had caused her to understand now why Benedict had never trusted his godmother.

"It need not have done," Rose argued. "But Lavinia chose to abandon her social contacts to punish Sir John. She never went to London after Isabel came here. By the time Isabel died, it was too late to alter that, for she was herself already wasting."

"How did she die?"

"She caught a fever in the village. Benedict had it, too. But I don't think Isabel wanted to live." Tears stood once more in Rose's eyes. "She had suffered so much for so long. I think she welcomed the end."

For a while they walked in silence, retracing their

steps back up towards the house. Theda waited for her visitor to compose herself before speaking.

"Very well, ma'am. Now I am suitably softened up, what more can you say to persuade me to give everything up to Benedict?"

"Not *everything,*" Rose said, apparently impervious to Theda's irony. "I would not expect that. Nor advocate it, indeed."

"No, foolish beyond permission! And so *wasteful* of me, don't you think?"

Mrs Alderley stared at her, nonplussed. "I don't understand you."

"My dear Rose," Theda said with a smile, "you have so espoused Benedict's cause that you imagine it is enough to tell me all his unfortunate history to make me realise what I already know. *None* of this belongs to me. By rights I *should* give it up. But whether to Benedict or Araminta remains a matter for dispute."

"Araminta! Good God, Theda, you cannot be serious!" gasped Rose.

"Certainly I am. She may be a spiteful piece, but there is no doubt that she has been very badly treated. At war both with mother and father! Her life has been quite as miserable as your Isabel's, I fear. I only hope she may find happiness with Saul Quatt."

"Well, hope it no longer! I declare, I could shake you, Theda! She had her chances and she threw them away. She would not know *how* to be happy."

"And I?" Theda cried. "Am I also to have no happiness?" She saw the quick remorse in Rose's face and stretched out a hand to her. "Never mind!

Rest assured I will not buy my own happiness at the expense of...of another's."

"Then you *will* give it to Benedict?" Rose said eagerly, turning to grasp Theda's hands. Without giving her an opportunity to reply, she went on, "As for yourself, I have the most splendid notion! You will retain enough of this fortune for a decent dowry and come to London to find a husband. And I will sponsor you. There!"

There was no echo of her radiance in Theda's face. She looked, if anything, paler than usual, her grey eyes dark with some unfathomable emotion. Mrs Alderley's own eyes dimmed.

"Theda?" she said uncertainly.

Removing her hands from Rose's grasp, Theda responded quietly, "That is quite impossible."

Mrs Alderley frowned in perplexity. "Impossible?"

"Utterly. Don't let us talk of it. Besides, until probate is granted, all is conjecture. I shall simply remain here until I know for certain what my situation really is."

"I suppose you must," Rose said reluctantly, and Theda wondered if she had imagined all might be settled at once. But her mind appeared not to be on that at all. "You can't stay here alone, Theda. You will have to hire a companion."

"A companion!" echoed Theda. "For *me?*" The irony of it struck her forcibly and her gurgling laughter broke out. "There is your answer. I shall hire Benedict to live with me and leave him the place in my will!"

* * *

In late July, Mrs Rosalia Alderley, accompanied by her husband and her son—on holiday from school—in addition to her remaining daughter, made a belated appearance in the seaside resort of Brighton, made fashionable by the young Prince of Wales and his followers.

Among the gentry residing there was to be found Mr Benedict Beckenham, riding as hard as he could to the devil. He responded to an imperative summons with an ill grace, and presented himself in the drawing-room of Rose's hired house in a mood of ill-concealed annoyance.

"What do you want, Rose?" he demanded truculently.

"You look terrible!" she exclaimed, taking in the blue shadows under his bloodshot eyes and the air of decadence that hung about him.

"What did you expect?" he returned. "To find me in rollicking good humour, basking in my good fortune?"

"Oh, Benedict!" Rose sighed.

She held out a hand to him and patted the sofa beside her. Benedict looked at the hand, and pointedly took a chair on the other side of the room, lounging in a stance of deliberate contempt. The colour in Rose's cheek heightened.

"Good God, Benedict! It is not *my* fault that your godmother chose to cut you out."

"No," he agreed. "But you need not expect my goodwill if you choose to consort with the enemy."

"Enemy? Don't be foolish! Theda is nothing of the sort."

"What, then, is she? Other than a double-dealing traitor who has chiselled me out of my dues, while throwing out lures to throw dust in my eyes!"

Rose fairly gaped at him. "You don't know what you're talking about!"

His eyes narrowed. "So she has beguiled you, too, has she?" He gave a short, ugly laugh. "It was to be expected. She would fool anyone with that play of honesty, that—" his voice thickened, passion suddenly rife within it "—that damned shining *innocence.*"

He seemed to explode out of the chair, pacing to and fro as if he could not be still.

"How could she do it to me? How *could* she? Oh, she bowled me out, all right! With that luminous cheek of hers, that flame she used to *enslave* me. Taunting me with digs at my honour, when all the time..."

He broke off, almost grinding his teeth, and flung over to the window to stare out.

Mrs Alderley gazed stupefied at his rigid back. Good God, there was more here than she ever dreamed! Theda, too. What *was* there between them? For Benedict had not spoken rationally, nor like a man whose hopes had been disappointed. He raged like a man betrayed, like a man whose trust had been smashed. The next thought came only to be dismissed: like a man *crossed in love?* No! Absurd. Yet if it was so...

"Benedict!" she said imperatively.

He turned. He had regained command over himself, for there was no trace now in his handsome features of the recent turmoil, only the too evident ravages of dissipation.

"Yes?" he said, raising his brows. He noted the determined air about her, and a cynical smile curled his fine mouth. "Pray save the lecture, Rose. You know I am free to gamble my way into a debtor's prison. Allow me to go to perdition in my own fashion!"

"There is no necessity for you 'to go to perdition'," Rose said crossly. "You are an improvident fool, Benedict, if you cannot see the answer."

To her surprise, the cynical look became more pronounced than ever. "Marriage? Save your breath! She has already refused me—in no uncertain terms."

Mrs Alderley gasped. "You mean you *asked* her?"

"Not exactly. It was my beloved godmother's idea, but..." He stopped, an arrested look in his face. "Dear *God!* So that was it. The cunning old witch!"

"What in the world...?" began Rose, feeling quite bewildered as he let out an amused laugh.

"I see it all now," he said, a perfectly genuine smile crossing his suddenly lightened features. Then he frowned again. "Yes, I see it. But will *she?*"

"Benedict!" uttered Mrs Alderley, exasperated. "What are you talking about?"

He grinned at her. "Just what you were talking about, Rose. Marriage. Forgive me! I must go. I have a most urgent appointment—at Merchiston Lodge."

It was in fact more than a week later that he finally arrived in Switham. At first sight the house seemed very little changed, except that the area of grass about the porch had been scythed. It was a bright day and the early August sun picked out the myriad windows across the front, which winked at him as Benedict took his curricle down the drive. But the significance of this did not strike him at the moment.

Forgetting his altered status here, he drove around to the stables and, as he had always done before, saw to his own horses before entering the house via the kitchen premises.

"Mr Benedict!" uttered Agnes Diggory, looking up from the pastry she was rolling. "I took you for Adam, for he's gone down Mountsorrel to fetch in some supplies."

"Hello, Taggy," Benedict said, smiling at her. "Are you cook, too, now? Where's Mrs Elswick?"

The housekeeper clicked her tongue. "Gone off to serve Miss Ara, she has—or rather, *Mrs Quatt,* I should say. Tried to get me and Adam away and all, but we wasn't to be budged!"

"I am glad to hear it," he said, thinking how like Araminta it was to try and leave Theda totally unattended. "Where is Miss Kyte?"

"I don't rightly know, Mr Benedict. Could be anywhere, Miss Theda could. Always busily employed." She wiped her floury hands on her apron. "I'll go and find her, shall I?"

"No, don't trouble yourself," Benedict said quickly. He came up to her and planted a kiss on her cheek, grinning. "I'm glad to find you at least don't hold my bad temper against me!"

"Oh, go on with you, Mr Benedict! If I was to have done that in *this* house, I'd have packed my bags long ago!"

"Very true," he agreed. "Where's Hector, by the by?"

"Likely he'll be out roaming, if he's not with Miss Theda. Regular wanderer he's turned out, now the mistress is gone."

"Well, his *new* mistress does not keep her bed." He saw Agnes fold her lips together and put her attention back on her pastry. "What is it, Taggy? Miss Theda *is* the new mistress of this house."

"That's as may be," Mrs Diggory said shortly.

Benedict frowned. "You don't approve?"

"Ain't for me to say." She paused, but the vexation would not be contained. "But I'd be the better pleased if she'd take on and *be* the mistress!"

"What do you mean, Taggy? She can't do much with the place until probate is granted."

Mrs Diggory shook her head. "You don't know her, Mr Benedict. And as for not doing much, you'd hardly recognise the place!"

Benedict laughed. "It looks much the same to me."

"That's because you're a man, sir," scoffed Agnes. "And I don't know about all this 'probate' flummery, because it ain't stopped Miss Ara and that there reverend husband of hers from taking all they want."

"What?"

"Well may you stare, sir! I wish you could've seen them," said the housekeeper, her arms akimbo, her plump face flushed with indignation. "Going round the place arm in arm, the two of them, picking and choosing. *He* as bad as she, let me tell you. Twice they've been with a cart, and Miss Theda let them take it all without a word said!"

"Well, they are premature, but Araminta is entitled to it," Benedict commented, surprisingly unmoved.

"Humph!" grumbled Agnes, by no means convinced. "Not a stick of silver is there in this house, Mr Benedict. And if they'd a bigger place than that there little rectory, there wouldn't be a stick of furniture neither!"

"I would not bank on that, Taggy," Benedict said cynically. "Araminta will very likely make the wretched man stuff it all into his church."

"Mercy, *no,*" gasped the housekeeper. "Though I dare say Miss Theda wouldn't fret. She ain't even moved out of that there little room next the mistress, and all those lovely bedchambers up there standing empty."

Benedict left her, armed with food for much thought, and a recommendation to try the library. As soon as he entered the hall, it was immediately apparent that there *was* a change. Sunlight streamed in from the windows above the gallery, bathing the polished panels of the walls in a warm glow. The staircase gleamed, and the banisters and railings all around the gallery gave off the same sheen. There was a new smell in the air—the fresh scent of flowers, a hint of lemon, and a drowsy aroma that reminded him of honey.

Beeswax! he realised, looking about in wonder. The place was *clean.* The windows were sparkling, the ivy stripped away to let in the light. All at once he pictured again the sun striking the glass and understood why it had done so. Moreover, the doors to the ballroom and library were open, letting in the air. So this was all it took! A little spit and polish, and a pair of determined, busy hands.

He crossed to the library and entered, assailed at once by warm memories of the man who had been to him the nearest thing to a father. He had worked at his books in here as a boy, shared port with Sir John as a stripling in his callow youth, sitting across from him before the fire in this male stronghold, deep in the leather chair. Here had he buried his face in Sir John's broad chest to weep for the loss of his mother.

Something swelled inside him. *He must have this house.* Hell and the devil confound it, this was his *home!* And it had been taken away from him.

All the resentment came flooding back. Wasn't it enough that he had been so humiliated? Must he now grind his pride in the dust and sue for the hand of she to whom he owed that indignity? For whether or no she had been instrumental in the making of that despicable will, it was her presence here that had caused it to be made. Had she not come, it would have been himself against Araminta, and he would have *won.* Even had he not, he might have supported with more equanimity *that* defeat. But *this*...no, by God, it was too much to expect of him!

About to leave the room with the intention of driving immediately away, he checked at a slight sound by the open door to the outside and looked around.

In an old cotton gown of striped dimity stood Theda, just outside on the shallow step, so that the bright sun glanced off the uncovered copper hair, which was piled untidily on top of her head, a few strands breaking loose and waving into the bare expanse of pale, glowing flesh above her bosom. With her back against the sun, her face was shadowed so that he could not see her eyes. But he knew that she stared at him, and felt rather than saw the hostility there.

Chapter Eight

Benedict's pulse began to beat in his throat, and he fought vainly against that familiar rush of heat to his blood that invariably engulfed him at the sight of her. His mind blanked. He was dumb.

"Why have you come?"

It was the thread of a voice, for Theda, too, fought against the giddy pounding of her heart in his unexpected presence. She had heard the arrival as she weeded in the walled garden, but, like Taggy, she had taken it for Diggory. Only now did she recognise that there had been more than one horse. It could not have been the gig.

He did not answer. He did not even move. Only stood staring, unaware of the mix of emotions in his face: double fire in his eyes—anger and desire both; the sneer on his lips that was almost a smile; and the still-present evidence of his recent excesses—a pallid complexion and the darker skin beneath his eyes, the deeper carved lines down to his mouth.

Distress smote Theda as she took in his condition and knew herself to be the cause of it. Tears stung her eyes, and she turned as from an unbearable sight to vanish back into the garden outside.

Benedict found his tongue. ''*Theda*...Theda, wait!''

With swift steps he crossed to the glazed door and saw her crouched before a flowerbed, apparently engrossed in the task of tugging weeds from between the flowering rose bushes.

''Confound you, can't you even face me now?'' he growled, and, walking up to her, he bent to seize her arms and drag her to her feet. ''Get up! *Look* at me!''

''Let me go!'' she snapped, wrath drowning out both her guilt and the unconscious soaring of her heart at seeing him again. But she *was* looking at him, the deep grey eyes blindingly furious. ''How dare you manhandle me like this? What do you want?''

His grip on her arms did not relax. ''I came here to apologise, but if this is your attitude I'm damned if I do!''

''*My* attitude? Look to your own, you unmitigated bully! *Let me go.*''

She brought up her clenched fists to beat at him, and as he saw the dirt on them Benedict did let her go, stepping back out of the way.

''Why the devil can't you employ a gardener on such work?'' he demanded irascibly.

''Because I can't afford one!'' she threw at him, automatically dusting off her hands a little.

''Don't be ridiculous! I know how much my godmother was worth. And don't tell me probate is not yet granted, for I know that too. I'm waiting for my own funds.''

"Then you should know there's not a penny in the house," Theda retorted. "We are living on enough credit as it is."

"My good girl, don't you know *anything?* Ask Aycliffe for an advance."

"I don't *need* one," Theda returned, brushing the back of her hand at a lock of hair which was blowing across her face.

A frown came into Benedict's eyes and he reached out, his fingers closing about her wrist. Theda resisted, pulling away.

"Be *still,*" he growled. "Show me your hands!"

Unthinkingly, Theda held the other out to him as he turned the one he had entrapped palm up. Under the brown stains could clearly be seen the white bumps of calluses.

"You confounded little fool!" Benedict uttered, somewhere between a scold and a caress. "You've been slaving like a scullery maid."

Theda snatched her hands away. "What is it to you?"

His eyes blazed. "Do you think I've lost a fortune only to see it salted away in the same nip-cheese fashion as before? For God's sake, *live* a little, woman! Haven't you had enough of drudgery?"

A gleam of humour irresistibly lit Theda's eyes. "Am I to spend it for *your* pleasure or my own?"

"Both," he said instantly, and suddenly his voice was urgent. His fingers again grasped her shoulders, pulling her closer. "Theda, don't you see? *This* is what Aunt Lavvy intended! You *know* she meant us to marry. This is her way of bringing it about."

Theda's lip trembled and her eyes darkened, while the amusement drained out of her face. "Let me go, if you please, Benedict. What you suggest is—is quite impossible."

His eyes burned into hers. "Don't say that, Theda! We must *make* it possible. It's the only way."

"I *cannot,*" she uttered in a stifled voice, trying to pull away.

Benedict imprisoned her closer, oblivious to her grubby hands caught against the pristine whiteness of his neckcloth. His voice was hoarse.

"I didn't mean the things I said that day, my lovely witch. I *want* you."

His lips pressed against her hair, ran across the brow, all damp as it was with perspiration. Theda felt the warm ache inside her, and resisted the more.

"*No.* Pray, pray, let me *go.*"

His breath was warm on her cheek, closing in. She turned her face away, desperate to avoid his kiss. His voice came huskily in her ear.

"Theda, don't deny me!"

"I *must,*" she cried, and wrenched herself out of his hold, stepping back and holding one hand up in a pleading gesture. "No, don't *touch* me, Benedict! You may *have* the house. You may have the *money.* I don't *want* them. But we must find another way. I *cannot* marry you!"

His lips formed the "why?" but he did not speak. His breath ragged, his eyes near wild, he stared at her, and it came to him then that he wanted it *all*: the house, the money, and Theda, too. Nothing less would satisfy him!

About to speak, he paused as a distant squealing came to his ears. Theda heard it, too.

"What in the devil's name is that?" he demanded, following her as she crossed quickly to the gate and moved out into the grounds.

The squealing became slightly louder, and clearer—the yowls of an animal in pain. They glanced at each other, and the same recognition struck them both.

"Hector."

Then Benedict was running, with Theda in hot pursuit, around the corner of the house towards Switham Thicket. Panting, Theda groped her way through the thick undergrowth, her direction signalled by Benedict crashing through ahead of her, and the howls of the dog growing ever louder.

She heard Benedict swearing and knew he had located the animal. Hurrying, she came upon him kneeling by Hector, whose howls had reduced at sight of rescue to pathetic whimpers.

"What is it?" she gasped out. "What has happened to him?"

"Can't you see?" snapped Benedict angrily. "I hope to heaven this leg is not broken!"

He moved behind the dog as he spoke, and Theda could see that Hector had caught a front foot in a trap.

"Oh, dear Lord!" she exclaimed, dropping to her knees.

Benedict was casting about. "I need a stout stick. Hold him!"

He found a thick piece of deadwood, and broke off

the twigs. This he inserted under the spring and put his own booted foot on the trap.

"Keep him still!" he commanded, heaving at the lever.

"Hush, Hector! Hush, now," Theda crooned, grasping the animal tightly to her, and avoiding the sight of his trapped foot.

Hector squealed as the trap lifted a fraction, but Theda quickly drew the foot out and the trap sprung back with a clang. Gritting her teeth, she tried to examine the hurt, but Benedict was before her, throwing away the stick and gently taking the dog's paw in his hands.

"Is it broken, do you think?" Theda asked fearfully, still clasping Hector's shivering body to her.

"No, but badly cut. Fortunately it was only meant for rabbits." Suddenly he turned a face of fury on Theda. "What the devil possessed you to set traps here, when you knew the dog was roaming?"

"*I* set traps?" she repeated, stung. "I did no such thing!"

"Well, someone must have."

"Oh, use your wits, Benedict! It is poachers, of course. We shall have to inform the Alderleys' gamekeeper."

"Never mind that!" he said impatiently. "Let me take Hector. That wound must be dressed."

Picking up the dog, he carried him, still whimpering, to the house, while Theda ran ahead to find basilicum powder and linen for a bandage. In a very short time, the two of them, together with Mrs Diggory, were fussing about the dog in the library, with bowls of warm water, blankets, an old sheet torn in strips, and even some milk laced with laudanum unearthed from the late Lady Merchiston's store of medicines in the attics.

It was early evening by the time the house settled down again, and Theda and Benedict, exhausted, found themselves alone together, one in each leather chair either side of Hector, asleep on a blanket before the fire that Adam Diggory, back from Mountsorrel, had lit in the grate in spite of the warmth of the day. Either one or the other had remained with Hector throughout the afternoon, taking turns, at Mrs Diggory's insistence, in going to the breakfast parlour to eat.

Theda had washed the dirt off her hands, but she was still attired in the old cotton gown, now stained with blood as well as dirt. She sat, leaning her cheek on her hand, gazing down at the dog, her flaming hair falling untidily down her back, and over her shoulders, and glistening in the light from the candelabrum on the mantel and the glow of the fire.

Benedict, quite as dishevelled as she, if not as dirty, sat and watched her. His heart contracted and the thought struck him that this domestic scene encompassed all he could ever want of life.

She seemed to feel his scrutiny, for she looked up, smiling involuntarily. Their eyes met and held. Time seemed to lie in suspension. When they began to speak, so softly, it was as if their mouths uttered words that did not match their thoughts.

"So much work! Why, Theda?"

"I am used to work."

He smiled. "The ghost passes through, cleansing the place of shadows."

"Soon there will be nowhere to hide...and she'll have to move on again."

"No," he protested, and his voice sharpened. "Why won't you marry me, Theda? *Tell* me."

At once she broke the contact, looking away and rising. The intimacy was gone. A sense of loss invaded Benedict's breast, and he rose as well, taking a step towards her.

"You owe me that much!" he insisted, vehement now. *"Why?"*

"Because of what I am!" she burst out, facing him squarely. "Let that be your answer, and ask me no more."

"It isn't good enough!" he told her, his ire rising.

"Pray, hush! You will wake the dog," Theda chided in a low tone, moving away to the other side of the room by the desk where they had ministered to Hector's hurt. On it lay the remnants of bandages, the scissors and a tin of basilicum powder, lit by another candelabrum.

Benedict followed her, lowering his voice, however. "You cannot fob me off so. I *will* learn your confounded secret."

"By what right do you demand it of me?" Theda said, turning on him. "You are very free with your plans and schemes for *my* future. I will not be coerced! You and Lady Lavinia, you are two of a kind. If *she* thought by this means she might bend me to her will, she was as mistaken as you are now. As for you, Benedict, neither your cajolery nor your hectoring will work with me. I know that you want me, and I know why you would marry me. But I don't choose to sell myself, do you see?"

"I thought *I* was the one up for sale," sneered Benedict. "This is as much foisted on to me as on to you."

"Then there is no need to pursue it! Rose suggested a deed of gift, and that will suffice."

"A deed of gift? So that you may vanish away and hide yourself from me? Never!" He took her by the shoulders and shook her. "Do you hear me, Theda? You are mine and I will never let you go!"

Her hand came up to strike him, but he was quicker, seizing her wrist. "No, you don't, termagant!" He turned her about and held her imprisoned against him, the better to control her, and the better to feel her body against his own. He buried his face in the untidy tresses coursing about her twisting neck.

"Release me at once!" she panted, struggling madly.

"Never," he repeated huskily. "By God, you kept all your fires so well hidden, didn't you, witch? That passion that you know you share with me, and that fiery temper to match your glorious hair! God, how you *inflame* me!"

Theda groped about the surface of the desk as she felt his lips burning into her neck, sending the betraying heat flittering through her.

"If my hair is responsible, then I shall be rid of it!" she cried, and swung aloft the scissors which her fingers had found.

"The devil you will!" he snarled, and seized the

scissors from her. "You will never cut it, not while I'm alive!"

"Then it will *fade,*" she told him in triumph. "So Lady Lavinia told me, and so I have seen. Give it up, Benedict! You cannot keep it thus forever."

"Then, confound you, I'll cut it myself," he threatened, raising the open scissors before her face, and seizing a handful of hair in his fingers, "and *keep* it so."

Theda froze in his grasp. "No, *don't.* Benedict, I beg of you, *no.*"

He pressed her head back so that it rested on his shoulder. His voice gentled her, caressing. "Still, my fearful ghost, be still! I won't hurt you."

"Then let me go," she begged.

"Presently." His lips were in her neck and she shivered involuntarily at their touch, her eyes still on the scissors in his hand. "Theda, why are we fighting? Where's the purpose in it?"

She almost cried out as his mouth traced a path of fervid heat across her cheek. She felt his fingers in her hair and his arm tight about her, and her bones turned to liquid. Then his mouth was on hers and she groaned, turning unconsciously into him a little.

"Look at me!" he whispered as his lips left hers.

Her eyes opened and she saw that he had tugged a long strand of hair free and was playing it between his fingers. Was that all she was to him—a head of sensuous hair?

"I'll have this, Theda," he said huskily. "Mark me well, for I'll have you and your crowning glory, and the house, and the money, if I die in the attempt!"

A sense of hurt and outrage welled up inside her. Pain gnawed at her. What was she, that he could lay claim to her like this? Had she become part of his vaunted inheritance, too?

Benedict saw the change in her face and a frown came into his eyes. "What is it?"

Her fingers seized the scissors from his slackened grasp, and she snipped at the strand of hair he held. He was so surprised that he let her go, as if she had cut herself free of him.

"Take it, then!" she almost spat at him. "If that is what you want of me, take it. You may have the rest that you covet as soon as I am able to make it over to you."

She threw the scissors down on the table, glaring at him. His eyes narrowed, and he curled the hair about his finger.

"I'll take it," he said curtly. "On account. Keep the confounded house. And the money. Until you're willing to give yourself with them, I don't want any part of either!"

"Why should you dare to try and strike such a bargain?" she demanded frustratedly.

"Why should you dare to refuse me without giving me a reason?" he countered.

She caught the echo of pain in his voice. But her own was too strong to be set aside. "I'm not to be a pawn in your game, Benedict!"

"Then be queen to my king!"

"I cannot, I cannot, I *cannot!*" she almost screamed.

"Then you can burn in hell for all I care!" he burst

out, and, turning on his heel, he marched to the door and flung it open.

For a moment Theda stood where he had left her, hardly aware that he had gone. Dear Lord, he did want her! Would he really give everything up? She did not believe it, but all the same she ran to the door. He was already halfway down the hall.

"Benedict!" she called out after him, her voice rampant with the passion she could no longer control. "Where are you going?"

"To the devil!" he yelled back, without turning round. Next moment he was gone.

Mr Beckenham, partaking of his friend Woolacombe's hospitality in that gentleman's absence in Brighton, sat over his dinner fighting the urge to go back to Theda and press his suit once more. Why the devil was she so stubborn? What was there in her murky past to raise this barrier between them?

The memory of their first meeting haunted him. They had slipped, right then, all unknowing, into an unconventional intimacy that had led them, he was convinced, to this present pass. In ordinary circumstances, persons of their order would never be permitted sufficient licence to be alone together, and so enkindle the fire that sparked between them. Had she been of any other class, he would long ago have stormed her defences and conquered.

He frowned over the glass of brandy in his hand—his fifth or sixth? He had half emptied Woolacombe's decanter, and yet his head was scarcely touched. *Was* it because of her quality? He had not thought himself so chivalrous. The *devil* it was! He slammed the glass to the table. *She* was responsible.

She knew, for she had told him so that first night, that her situation, alone, unchaperoned, *unprotected*—and that was the worst of it!—laid her open to advances. No doubt she'd had ample proof of it. The thought made his jaw tighten and his hands curl and harden into fists that might smash the unknown male faces of those who had *dared* so far! But had they, too, come up against that indefinable barrier that had stopped him?

She, contained spirit, all her fires damped, had put out to him the message that said "stop!" And he had. But now, with her fires so stoked that she could no longer contain them, her messages were confused. And she had him in turmoil! *Confound* her.

Snatching up his glass again, he tossed off the liquid it contained and stood up. He *would* have her. He had toyed with the idea of marriage, flirted with it only to tease her before his godmother's death. It was different now. He would have her—to *keep*—and she would put him in possession of his disappointed expectations.

The following day he drove to Mountsorrel to seek out Aycliffe.

"I had expected you before this, Mr Beckenham," said the lawyer with a twinkle, setting a chair for his client to sit down in the drawing-room of the small house that served also for his office.

His clerks worked next door in what would have been the library, and his family used the upper floors for their own apartments. It was, he felt, one of the advantages of living and working in a small town. In London, where he had been apprenticed as a young man, the poky City offices had been suffocating.

"I was otherwise engaged," Benedict answered shortly. Then he grinned. "To tell you the truth, Aycliffe, I was so devilish put out that I had determined to shake the dust of this place from my heels forever!"

"That was rather the impression that I gathered, sir," the lawyer said with a lift of one ironic eyebrow. "What changed your mind?"

Benedict hesitated, eyeing the man. The devil! Theda would not hesitate to speak her mind. By God, she could teach him a thing or two yet! He leaned forward, resting his elbows on the table, lowering his voice confidentially.

"Aycliffe, I'm trusting you with this. I mean to marry Miss Kyte, and so gain possession of Merchiston Lodge and Aunt Lavinia's fortune." He held up a hand as Aycliffe pursed his lips. "Pray don't look austerely upon me. If you knew the full sum of the doings before she died, you would see that this is the result my godmother intended."

"Is it the result *Miss Kyte* intends, sir?" asked the lawyer shrewdly.

"Confound your impudence!" Benedict hit the surface of the desk with the flat of his palm.

"I beg your pardon, Mr Beckenham, but I am, you will recall, Miss Kyte's man of business in her new capacity."

After a moment's glaring silence, Benedict sighed, relaxing. "You are right, of course. It is *not* Theda's intention. But you must understand that her refusal has nothing to do with her *wishes*. There is some impediment. Or at least, so she believes. And this is where I think you may be able to be of service to me."

"Indeed?" frowned Aycliffe.

"Yes, in point of discovering information. Miss Kyte is not, you must have realised, any ordinary female. There is a mystery surrounding her background, which she will not reveal."

"That is her prerogative, surely?" objected the lawyer.

Benedict was leaning forward again. "Aycliffe, this is no indigent genteel girl, forced into such a life by poverty! She has been wandering from post to post for six years, having left her home in, I suspect, scandalous circumstances. Now what does that suggest to you?"

In spite of himself, the lawyer was beginning to be interested. "There are several possibilities for such a flight. All would almost certainly involve another party."

"Precisely—a man!" said Benedict grimly. "Whatever happened to part them, she considers herself so tainted that marriage is out of the question."

Aycliffe looked appalled. "And you would *override* that belief?"

Benedict rose from his own chair so hastily that it almost tipped over. "Don't *dare* impugn her! Override it? Of course I shall override it! What, am I to condemn the girl for one silly mistake to a lifetime of slights and abuse? She has been punished enough, by God, by her own dread conscience! Am I to watch *another* woman sink into her grave for want of a little *compassion?*''

Suddenly, he threw a hand across his eyes for an instant, and, turning, strode to the window and stood with his back to the room, his shoulders rigid.

Mr Aycliffe watched him in silence, his own eyes full of pity. He knew the man's history, and could not but be moved by his appeal.

Benedict spoke without turning round, his voice gruff. ''You must pardon my intemperance. It is not a subject upon which I can speak with any moderation.''

''I am aware, Mr Beckenham,'' said the lawyer gently.

Turning at last, Benedict smiled a little. ''Of course you are. I had forgot.'' His voice hardened again. ''But don't *you* forget this: I will never tolerate one word in disparagement of Miss Kyte's honour!''

Aycliffe bowed. ''Your sentiments do you credit, sir.''

A little shamefacedly, Benedict laughed, his colour heightened. ''In fact they don't. Not towards Miss Kyte, in any event.'' Something struck him all at once, and he smote his own forehead. ''What a dolt I am! *Kyte*. It must be a false name.''

''Jupiter!'' ejaculated the lawyer involuntarily. He was suddenly very alert. ''Do you really think so, Mr Beckenham? That would alter things indeed!''

Benedict stared at him blankly. ''How do you mean?''

''The will, sir! If Miss Kyte—if that is not indeed

her real name, then the matter is up for dispute at once.''

''You mean it may be contested successfully?'' demanded Benedict, coming swiftly forward.

''I don't say that, sir, but it certainly opens up the prospects. If she is not the person she purports to be, it may be argued in law that the will is invalid. That there is no such person as Miss Theodosia Kyte, and therefore—''

''But it is not *automatically* invalidated?'' interrupted Benedict anxiously. ''*That* would serve Araminta, and neither myself nor Theda would benefit.''

Aycliffe frowned portentously. ''I think it would rather be a matter of *relinquishment* of the claim. Voluntarily, you understand.''

''Oh, the devil! A day or two ago I would have welcomed this,'' Benedict said irritably, beginning to pace. ''Now it seems only to worsen the coil!''

''Calm yourself, sir, I beg of you,'' Aycliffe said soothingly. ''This is all conjecture. Until we have facts at our fingertips, there is no use in speculating.''

''Yes, but how are we to get these facts?'' demanded Benedict, turning to him. ''Not from Theda, I'll be bound!''

The lawyer pursed his lips. ''In a legal matter, sir, she will have no choice but to reveal the truth.''

''Don't you go threatening her!'' warned Benedict angrily. ''You'll leave her be, man, or you'll answer to me!''

Aycliffe sighed. ''Mr Beckenham, you are really making matters very difficult.''

"Never mind! Don't trouble *her,* I tell you. Not at this present, in any event."

"Since the matter has been raised, sir, I have no choice but to pursue it," explained the lawyer. He held up a pacifying hand as he saw the other prepare for battle. "Have no fear! I may be able to institute discreet enquiries. I have a previous address. I may work backwards from there."

"And if probate is granted meanwhile?"

"I will have to halt the proceedings, I am afraid," Aycliffe said regretfully.

"Oh, my God! And I had it in mind to ask for an advance."

"I can still advance you funds, sir. Although your portion would also be affected, there is still a considerable sum in trust from the late Sir John Merchiston's will. How much do you require?"

Benedict settled his own needs and the lawyer gave him a draft on Lady Merchiston's bankers.

"By the way, Mr Beckenham, I have something for you," he said when he had done, opening a drawer and locating a small visiting card. "I had almost forgot it."

Benedict took the card and glanced at the name. "It is unknown to me. Who is it?"

Aycliffe coughed. "I believe it possible he may be an agent for one of your creditors. He would not state his business, but he had come here to find you, and came to me as having been advertised as executor of Lady Merchiston's will."

"The devil! You are probably right, Aycliffe. Perhaps you had better increase the sum you are giving me. I must go to London, for I brought very little gear with me, so I will see him then." He studied the card. "This address is in the City, is it not?"

"Yes, sir. Quite a respectable neighbourhood, although he did not seem like a man of business. That is why I took him for an agent. Or perhaps a clerk."

"Well, we shall see. I'll come straight back to you when I return to find out how you have fared."

Aycliffe frowned a little. "It may take some time to discover anything—if I *can* discover anything, that is."

"Well, don't dawdle on the matter, man!" said the other, tucking both card and bank draft into his pocket book. "My whole future is at stake."

There was an odd glint in the lawyer's eyes as they rested on Benedict. "Naturally you will be concerned. It may be that you need not, after all, tie yourself up in matrimony."

Benedict's head came up from his pocket book and his eyes glowered. "That's as may be. In any event, Miss Kyte—at least Theda, for that I *know* to be her real name—is not to lose by this. You will please to see that she has enough to cover her present needs. She will tell you she has none, but pay no attention to that! She needs help in the house, for a start, and you will inform her she is *not* to be acting like a servant. And make her buy some new clothes, for heaven's sake! *My* orders. And if she is to lose the inheritance, you may set it all to my account. But don't tell her that, or she will refuse it all!"

Aycliffe smiled. "You may rely on me, sir. It will

be better, perhaps, if she does not wholly know that the will is in question."

"No, my God, don't *dare* reveal that to her!" Benedict said, alarmed. "She will be off at once and I shall never be able to find her!"

Before Mr Aycliffe went to see Miss Kyte to fulfill his promise to Mr Beckenham a week or two had already gone by. He was surprised that he'd had no word from that gentleman, and even more so to find that Theda had not either.

"I had expected Mr Beckenham would have been in contact with you at least, ma'am," he said with a frown.

Theda gave him a suspicious look. "Why should you expect that?"

Aycliffe coughed, and his glance drifted away to rest unseeingly on the shelves of books as he spoke. They were standing by the desk in the library, where Theda had been going over the household accounts when the lawyer arrived, Hector, his wound still troublesome, laying at her feet.

"Mr Beckenham was good enough to confide his intentions to me, ma'am."

"Oh?"

Aycliffe's eyes came back to her face. "He was most anxious for your comfort."

"Oh?" said Theda again.

Although her tone was non-committal, and her face gave nothing away, there was a tell-tale glint in the deep grey eyes. Tread warily, the lawyer told himself. He indicated the room with a sweep of his arm.

"You have done wonders here, ma'am! I have not seen the house look so well since Sir John's time." He glanced out of the open door to the garden. "If you should be in need of assistance, I can recommend an excellent gardener, for instance."

"I thank you, Mr Aycliffe, but I have no intention of wasting money which is not my own and may never be so."

"It is surely hardly a waste to put the place in order? Whoever comes here can only be grateful to you," argued Aycliffe.

"Indeed? Do you include Mrs Quatt in that category?" asked Theda with a humorous look.

"Mrs Quatt is not contesting the will, ma'am."

Theda shrugged. "Then it can only be Benedict. Well, he said he was determined to have the place."

"Miss Kyte, there is *no* contestant just at present," said the lawyer firmly.

"Then why is probate delayed?" demanded Theda. "And don't tell me it is merely a legal hitch!"

"Let us say a quibble," amended the lawyer, smiling.

"And you cannot tell me what it is?"

"Not just at present, I am afraid."

Theda sighed and moved to the garden door, looking out in silence a moment. Hector rose from under the desk and limped after her. As he went out, drawn irresistibly by the fresh air, Theda, with a determined air, came back to the lawyer.

"Mr Aycliffe, let us suppose that all goes through safely. How much do you think I might retain, in all fairness?"

The lawyer raised his brows. "You intend to be rid of the main part of it?"

"Of course I do. You don't imagine I would dream of keeping what does not belong to me?" She smiled a little. "But I am neither so foolish, nor so quixotic—nor, I may add, is my mind and resolution of so high an order!—as to deprive myself entirely of the opportunity to better my own lot. The fortune is large enough to satisfy anyone, I believe. To share a little could not be other than beneficial to the recipient's soul!"

There was an answering twinkle in the lawyer's eye, but he spoke quite seriously. "It must depend upon what you would like to do with your share."

Theda threw up her hands in a despairing gesture. "Oh, but a tithe of what is in my heart! But, alas, one's head must be permitted to rule, and so I will say only this: a little house where I may be safe, with an income to enable me at least to enjoy the comforts of life, if not its luxuries. Just a simple place, somewhere...somewhere *far* from here!"

The lawyer pursed his lips. "Your needs seem to be modest, Miss Kyte."

"Not by comparison with what I have endured up to now," Theda said quietly. "Do you think sufficient to derive an income of two hundred a year would meet the case?"

"Two hundred!" echoed Aycliffe, startled. "I was going to suggest five at least."

Theda blinked. "Lord above, Mr Aycliffe, I am not in the market for a husband, you know! What in the world could a single female want with such a sum?"

The lawyer smiled. "A *companion,* perhaps?"

She had to laugh. "Not that again, pray! But certainly a servant or two."

"Speaking of which," put in Aycliffe quickly, recognising his cue, "it is quite absurd in you to be refusing to employ anyone to help improve the place." He held up a hand as Theda opened her mouth to protest. "The household expenses may be met by funds in trust, you know, and *not* your expectations from the will."

"Do you take me for a fool, sir?" Theda demanded, a fresh glint in her eye. "I am perfectly aware that the only *trust* is in Mr Beckenham's name." She raised her brows. "Has he told you to make me hire help? Is that it?"

The lawyer hesitated. She was extremely sharp. He must prevaricate a little. "I think perhaps Mr Beckenham is anxious to protect his own interests, rather than yours."

"Because he means to come by this house by hook or by crook?" She sighed wearily. "You have it wrong, but no matter. Very well, let him bear the cost of extra servants. Will that satisfy him?"

Aycliffe shook his head, and the twinkle was once more visible in his eye. "You must also kit yourself out more suitably, ma'am."

"Oh, indeed? Suitably to *what?*" She threw up a hand in a gesture of exasperation. "No, don't answer that! Yes, I shall buy clothes, for I need them. But they are to be paid for out of my eventual share. You will keep a strict accounting, if you please."

"Certainly, ma'am," agreed the lawyer, relieved to

have accomplished his task as easily as this. But he had still a trick or two up his sleeve. "Have the bills sent to me, and I shall settle them and deduct the monies when the time comes."

"You are very good, Mr Aycliffe. I will wish you to draw up a deed of gift in Mr Beckenham's favour when once probate is granted, if you please."

"We will tackle that at the appropriate time," said Aycliffe, adroitly side-stepping this issue. "If you should hear from Mr Beckenham in the meanwhile, perhaps you would be so kind as to inform me."

"I will do so," Theda said, but with a puzzled frown. "Are you so anxious to see him?"

"Not at all. Only he said he would return forthwith and I was surprised at his continued absence."

Theda's frown deepened. "Do you know where he went?"

"To London. He was only going to see a man whose address I gave him—a creditor, I believe."

"A *creditor!*" Sudden alarm gripped Theda. "And he is not back? Oh, dear Lord! Mr Aycliffe, have you not thought that he could have been *imprisoned?*"

Chapter Nine

The lawyer blenched. ''No, I had not! Do you indeed think it possible?''

''How much was the debt?'' asked Theda swiftly. ''Had he funds?''

''I advanced him a goodly sum, yes. But if the debt had been greater—''

''Lord in heaven!'' The grey eyes were stricken. Theda grasped the lapels of the lawyer's coat. ''Mr Aycliffe, you must go to London at once! Pray, *pray* seek him out. Go and see this man, if you will, and search the prisons! Anything, anything, but *find* him!''

''Yes, yes, Miss Kyte,'' he said, infected a little by her agitation, and putting his hands over hers in a fatherly way. ''Don't disturb yourself. If there is indeed any foundation for these fears—which I do not at all suppose, for why should he not have contacted me if he was in such trouble?—I shall settle the matter at once. A debtor's prison! I cannot credit it. I had never supposed, by Jupiter, that *that* part of the will would ever come to pass!''

* * *

The damp hair lay like a dark shroud about Theda's head, flowing down behind the chair where she sat with Hector at her feet, her back to the sun, on the terrace outside the ballroom.

"Just you take the weight off your feet, Miss Theda," Taggy had insisted. "Rest easy, and don't *think!*"

But how could she rest easy, Theda thought in despair, beset as she was by hideous visions? Near a week, and not a *word* from Aycliffe. And daily, hourly, the picture came to haunt her: Benedict, cold and lonely. Benedict, weak from hunger, his golden hair bedraggled and grimed, his fine clothes unkempt and dirty, and, in all probability, his head foggy with the fumes of cheap gin! For there would be no silver flask of brandy. Oh, no. That would have gone to pay some meagre way towards the debt. That, and his watch and chain, and the pin he wore in his cravat. There would be no succour for Benedict if—*if*! Pray God that her fancy prove untrue!—he was immured in one of those gruesome buildings where only ready money could save its unwilling patrons from abject penury.

Oh, lord! *Unendurable.* To banish the visions, Theda had thrown herself into work—work that would at least welcome Benedict home again to a house of warmth and light.

She had not abandoned her own efforts, but she had got Mrs Diggory to fetch up a couple of girls from the village. The ballroom was now immaculate, its inlaid decorative wood floor gleaming, all the facets of the chandeliers sparkling in the sun that was permitted to stream through the clear glass of the French windows. Now they were all busily employed in setting to rights the big front saloon—a difficult task, for all its furniture was large and heavy and the carpets had not seen even a brush for years and years.

Theda had been obliged to retire from the room after receiving a deluge of dust over her person when attacking the top of a wide dresser. Coughing and spluttering, she had been dragged upstairs by Agnes Diggory.

"Out of them clothes you get, Miss Theda! I knew how it would be in that room. Just you leave them wenches to do it now. I'll fetch up the bath to you straight, and have Adam bring cans of water up here."

Bullied into bathing, Theda allowed Agnes to wash her long hair for her, and acquiesced when that redoubtable dame dragged a chair outside that she might sit and dry it in the sun.

The surface had just begun to shimmer in the light when Mrs Rosalia Alderley came out through the French windows of the ballroom and stopped, staring in thunderstruck amazement.

The dog rose, growling under his breath. Theda, her attention caught, put up a hand to shade her eyes. "Rose? Is that you?"

"Theda," gasped the visitor. "Good God in heaven, I thought I was seeing ghosts!"

Theda almost burst into tears, as she recalled Benedict's endearing name for her that had stuck from their first meeting. She fought down the lump in her throat, and summoned a smile as Rose came quickly forward, drawing the animal's bark.

"I assure you I am not dead," Theda said, with an assumption of humour. She laid a hand on the dog's woolly head "Quiet, Hector!"

The dog looked at her, and back at the visitor. Then, apparently deciding that the idyll was over, he wandered away, his limp much less apparent now that his wound was healing well.

Theda glanced up at Rose. "Forgive my not rising, but I dare not move out of this chair until this wretched hair of mine is dry."

Rose took the hand she held out, but her eyes were on Theda's copper crown. "Of course there is really no resemblance at all, but for the hair. I was startled for the moment all the same. Has Benedict seen this?"

Theda's smile went a little awry as the memories pierced her. "Why, yes. It has—*had*—a profound effect upon him."

"I'll warrant it did!" Rose exclaimed. "Good God, there was a time I saw him—still but a child, to be sure—playing his fingers in her hair with such warmth and love in his face, such concentrated attention, as if it so fascinated him he could not leave it alone. I have never forgot it!"

Theda was staring at her, a pulse beginning to beat in her throat. Benedict and red hair? Had not Lady Lavinia said something of this? Could it have been...? Was it possible that it was not, after all, some long-gone love, but...?

"Rose, are you telling me that *Isabel* had hair this colour? His *mother?*"

Mrs Alderley looked surprised. "Did I not say so? Though I fancy it was not as fiery as yours. It tended more to gold than copper, but it *was* red. Sadly, the colour faded as time went on." She stopped, frowning. "Why do you stare at me so, Theda?"

Theda shook her head a little, sending the fire rippling down the tresses, and looked away. "I beg your pardon. I had not realised—it did not occur to me..."

Her mind was all chaos. She had never thought that her hair stood for anything other than passion and desire to Benedict. And it did do so. But so also must it stand to him for warmth, for...*affection.*

She touched on the word with delicacy, as if she dared not think of it. A pang went through her. Then another, of a different sort. Her eyes pricked. Might it stand also for *pain?* For had he not lost that woman's love in death? Oh, Benedict! Have I hurt you, too? What had they said at the last? "Where are you going?" she had shouted. He had answered, "To the devil!" Now, perhaps, the devil *had* taken him—if prison was his shameful abode. And all to be set to her account, for she had driven him away!

"What is it, Theda?" Rose was asking, concerned at the other's silence, at the distress in her face. "What have I said?"

"Nothing, nothing, upon my honour!" Theda cried, reaching out a hand to her. She must pull herself together, make an effort. Where was that hard-earned gloss of calm efficiency that she had cultivated over the years? She tried for a brighter smile. "Rose,

I am so happy to see you! How was your stay at Brighton?''

''Never mind that,'' Rose began, by no means deceived. ''What has occurred to distress you? It is to do with Benedict, I'll be bound! What is amiss?''

Theda's eyes clouded. ''Don't ask me, Rose!''

''I thought he intended matrimony,'' pursued her friend, unheeding. ''I had expected to find the banns posted on my return.''

''There will be no banns,'' Theda said quietly.

''Why not? Forgive me, but we *are* friends, are we not?''

''Assuredly.''

''Then I will ask you again; why not, Theda?'' Mrs Alderley's eyes narrowed. ''You surely cannot hope for better?''

''Better than Benedict?'' uttered Theda on a sudden half-sob. *''Never.''* She covered her eyes with one hand. ''Ask me no more, Rose, I pray you!''

Rose stood looking down at her, a worried expression in her eyes. What had gone wrong? she wondered. And where *was* Benedict? For he had certainly not returned to Brighton. Not that she approved of his plans. Far from it. She liked Theda, yes, she did, but she felt Benedict could do better for himself, even if Theda could not.

An idea occurred to her. She was fully determined that the Merchiston fortune must end with Benedict—that much she owed to Isabel's memory—but at least some provision might be found for Theda. Something better than that little house of which they had once spoken. And with that hair…!

"Theda!" she said imperatively.

The copper head moved and Theda's hand dropped. She was in control again, Rose saw, but her eyes were still eloquent of some turmoil within her.

"I beg your pardon, Rose," she managed, a faint smile crossing her face. "I was miles away."

"Never mind that! Theda, listen to me. You must cease this nonsensical life of yours, slaving away as if you were a servant! Oh, yes, Taggy told me how you have been working your fingers to the bone."

"She exaggerates," Theda said.

"No, she does not! Why, I can see for myself what has been done." She reached out to grasp one of Theda's hands, touching the calluses. "*These* show who has been doing it."

Theda snatched her hand away. "What does it matter, to anyone but me, and—?"

"And *Benedict,*" Rose supplied. "You need not tell me, Theda. You are doing it for him, are you not?"

"I had to do *something.* I cannot sit idle," Theda said with spirit, evading the question.

"What is the use of doing up the house, if you are to leave yourself in the same poor condition?" demanded Rose.

Theda blinked at her. "I don't understand you."

"Good God, Theda! If you mean to put everything to rights between yourself and Benedict, you must make an effort on your own account. Buy some clothes! Show your beauty—for with your hair uncovered you *are* beautiful. You will never catch a husband if you persist in looking like a dowd!"

"I have no desire to catch a husband," Theda said frostily.

"Then you are a fool! I told you I would sponsor you. There is a deal of social activity now for the hunting season. It is an excellent opportunity to introduce you."

Theda drew back in her chair, seeming to shrink within herself. "No! No, I cannot."

"Nonsense, of course you can. Even if you marry Benedict, you cannot skulk in hiding at the Lodge, you know."

"I am not going to marry Benedict."

"Certainly you won't, if you don't smarten yourself up!" Rose said tartly. "You have done the house for him. Think how much more appreciative he will be of your place within it when you are suitably arrayed to complement him."

She had struck the right note. Theda had no intention of marrying Benedict, even when—if—he returned. No, not *if,* she scolded herself. He *will* return. And yes, she *would* study to please him. For she could not *bear* him to be unhappy—even if it meant that she must…

She pushed the thought away. That was for the future. She remembered that Aycliffe had brought up the matter of clothes, that Benedict himself had scolded her for her nip-cheese ways. Well, then, she would buy some new gowns—just one or two, perhaps—that she might, as Rose said, fit better with the work she had done on the house.

She smiled. "Very well, Rose. You have convinced me. Where shall I go?"

Antoinette was the best of the Leicester modistes, run by a little French *émigrée* who had set up shop and named it in memory of her martyred Queen. The mantua-maker was horrified to see Miss Kyte's ridiculously outmoded attire.

"But it is *affreux!* You ask me to improve the appearance of *mademoiselle?*" she said, shuddering. "How can I not?"

Theda was more amused than offended, and when the assistants began scurrying about the little salon on the first floor, bringing samples for her to try, she very quickly fell into a mood of unqualified enjoyment. Nothing could better have driven her fears for Benedict temporarily from her mind.

It was very strange at first to have the tight constriction of a waist a little below her bosom, and the softly flowing folds of muslin seemed extraordinarily light about her legs. She felt almost naked, as if she were parading in her chemise. She had been too long used to plain dark colours to take easily to the frivolous sprigs and pastel shades, decorated with frills and bands, and artificial flowers.

But she fell in love with a gown set low over the bosom, and unadorned, but for a ribbon or two, in a soft peach that set off her copper tresses. She was staring at herself in the mirror in the curtained dressing-room, wondering what a certain gentleman might do and say if he were to see her in it, when she became aware of hushed voices in the salon outside.

"My dear, Antoinette positively said 'Kyte', I am certain of it," one voice was saying.

"Well, if it is indeed she," came another, harder

voice, "I can only say that Rose Alderley is most tiresome. Bad enough when she befriended Isabel Beckenham. And now this!"

Behind the curtain, Theda froze, stiffening. But the voices continued.

"For my part," argued the first one, "I am very glad of it. Do you not recall what Araminta Merchiston—?"

"*Quatt,* my dear Mrs Tiverton," interpolated her companion, with a titter. "So vulgar, but nevertheless true."

"Quatt, then. Do you not recall, Lady Danby, that she is supposed to have said that Miss Kyte has inherited *everything?*"

"Well, but how much is everything? You would not think from the way Lavinia lived that there was anything at all!"

"But there is!" protested the one addressed as Mrs Tiverton. "My son had it from Woolacombe—and you know how thick he is with Benedict Beckenham—that the boy had expected more than a hundred thousand."

"In-deed?" commented Lady Danby in quite a different tone. "And this girl has it all?"

"All, all of it! And a very unnatural mother I should think myself if I did not make a push to secure it for Gerald!"

"Quite right, my dear," agreed the other.

As Theda stood, rigid with wrath and dismay, the woman's voice came up in volume, and she spoke with a perfectly nauseous degree of sweetness.

"My dear Rose, we have been hearing of your protégé. So delightful to have a new face in our midst! You simply must bring her to my little soirée on Wednesday evening.''

Shock thrust Theda into a panic reaction. Flinging aside the curtain, she stepped forward.

''Oh, no!'' she uttered in a far from steady voice. ''I beg your pardon, but I cannot!''

The trio before her were stricken to silence. She beheld Rose in the act of taking the hand of a middle-aged battleaxe of a woman, very fashionably attired, whom she at once deduced to be the lady who had last spoken. The third, a skinny matron with popping eyes under a feathered bonnet, gaped at her.

''Dear me!'' she gasped out. ''Araminta never said you were so *beautiful!*''

Then she coloured up, as Theda's grey gaze came round to her, the mix of emotions there apparent. Mrs Alderley stepped smoothly into the breach.

''Lady Danby,'' she said, reaching for Theda's arm and bringing her forward to face the battleaxe, ''you will allow me to present Miss Kyte, and she will, I am sure, be delighted to accept your invitation.''

''Rose!'' broke from Theda desperately, and then she bit her lip, trying for some self-command.

''Mrs Tiverton you have also not met,'' Rose pursued, indicating the thin dame as if nothing at all were amiss.

''H-how do you do?'' Theda murmured, unable to help admiring Rose's social address, which enabled her to gloss over the incident so easily.

''So happy!'' gushed Mrs Tiverton, taking Theda's fingers in her gloved hand. ''You *will* come on

Wednesday, won't you? I know my son will be enchanted. He dotes on red hair, you know.''

''Indeed?'' was all Theda could find to say. She could only wonder at the woman. How disingenuous! She must *know* she had been overheard.

Mrs Alderley was delighted. This was better than she had hoped for! She must make it impossible for Theda to refuse.

''Have no fear! I shall bring her with me on Wednesday, trust me.''

''Excellent!'' smiled Lady Danby.

''Rose, I must speak with you!'' Theda said in a low tone.

''Presently, my love,'' was the only response.

''Oh, but I must have your promise, too, Miss Kyte!'' exclaimed Mrs Tiverton. ''For you know, we are obliged to try to amuse ourselves during the hunt.'' She tittered. ''The gentlemen are so very single-minded at this season. I have a *morning* gathering for those of us who do not care to ride. On Friday. Do say you will come. You *will* bring her, Rose?''

''Assuredly,'' said Mrs Alderley. ''But now Miss Kyte must leave you, or she will have nothing to wear for the occasion.''

So saying, she bustled Theda back behind the curtain, bidding her change quickly that they might visit a milliner, and prudently went away to confer with Antoinette.

Theda was left to stare again at her reflection, all her pleasure in the delectable peach gown destroyed. For dread—the old, quivering dread that she thought she had long left behind her—was settling in her bosom. She began to shiver, feeling sick to her stomach.

Seated between Gerald Tiverton and young Mr Finchingfield, Theda parried as best she could the barrage of effusive compliments with light banter. Finchingfield had turned out to be Lady Danby's nephew, which, Theda decided cynically, explained that lady's change of face. It had proved impossible to withstand Rose's cajolery, and, more importantly, her questions. Confession only would have served. But confession was too awful to contemplate, even with Rose.

Theda no longer knew whether Benedict's possible plight—for still no word had come from Aycliffe—or her own present one bore down on her nerves the most. Attired in the peach gown, she knew she looked well, but she felt thoroughly disadvantaged by the long years without usage of social graces. It had taken all her courage to come here with head held high, to converse with any degree of composure with the young men who interestedly flocked about her, thanks to Araminta's loose tongue. But that courage was becoming rapidly undermined.

On the other side of the room, an ancient dame was regarding Theda with a fixed stare while she slowly plied a fan before her face. Now and then she lifted an eyeglass up and peered through it for a moment, and, evidently finding it useless at this distance, let it fall again, shaking her head in a frustrated way.

At last Theda could stand it no longer. Interrupting without ceremony Mr Finchingfield's flow of compliments, she burst out, "Forgive me, but this is all nonsense! I wish you will tell me instead who is that lady over there." She added, as both gentleman turned to look, "The old one with the fan and the eyeglass."

Mr Finchingfield, a slight young man, rather floridly dressed for the country in a laced silk coat of purple hue, searched among the guests and had no difficulty in picking out the lady. He gave a short laugh.

"That old tabby? That's poor Woolacombe's grandmother. Dreadful woman! Devilish starched up. Always comes over for the hunting—don't know why, for she can't have ridden a horse for centuries!—and leads poor Woolacombe a dog's life."

Gerald Tiverton shuddered. "Don't she, though! And the poor devil can't hide a thing from her. Got a nose that wouldn't disgrace a bloodhound, and a phenomenal memory."

Theda felt suddenly sick. "A memory for what?"

"Gossip, mostly," said Finchingfield. "Remembers every morsel of scandal since Queen Anne, I dare say."

"By George, yes!" agreed Tiverton. "Poor Woolacombe says if he's had one story thrown in his face as an example of what bad conduct may lead to, he's had fifty. There was the devil to pay over his friendship with Beckenham."

"You mean Benedict?" Theda asked involuntarily.

Finchingfield looked round at her. "Of course, you know him."

Both young men then glanced at each other, clamming up in some embarrassment as they recalled that the fortune they were at this moment vying for had been lost by Benedict Beckenham, for the story of the will was naturally common knowledge among his intimates.

"Yes, I know him," Theda said quietly, and smiled sympathetically at both of them. "You need not look so downcast. The matter has not resulted in a bitter enmity between us, you know. We *are* still on speaking terms."

Finchingfield laughed a trifle self-consciously. "Yes, well, couldn't help but be sorry for the old fellow. Do you know where he's got to, by the by?"

"By George, yes!" exclaimed Tiverton again. "Woolacombe has been expecting him this age, and not a word from the man to anyone!"

Theda kept a tight control over the lurching of her heart. She spoke as calmly as she could. "No, I have not heard from him for a month now."

"Odd. Wonder where the old fellow has got to. Still, he was ever devil-may-care. Comes and goes as he pleases. Fortunate dog!" laughed Tiverton.

A shadow crossed Theda's face. Finchingfield, sensing embarrassment again, turned the subject.

"Never told us why you were so interested in old Lady Usk, ma'am."

"Lady Usk?" asked Theda puzzled.

"Woolacombe's grandmother."

"Oh." Theda shrugged with an assumption of ease. "It is rather she who is interested in me, I fear."

Both gentlemen once more glanced round to where the old lady was still staring, but now speaking to

Lady Danby, whom she had detained with a hand on her arm.

"Uh-oh!" uttered Finchingfield. He looked back at Theda and exchanged a knowledgeable glance with his friend Tiverton. "I'll lay you any money she's checking you out with my aunt."

"By George, yes!" assented Tiverton in his usual fashion. "There she goes to collar Mrs Alderley." He grinned at Theda. "Hope you ain't got any deep, dark secrets, Miss Kyte. Old dame Usk will ferret them out in a twinkling."

Theda managed an answering smile, but her heart was thumping like a drum. In a moment the young men were proved right as Rose came over to oust them from her side.

"Theda, there is someone who wants to make your acquaintance."

As she approached the formidable, although diminutive figure of Lady Usk, she had to fight to overcome the hollow throbbing in her chest. She was not helped by the unnerving sight of the old woman's hugely magnified eye as she held up her glass to inspect the girl coming towards her.

But then Lady Usk dropped the glass and held out a scrawny hand. "How de do?"

Theda took the hand, dropping a curtsy. "Lady Usk."

"You know me?" came sharply from the old lady.

"I asked your name, ma'am," Theda told her frankly.

The other nodded. "You noticed me watching you, I shouldn't wonder."

"Yes, ma'am," Theda agreed, adding daringly, "Why did you?"

Beside her Rose gasped, but Lady Usk said at once, "Your hair. I've only seen that precise colour once before."

Warily Theda eyed her. "Indeed? I believe it is not unique, though perhaps unusual."

The old lady nodded. "Very much so. Most of 'em are carroty or golden. Though, to be sure, in my day we used so much powder one couldn't always tell."

"That is true," Rose Alderley said, putting in her mite, and immediately came under the scrutiny of Lady Usk's interested eye.

"Remember anyone who *didn't* powder, do you, Rose?"

"Oh, yes, several," she answered, taking a chair next to Lady Usk. "But—"

"But only one redhead," firmly stated the old lady, her eyes going back to Theda's flaming crown, which she had dragged into a knot on top of her head and then allowed to fall behind. "You remind me of her very much."

Theda produced a smile. "Well, if she indeed had similar hair, I dare say that is not surprising."

Lady Usk was studying her face, as if she saw there more than she spoke of. "There is something about the complexion also," she said slowly. "Common to you redheads, of course. So pale, almost as if one can see through your skin."

You mean that you see through me, Theda thought. Lord help me! Does she really know *who I am*?

"It is very tiresome at times," she said rather desperately. "People seem often to think one is unwell. And the sun—the sun, too, can be troublesome. One feels easily...overheated."

She was speaking at random, saying anything at all, only to try to distract this acute old woman from saying what was clearly in her mind.

"Overheated?" repeated Lady Usk in an interested voice. "Yes, I see. Rather like seizure, I should imagine. Faintness and palpitations?"

"Some-something of the sort," Theda said in a rather husky voice, thickened with distress.

"Oh, I know what you mean," chimed in Rose. "One is subject to it when increasing."

But Lady Usk paid no heed to this interjection. Her eyes were on Theda's in a look so compelling that Theda felt as if her mind were being dragged out to be read.

"Something like, I dare say," went on the old lady, "that seizure that attacked poor Kirtlington at the end of last season."

Theda's eyes widened and she seemed to sway. In a hushed voice, she faltered, "You s-said...*Kirtlington?*"

Lady Usk's eyes never left hers. "Lord Kirtlington, yes. Though, to be sure, *he* has not red hair, so he cannot plead that excuse. However, his *wife* might have done so, if—"

"*Pray*" interrupted Theda in a thread of a voice, "you said a—a *seizure?*"

"That is correct. Dreadful thing to happen to any

man! His wife had to take him home to Cheshire. They say he may not live out the summer.''

Somewhere in the background, Theda heard Rose's voice exclaiming as she remembered the sad event for herself. But through the clogging pain in her breast, she could only seen the gaze of Lady Usk—dark and knowing. It was as if Lady Lavinia herself had come back to life, and sat staring at her out of the malevolence in her soul.

The protest floated at the back of her numbed mind: how could she have the heart to deal such a blow only to satisfy her own thirst for scandal? The deliberate cruelty of it gave Theda the strength she needed.

''I am happy to have made your acquaintance, Lady Usk,'' she said mechanically, and then, like an automaton, turned to her friend. ''Rose, it is extremely late, and I am not used to such hours. Pray may I take your carriage and go home? Unless you are ready yourself to go now?''

Mrs Alderley, aware that something had occurred which had escaped her, and conscious of the metallic edge to Theda's voice, and the look of...yes, triumph in Lady Usk's eyes, at once lost herself in indecision.

''Oh, I don't...well, yes, I suppose—but I did want...'' She drew a breath and pulled herself together. ''Yes, we will go, Theda. Lady Usk,'' she added, turning to the old lady, who had resumed fanning herself and was sitting back in her chair with a smug look on her face, ''I will certainly see you again. We *must* talk.''

How Theda kept her countenance throughout the drive home she never knew, but somehow, perhaps by dint of dwelling on the attention paid her by Finchingfield and Tiverton, she managed to divert Rose from the dangerous topic of Lady Usk's strange conduct.

Once back at the Lodge, however, all her fortitude deserted her. The Diggorys were long abed, and Hector shut up in her little room, but candles had been left for her by the front door. She lit one and carried it into the ballroom, where the silver light from a large moon cast shadows on to the wood floor.

Dropping to her knees, as if she could no longer stand on her trembling legs, and heedless of the new peach gown and the pretty fawn pelisse she had bought that covered it, Theda set down her candle on the floor with quivering fingers, and covered her face with her hands.

Lord in heaven, was there no end to the burdens she must bear? It needed only this! Now must the dagger she had long carried in her heart twist in an agonising dance. Dear lord, how was she to *endure* it?

Tears flowed down her cheeks, trickling through her fingers. She tried hard to hold them back, swallowing on her aching throat.

To her came, unbidden, a desperate longing. *If only Benedict were here.* But that was madness! She must not think of Benedict. For here, thrust on her out of the darkness of her past, lay the reason she could never be his. Now how much stronger had become that barrier!

She sighed deeply. If there was any justice, it was

she who should die. Not he! Not *he*. Dear lord, *no*. No, no, *no!*

Uncontrollable sobs broke from her and echoed on the night.

Chapter Ten

Viscount Dacre stood by the open window of an opulent upstairs saloon, gazing out upon the vast estates he had inherited. Visible through the trees was another, smaller building. Without turning round, he pointed, addressing the man behind him. "Is that the Dower House?"

The agent stepped forward. "No, my lord. That is one of Lord Kirtlington's houses."

The Viscount turned his head, a frown adding to the already sombre expression of his features. "I have heard the name in some connection, I think."

An explosive snort came at him from the centre of the room behind him. "Don't ye remember the name of your own neighbours, boy?"

Lord Dacre cast his great-uncle a glance of acute dislike. "No, sir, I do not. It is more than I bargain for to recall the names of my own...family." He brought out the word with distaste, as if it soiled his lips.

"Just as I foretold!" grunted the crusty old gentleman.

He was a spare, grizzled man, who limped with the gout that made him ill-tempered, so unlike the dandified figure of Lord Dacre's vague memory that he felt wholly disorientated in his presence. Not that this entire experience had not thrown him completely out of his stride! It was near twenty years since he had been here, and he had never, to his knowledge, so much as set eyes on any member of the surviving household.

"If I said to Robert once, I said to him fifty times," his great-uncle was grumbling. "'Keep the boy under your eye', I told him. Would he listen? No, he would not. Now see what has come of it!"

"Mr Robert could scarcely have anticipated *this* contingency, sir," ventured his lordship's agent.

"Ha! D'ye imagine any of us anticipated it?"

Lord Dacre's eyes narrowed. "Rid yourself of the notion, sir," he said on a menacing note, "that it is any more acceptable to me than it is to you!"

His uncle snorted again. "Gammon! Because you haven't chosen to show yourself, don't think we haven't heard of you. You may cut a fine figure—" with an approving glance cast up and down his great-nephew's fashionably tight-fitting blue coat over buckskins and top-boots "—but an expensive young profligate is what you are, Dacre, and if this inheritance don't come as a windfall you may call me a dunderhead!"

A sudden grin lightened the Viscount's features. "I should not dare, sir!"

"Humph!" grunted the old man, but a reluctant

twinkle entered his eye. "Ye've inherited something of my poor brother's humour, in any event."

"Have I? I remember very little of my grandfather, sir."

"Small wonder! If he'd been alive when Robert kicked up all that riot and rumpus, there'd have been a different story, I can tell you." The old man shook his head. "He was the only one who ever had any influence with Robert. It's to be hoped you've not come by your father's headstrong ways, boy."

"You will be the best judge of that, sir. I hardly knew my father." With that curt dismissal of the subject, Lord Dacre turned his back on his uncle.

But the word was not to be so lightly dismissed from his mind. *Father.* Unconsciously his hand reached for the pocket of the greatcoat he was not wearing, where he kept his silver flask. As well, perhaps. One did not take to the brandy at ten o'clock in the morning! Even if oblivion was the only way one could wipe that dread word from one's mind.

Almost harshly, he addressed his agent. "Before we go into the matter of how much of a 'windfall' all this may be, Bewdsley, where *is* the Dower House?"

Both the other men frowned, seemingly unable to understand his interest in a relatively unimportant subject. Dacre smiled rather cynically.

"Come, come, Bewdsley. Did you not tell me that all the surviving females of the family have fled there, to take refuge from my vengeance?"

A crack of laughter left the old man's lips. "Pack

of ninnies! Nothing of the sort, however. Your stepmother resides there."

"My *stepmother!*" echoed the Viscount, and set his teeth.

"Aye, and your half-brothers and sister. Your cousins, too," added his great-uncle, apparently unaware of his dangerous mood. "Went off there on your aunt's death. I mean your uncle's wife, young Dacre's mother, you know."

"It is a *little* complex, my lord," interposed Bewdsley apologetically, seeing the frown in his new master's eyes.

But Lord Dacre was not thinking of the odd circumstance that had resulted in his stepping into his cousin's shoes. For his predecessor had been a minor, the only surviving child of the eldest of three brothers. The estate had been held in trust by the second brother. But both he and the young lord had been carried off by smallpox, leaving this estranged son of the deceased youngest brother to inherit.

All this had been carefully explained to him by Bewdsley, who had been sent to find him. Although it had come as a shock, for he had never made it his business to enquire into the ramifications of his family, he had found a morbid humour in the situation. The gods were at their tricks again! But to hear now that That Woman was living in the Dower House, the very woman on whose account his mother had been incarcerated there, filled him with such distress that he could barely find the strength to be civil.

Vividly could he still recall his nurses preventing him from going to her there, and he knew he had stood at a window just like this, gazing with longing through the trees to the building where his mother was imprisoned.

But this was all in the past! There was a future now, brighter than he had ever hoped for. He must learn to *forget.* To give himself a moment to recover control, he looked again out of the window and spoke at random.

"You were going to tell me something of Kirtlington, were you not?"

The agent took the question to himself. "Was I? Oh, only that his estate marches with yours, my lord. You have met him, I dare say?"

Dacre shook his head, his mind still on his mother. "I've seen him, or heard of him."

"Heard of his brush with death, I dare say," interpolated his great-uncle. "Not that I paid much mind to it myself. Too many damned funerals of our own!"

"Dead, is he?" asked his lordship absently.

"No, my lord," Bewdsley told him. "He suffered a stroke, but I believe he is said to be recovering."

The Viscount nodded, although he had scarcely heard what was said, registering it somewhere at the back of his mind. He was more in command of his emotions now, and he turned back into the room.

"Well, Bewdsley, since I appear to be saddled with this place, perhaps it is time you told me precisely what I am worth?"

"Difficult to say *precisely,*" said the agent carefully.

"Don't be a nodcock, Bewdsley!" snapped the old

man. "Give him a round tale and a round figure at the end."

The agent coughed. "Your lordship will be pleased to hear that the estates have been well cared for."

"Aye, my brother saw to that."

"Exactly so, sir. And his sons, too."

"Bewdsley," Dacre said gently, "I am not a fool. I can see the land is in good heart, and I remember enough to know the extent of the estates. All I want is a yearly figure."

Mr Bewdsley looked him straight in the eye. "About eighty thousand, my lord. Excluding the investments, of course."

"Eighty thousand a *year?*" asked the Viscount faintly.

"Perhaps a little more," said the agent hopefully, and then his eyes popped open as Lord Dacre began to laugh.

For a moment the two gentlemen stared at him in perplexity, as he shook his head, bubbling over at some private joke, until he caught the puzzlement on both faces.

"Forgive me!" he said, his eyes still alight. "But if you only knew—it's hell's own jest!"

"Jest," echoed his uncle, affronted.

"On me, sir, on me," said his nephew soothingly. Dear God! He had been moving heaven and earth to gain what was now little more than a pittance, in the light of what he had unexpectedly inherited. Like a thunderbolt it had come, just when he looked like losing it all. His brows snapped together. *All?*

"Hell's own jest," he repeated aloud. "And with

a vengeance, too. Hell and the devil! Now I shall have no hold over her at all. How the devil am I to...?" He stopped, becoming aware of the glare from his uncle and the frank astonishment from his agent. "I beg your pardon. I was thinking aloud."

"Who in the name of God is *she?*" demanded the old man, shooting him a suspicious look from under frowning brows. "You're 'Dacre' now, boy. You've a duty to your name."

The Viscount's face changed, in another of his startling alterations of mood. "Indeed? And I must take care not to sully it, is that it? As my father did mine!"

"Now, Dacre—"

"Have no fear, sir! I have lived all my life in the shadow of scandal. I know the cost." Then he turned to the agent. "Speaking of cost, Bewdsley, can I afford to buy a hunting-box? There is a place I have an eye to—in Leicestershire."

Friday came, in spite of all Theda's wishes that it might not, and, with it, a resurgence of her fears. What should she do? No word had come from Rose, and surely she would have cancelled their arrangements at the least hint of scandal? Had that dreadful Lady Usk thought better of it, or was she out to torture her victim, playing a waiting game?

If so, she was succeeding admirably, Theda thought. What little peace there had been was quite cut up. She had not even the comfort of Hector's presence, for her nervousness upset him and he had taken to roaming again, now that his leg was healed. But the dog was the least of her worries. If she was not thinking about Benedict, and seeing the most dreadful visions, interspersed with the haunting—and piercingly sweet—memories, she was assailed by the picture which tore at her heart, of that loved face, laid in a coffin, devoid of life. It would have been better to have remained in total ignorance than to know, yet *not* know, and have no means of finding out.

With all that, must she also attend this gathering, where she might find herself exposed to public ridicule, to painful humiliation, by the dread words of that *evil* old woman? Lord in heaven, but it was too much to ask!

Nevertheless, some spark of remaining pride had driven her to array herself in a sprig muslin gown she had bought with the peach, topped by a pretty chip-straw bonnet that at least provided a little place to hide her face under its poking brim.

She heard the jangling of the bell, and hurried from the little chamber. Rose! What should she say? Should she confess all and refuse to attend at Mrs Tiverton's morning do? She heard Adam's heavy tread moving down the hall, and slowed a little, her heart shrinking within her. Next instant, the front door opened, and as she began to descend the stairs a most unwelcome voice smote her ears.

''Where is she? Where is that thieving, sneaking hag who thought to oust me from my rightful inheritance?'' demanded the strident tones of Mrs Araminta Quatt.

Pushing past old Diggory, she swept into the hall, cast one angry glance around, and found Theda on the stairs. Her mouth opened, and stayed so, as her pale eyes widened under the close bonnet she wore.

Theda, stock-still on the stairs, her heart sinking, saw the discontented features pinch and harden into a mask of sheer fury.

"So!" hissed Araminta, finding her tongue. "I catch you in the act, do I?"

"I have not the remotest idea what you mean," Theda said coldly, all her old resentment flaring up at the woman's tone.

"Oh, have you not?" snapped the other, coming hastily forward to confront her as Theda came down the rest of the stairs. "Have you not, Miss Thieving Kyte? And I suppose you have not chosen to *flaunt* yourself as an heiress in society. I suppose you have not squandered money which is not your own on gowns like that you have on!" Closer she came, almost spitting into Theda's face. "And you have not removed your cap, I suppose, and displayed your *whorish* tresses that the men might be dazzled!"

Theda stepped smartly back, away from her, distress catching at the breath in her throat.

"*What* did you call me?" she managed faintly.

"I called you what you are!" Araminta almost screamed. "Just like that *other* bitch, with her oh, so *glorious* hair that my father doted on—to *my* disadvantage! That scheming, cheating harlot, whose son you have consorted with like a cheap jade. Stealing affection, just as *she* did, as well as this house, and the money that could *never* be yours! Thief! Whore! I shall shout it to the world, if I have to!"

"You are insane!" Theda uttered fearfully, backing

away towards the library, aware vaguely of the bell again jangling and of Adam shuffling reluctantly off to answer it. "You don't know what you are saying! What do you want from me?"

"I want my dues, Madam Adventuress, that's what I want!" stated Mrs Quatt angrily. She moved forward, driving Theda before her into the library itself. "And I'll get them! Aycliffe may not be there, but I got it from his clerks. Probate is delayed, is it not? And do you know why? Because he has set his clerks on to find you out, Miss Theodosia Kyte! Or is it some *other* name?"

Theda paled. "He...*what?*"

"Oh, yes, Madam Thief! *That* is why probate is delayed. No doubt Benedict means to contest the will. But he won't succeed, because I shall contest it. And I have by far the better claim. So how do you like that, you scheming wretch?"

"I don't imagine she likes it at all," said Mr Aycliffe's level voice from the library doorway.

Araminta swung round on him, and Theda looked past her, distress and reproach in her face as she met the lawyer's eyes.

"How do you do, Miss Kyte?" he said in matter of fact tones. Then he bowed to the other lady. "Mrs Quatt. Do I understand that you wish to take legal action in the matter of the will?"

"What are you doing *here?*" Araminta demanded suspiciously, ignoring his question.

His brows rose. "I have business with Miss Kyte."

"Pah! She is as much Miss 'Kyte' as I am, the wretch!"

"You know that for a fact, do you, ma'am?"

"Of course I don't, but—"

"Then I suggest that you keep your tongue, unless you wish to render yourself liable to an action for slander."

Araminta gasped, her cheeks flying two spots of colour. "How dare you address me in such terms?"

Mr Aycliffe bowed. "As your legal adviser, Mrs Quatt, I conceived it to be my duty to warn you of the possible consequences of your words."

"Pah! Don't come that nonsense over me, Aycliffe! You are on *her* side, I suppose?"

"I endeavour to serve all parties to the best of my ability," the lawyer said repressively. "It is not in my brief to take sides."

"Legal jargon!" scoffed Araminta. "Well, if you don't favour her, I dare say you would do more by Benedict than by me." She smiled maliciously. "That is, if he is ever to come out of *prison.* Oh, yes, I have that tale also. You went to find him—didn't you?—for his creditors have caught up with him at last. How well my mother knew him!"

"Mr Beckenham," stated Aycliffe in a level tone "is *not* in prison."

There was an intake of breath from Theda, and the lawyer glanced round at her, but it passed by Araminta.

"Pah! Much I care! Let him be in or out of prison, he will get *nothing* of mine. I am used to being ignored and slighted, but mark this well! If there is any attempt to bypass me in *this* matter, you shall all know of it!"

With which she stalked past him and into the hall without so much as a backward glance at Theda, standing by the desk, a look of new hope in her eyes. All Araminta's spite, her flooding jealousy, paled into insignificance beside this momentous news.

"Miss Kyte—" began the lawyer.

"She may not care," Theda interrupted, coming forward eagerly, "but I do, Mr Aycliffe." She gave him an almost pleading look. "He *is* safe? You were not lying?"

"Certainly not."

"Thank the lord! Oh, you do not *know* how great a relief that is!" Her body seemed to droop all at once. "But it seems it will avail him little. Why, oh, why did you set such enquiries in train? Could you not just have asked me?"

"To tell you the truth, ma'am," Aycliffe said, with a wry twist of the lips, "I would have done so. Mr Beckenham, however, would not have me disturb you on the matter."

Theda's stomach seemed abruptly to fall. "He *knew?*" Suspicion kindled in her breast. "Mr Aycliffe, was it Mr Beckenham's idea that you should delve into my history?"

The lawyer grimaced. "I should rather say it was something he inadvertently let fall that led me to believe there might be a legal case to answer."

"*What* did he let fall?"

Aycliffe cleared his throat. "Mr Beckenham merely wished, if he could, to find and remove that impediment which he believes to stand in the way of a—er—union between you."

"I see," Theda said quietly, biting her lip. She had been foolish, had she not? She had allowed her own feelings to cloud her judgement. Ever since she had learned from Rose of his mother's red hair, she had fondly permitted her idle daydream, her secret wishes, to grow and flower as if indeed they existed.

But Benedict cared only for Merchiston Lodge and the money. In his frustration and anger, he had told her that she must give herself as well before he would take them. Yet he had since seen Aycliffe and told him of his unaltered intention to come into possession of them by wedding her. Why else should he be seeking to eliminate her past to his own advantage? Her heart twisted.

"Poor fool!" she said aloud. "You have dug your own grave!"

"I beg your pardon?" the lawyer said blankly.

Theda shook her head. "I was thinking aloud. It is scarcely in Mr Beckenham's interests to invalidate the will, I believe."

"Assuredly not. He will lose everything."

"Oh, lord in heaven! Then Araminta was right! For you are obliged to pursue your enquiries, are you not?"

"Unfortunately, yes."

"Unfortunately?"

"Why, I believe so, ma'am," said Aycliffe, smiling a little. "I may have told Mrs Quatt that my position demands that I remain impartial, but one cannot entirely prevent oneself from having human feelings and preferences!"

"Very true." Theda sighed. "And so it is over. I

am not concerned for myself. But what will poor Benedict do?''

''Your pardon, ma'am,'' said the lawyer, ''but you speak as if the battle were won! So far my enquiries have drawn a blank, your tracks are so well covered. But you suggested I might have asked you outright for your—er—credentials. Do your words now mean what I think they mean?''

Distress was back in her face and her eyes widened. ''Pray, Mr Aycliffe, don't ask me!''

''I'm afraid I must,'' he said, but with sympathy in his voice. ''Are you, or are you not, Miss Theodosia Kyte?''

Theda hesitated. Dear lord, what could she say? Suddenly here it was again! Had Lady Usk not been sufficient? But that was malicious. This—this was different. A legal necessity. If she did not speak the truth now, she was guilty of perjury. If she did, she was putting the knife in Benedict's back.

From the hall came a welcome interruption. Mrs Alderley's voice. ''Theda! Where are you? We shall be late!''

''Rose!'' Theda uttered quickly. All of a sudden, the morning gathering at Mrs Tiverton's had lost a little of its terror, for just at this instant it seemed less threatening than Mr Aycliffe's serious face, demanding of her this fatal choice.

''Ma'am,'' he said, ''I must insist—''

''Pray, sir!'' Theda interrupted, throwing out a hand. Necessity forced an urgent solution—*perhaps* a solution. ''Draw up the necessary papers. I shall relinquish my claim. Will that serve?''

* * *

Contrary to the impression given by Mrs Tiverton, there were in fact several gentlemen present at her morning gathering. Although there was no hope that her own son and his intimates would forgo their day's sport, there were those less inclined for the hunt than they had been in their younger days. Their small number, however, made them more noticeable.

Theda was therefore acutely conscious of one gentleman, rather stout and red of face. *Was* it he? He must be past thirty now, but she would never have believed he could have grown to make such a gross figure of a man. He looked to be peevish, the corners of his full mouth turned down, and an irritable look in his face each time he answered some remark addressed to him by the woman at his side. She was some years his junior, not pretty, but personable enough, with brown hair, neatly dressed and a good figure.

A sharp pain twisted in Theda's guts. Had she *gold*, poor woman, so to entrap for herself that monstrous lump of selfishness? Had she thought herself fortunate to capture a thing of beauty? For if it was indeed *he*, he had been beautiful—full of lip and sensuous of eye, and reed-slim he was, six years ago. Could a man change so much?

She tried to picture Benedict thus, but the image would not form. Benedict was near thirty, and yet his face and form had withstood the ravages of time and circumstance. Perhaps because Benedict was at heart honest and true, whereas *this* man…

''My dear Miss Kyte,'' said Lady Danby's voice, interrupting her reverie, ''I am certainly going to take you to task for leaving my party so early. Finchingfield was devastated.''

''I am sorry to hear it,'' said Theda, dragging her attention back and focusing it on the lady.

''He has taken a marked fancy to you, my dear,'' pursued the other.

''Indeed?'' The cynical glint appeared in Theda's eye. He has taken a marked fancy to my expectations, she might have said. ''I dare say he will get over it.''

Lady Danby frowned. ''Don't say you prefer Gerald Tiverton!''

The glint was angry now. ''My dear ma'am, I assure you I don't look for matrimony. As for my preferences, I believe they are my own concern.''

She then rose from her seat and bowed, leaving Finchingfield's fond aunt seething. Behind her back she heard a mutter. ''Such impertinence!'' But the boot, Theda thought, was on the other leg. Why had she come? She could curse Aycliffe and Rose both! Between them she had made a decision based only on panic and no common sense. Now, to confound her, there was *that man*—if she truly had recognised him in the wreck she had seen.

Passing with a smile and a bow through the predominantly female guests, she made her way through an open doorway to take refuge on the terrace outside, in spite of the slight September chill in the air.

She wished very much that Lady Lavinia had not practised this jest upon her. By now she would have been safely hidden in some dull merchant's house, forgotten by all the world—and Benedict himself. For had he not already forgotten her? If not, where *was* he? Oh, but she should have known. Men, especially handsome men, were not to be trusted!

The reminder, so sharp and painful, in the sudden appearance of that man now threw her into aching grief. Enough! She had borne enough. Better perhaps that Benedict should not return—though God send nothing had happened to him, for she could bear anything but that!—for that his lost inheritance, through her fault, must prevent his *ever* regarding her with anything but hatred. The sight of his face alone must be a reproach to her already tormented conscience. As if she were not sufficiently torn inside already by the dread news thrown at her by old Lady Usk. News that had left her prey to ancient longings added to the guilt, and a nagging anxiety that could not be relieved.

As she paced, unaware of the picture she presented of extreme agitation, she looked only at the ground, and so did not know that she was observed. She might think her identity concealed with her tell-tale tresses under the poke of the new chipstraw bonnet, but by a window overlooking the terrace a gentleman stared in horrified disbelief, his once sensuous eyes almost popping from his head.

A voice spoke at his elbow. "D'ye not know Miss Kyte, Caswell?"

Warren Caswell turned sharply to find old Lady Usk's eyes staring up at him from her diminutive height.

"Who?" he demanded brusquely.

"Miss Kyte," repeated the old lady, raising her eyeglass and staring through it at his face.

The man's florid complexion deepened. "Never met her," he said hastily. "Don't know the name."

"I dare say you don't," agreed Lady Usk with a knowing smile. "But do you know *her?*" One small finger pointed through the glass. "Like a cat on hot bricks, ain't she?"

Caswell shuffled in obvious embarrassment. "Never seen her before," he muttered.

The eyeglass came up again. "Haven't you? Pity she's covered up that copper head. You might recognise her then."

At this there was no mistaking the alarm that leapt into his eyes. In a strangled voice, he echoed, "Copper?"

"*Bright* copper. Most unusual." The old lady's smile was mischievous. "Would you care for an introduction?"

"No, no...I mean, my wife—must find her—," stammered her unfortunate victim. "Not too well lately."

"I'm sorry to hear you say so," said Lady Usk sympathetically. "Let us hope there won't be anything untoward to *worsen* her condition."

Warren Caswell paled a little now, his eyes quite frantic. Muttering something incoherent, he moved away. Lady Usk watched him wend a hasty path towards his wife and turned back to the window to find that Miss Kyte was standing stock-still on the terrace, staring in at her.

Theda was shaking, a river of ice at her back. She had been mad to come! Dear lord, one word from that dreadful old woman, and she was undone. There could be no doubt now. It *was* Warren Caswell. He had been standing large as life beside Lady Usk, and it was plain that he knew her identity. Not that she need fear him. She was sure he was no more anxious for the tale to break than she. Particularly if, as she suspected, that poor woman was his unfortunate wife. But Lady Usk had no such reticence. She was gone from the window now. Where to? Had she gone to spread the word? Well, Theda was not going to wait to find out. Let society say what it would. She was not going to stay to hear it!

Already making her way around the house, she came to the front and asked a footman to carry a message to Rose Alderley. Then she sat on the parapet atop the wide stairway and waited.

''What in the world is the matter?'' Rose demanded, running out to her in bewilderment a few moments later.

''Rose, I have to go home,'' Theda said urgently, jumping up from her perch. ''Pray lend me your carriage.''

''Good God, are you ill? As if I have not had enough to worry me with all this talk of Benedict!''

''What talk?'' Theda asked in quick alarm, at once diverted from her own concerns.

''Why, they say he has been thrown into prison for debt!''

''Araminta!'' Theda said instantly. ''Don't fear, Rose, wherever he may be, he is *not* in prison. That much Aycliffe knew.''

''So that is why he came to the Lodge!'' Rose was

eyeing her frowningly. "And why you are looking as blue as megrim."

Theda glanced away. "That—and other things." She looked back. "Rose, I *cannot* stay here, in company. I cannot explain it to you now, but I *must* go."

Rose's frown deepened. "Does this have anything to do with that scandalmongering Lady Usk?"

"Everything, I am afraid," Theda said with a pathetic attempt at a smile. "Let me go, Rose! I will not blame you if you refuse to recognise me, but *let me go.*"

Mrs Alderley was not proof against the desperation of her tone. She ordered her carriage, but assured Theda that she would never desert her. "Good God, if I weathered poor Isabel's friendship, I am sure I may weather yours!"

But no sooner had Theda left in her carriage than she immediately sought out Lady Usk.

"Ah, Rose!" said that bright-eyed old lady, on catching sight of her. "Just the girl I want to see!"

"And I want to see you, Lady Usk!" said Rose pointedly.

The other's delicate brows rose. "You do, do you? Good. Let us remove to somewhere more private."

"Willingly," Rose agreed, and led the way to a small antechamber that led off the main saloon.

It was deserted, and the two ladies settled together on the small sofa.

"Now, ma'am, what is it all about?" demanded Rose without preamble.

Lady Usk's eyes were eager. "Well, my dear, it is

an old tale now. You know Warren Caswell, do you not?''

''Of course I do. He is here with his wife this morning. But what has he to do with it?''

''Everything!'' announced the old lady gleefully. ''There was a rare scandal a few years ago, though to be sure it was hushed up very swiftly—but *some* of us heard of it, naturally.''

''Naturally,'' echoed Rose drily. ''Do go on!''

Lady Usk lowered her voice. ''Yes, a rare scandal! And Caswell was at the bottom of it...''

Theda's hands rubbed furiously at one of the posts of the bed in the second of the chambers she had tackled in the last unnumbered days. For she had no longer any mental account of time. She rubbed as if she would erase the images that flitted through her mind as she worked, like an unconnected pageant—the images, and the thoughts that crowded her mind around them.

Aycliffe's face, kind but serious, demanding of her the condemnation she *could* not give. What, was she to strike from Benedict all his hopes at one blow? She did not know if her efforts would save for him at least something from the wreck, poor Benedict.

Benedict. The smiling, classic features, topped by the golden hair. Oh, but he was so handsome! Yet, handsome? No, no. Not to be trusted. For had not *Caswell* been beautiful—his full, sensuous lips, whispering honeyed words. Love and romance to gull the wench at seventeen. For what? For her flaming tresses—burning like Isabel's on her son's sweet lips as he drew them through his fingers, drowned in them...

No. *No.* She shook her head, resting it against the wood, as her hands stilled. That was Benedict, not Caswell. Benedict, who wanted her for her hair. The *scissors.* She had snipped, and he had taken a lock. "On account," he said. But that was all there was, Benedict. *I have no more.*

A sob rose in her throat. Fool! *Fool* to weep. Angrily, she thrust herself away from the bedpost and her hands began again their energetic dance on the brightening wood. Would she could rub out Warren Caswell's loathed features! Curse him! Furiously she rubbed, unknowing that she passed and repassed over the same bright spot, while the images came and went, flitting through.

Araminta. Thin, pinched features, triumphant eyes. Words that flayed and scorched coming from her lips. For had she not earned such curses? Whore and thief, was it? A shiver ran through Theda's body—the frame that was near a shadow of itself, just as it had been that long-gone day in March. *Whore?* If not in body, then in mind. No, Theda, you are mad to talk so! Mad? True, she was not Warren's courtesan, but what of Benedict?

Benedict...Benedict...would he snarl and curse at her now, as once he had? Blenching, she closed her eyes, her fingers grasping the post. Was she not a thief? Lord help her, this was not the result Lady Lavinia had intended!

Lady Lavinia...The picture in her mind changed, and the glaring, venomous eyes looked out of the wasted features...to be succeeded at once by the smug face of another old woman. Lady Usk! With her barbed speeches and her veiled remarks. And her victim had run away, and thus *given* herself away.

The now familiar palpitating flutter in her heart made itself felt and the blood drummed unpleasantly in her head so that she feared she might lose her senses. Her eyes closed tight shut, and her forehead came to rest on the hands that gripped the bedpost.

There it was again! The threat of exposure hanging over her, so close that she had dwelled since—since when?—as if she inhabited a thick cloud of suffocating fog. How long had it *been?* Had anyone called? Had anyone written? Was Rose still her friend? Did they know now...everyone here...about her...where Benedict was...and that other, Kirtlington, was he...?

But that was a question she could not think about. That was a picture she *must* not see. Who had come here? She did not know. She had told Taggy—she *thought* she had—that she could see no one, speak to no one.

She had worked...yes, yes, she was working *now.* Her eyes opened and she made an effort to resume her futile polishing. If only she could remember...If only she could *cease* to remember. Lord in heaven, what *memories!*

Like a drowning woman clinging to a frail piece of wreckage, she hung for dear life on to the bedpost while the images cluttered her mind: Benedict smiling; Caswell shocked; a loved face dying; the wasted face of Lady Lavinia dead, eyes open; Araminta's bitter, hating mouth; Rose's pleading smile for Benedict.

Benedict. What have I done to you? *What have I done?*

Her heart felt as if it must burst. Her head was on fire, as if the copper flames outside were licking within. But she clung on to the post, her body sinking to the floor, oblivious to the groans that issued from her own throat, and the words that formed on her lips.

"The witch is *burning,* Benedict. Witch...ghost... oh, that she were a ghost indeed!"

With that came blessed oblivion.

Chapter Eleven

Theda came to herself to find that she lay in a large four-poster bed, with the curtains drawn back, and the weak autumn sun coming in at the windows. She could feel a coolness on her brow, and would have reached up her fingers to find out what was there, but that she was possessed by a lassitude that prevented her moving at all.

"Ah, that's better!" said Agnes Diggory's voice. "Quite a turn you give us all, Miss Theda!"

Theda's eyes focused on the face hovering above her, and she tried to speak. But the face shook from side to side.

"Don't try to talk, miss! Dr Spilsby said as how you're to rest, and rest you will. Knocked yourself up proper, you have. All that fretting and fuming, working yourself to flinders! You lie still now, for I'm to fetch you up some broth."

"Thank you," Theda said faintly. "I'm n-not very hungry."

"Never mind not being hungry," Taggy said firmly. "You'll eat it!"

However, when the housekeeper brought the thin soup, Theda found she was hungrier than she had supposed. She was too weak to feed herself, and Agnes had to spoon the broth into her mouth.

"How long have I been like this?" she asked in one interval.

"Too long!" snapped Taggy. Then, as Theda's eyes clouded, she relented. "You've only been abed these two days."

"Two days!" echoed Theda in shocked tones. "But I was cleaning the bedchamber…the post…I was polishing the bedpost."

"That's where I found you," confirmed the housekeeper, presenting another spoonful to Theda's mouth. "And a rare taking I was in, I can tell you! I sent Adam for Dr Spilsby straight, while the maids and I put you to bed in here. Been overworking, that's what. There's to be no more of it, Dr Spilsby says."

Theda half smiled. "It's not just the work, Taggy."

"I know that, Miss Theda. I'm not daft. But there ain't nothing for you to worrit your head over, do you hear me? You can't do nothing about any of it, in any event, so what's the use of banging your head on a brick wall? That's what I say. You rest easy, and get back your strength."

Fortunately, probably due to the doctor's potions, Theda found the kaleidoscope of worrying visions had ceased to run in her brain. It was easy to sink into a sort of limbo, where nothing seemed any longer to be as important as it had been. She took little account of time, and was hardly even aware that she had been placed in Lady Merchiston's old bedchamber. She ate as directed by Taggy, and made no fuss when that dame looked after her much as she had herself done for her deceased employer—nursing her and acting as lady's maid, and combing out her troublesome copper hair, until Theda felt strong enough to perform this office for herself.

She was sitting up in bed, some few days later, tugging a recalcitrant comb through her long tresses, when a commotion from downstairs made her pause, her fingers still.

Hector, who came and went at will through her open chamber door, was in turn barking and yelping, and she could make out Mrs Diggory's voice.

"Very poorly she's been, sir, and she's still abed."

"But what is amiss with her?" demanded a familiar male voice.

Benedict! A rush of warmth swept through Theda's body.

"Exhaustion and worry, that's all!" stated Agnes in a belligerent tone.

"*All?* Hell and the devil!"

Without thought, Theda threw off the covers and swung her feet to the floor. Through the sudden fierce pulsing of her blood, she could hear Taggy describing how she had found her mistress clinging to a bedpost in one of the spare chambers. Theda hardly took in the words. None of the thoughts that had so oppressed her came into her mind. His very presence banished them, and she responded to it with all the fire in her heart.

Her limbs were unsteady as she padded on bare feet, staggering a little, towards the door, oblivious to the fact that she was dressed only in a thin nightgown, that her half-combed hair flared untidily about her shoulders.

"Go up, Taggy!" she heard Benedict's urgent voice. "Go up and see if she will receive me!"

Receive him? Dear lord, when she had so longed for him!

She heard Agnes begin to protest as she came through the doorway, and called out, "Benedict!"

Sudden silence struck the voices downstairs and, as Theda reached the railings and leaned over them, she saw his handsome features turned up to stare at her from the bottom of the stairs.

"Benedict!" she cried, and did not know that she stretched out her arms to him.

"Theda!" he uttered throatily.

Next moment, he was racing up the stairs two at a time, and Theda was stumbling along the gallery to meet him, clinging to the railing for support.

But a few instants later, she needed no other support than the strong arms that seized her and gathered her to a broad chest, the lips in her hair uttering the words that sent the blood rushing through her veins.

"Oh, my witch! Dear ghost! I've missed you like the devil!"

"And I you," she managed to say through the tears of relief that choked her. "Oh, Benedict, are you *real?* Is it indeed you? Lord help me, I love you so very much!"

His hold about her tightened so suddenly that she winced and cried out. But the arms did not slacken, for his lips found hers and silenced the protest in a kiss so hard that she sagged, half fainting in his embrace.

In a moment he let her go, but only so that he might lift her bodily from the ground. With a sob, Theda flung her arms about his neck and buried her face in his shoulder. Benedict carried her through the bedchamber door, and, with one booted foot, kicked it to behind him.

Downstairs Mrs Diggory, holding fast to the protesting Hector's collar, smiled to herself with grim satisfaction, and went off to the kitchen.

Benedict laid his burden gently on the bed, and sat down himself on the edge of it. Theda's hands groped towards him, grasping at his greatcoat.

"Don't leave me!" she begged hoarsely.

His fingers closed reassuringly over hers. "No fear of that!" He drew one hand to his lips and kissed it, but his fingers left her other hand to trace the wet that trickled over the blue smudges under her eyes.

"Don't weep, dear ghost! What the devil have you been doing to yourself? You're skin and bone again!"

Tremulously, Theda smiled. "It is a long story. But you, Benedict! Where have you been? All this time and no word to anyone. Do you know that you are thought to have been imprisoned for debt?"

He grinned. "No, am I indeed? In obedience to Aunt Lavvy's will, no doubt!"

"Of course," Theda agreed, laughing a little. But her eyes clouded almost at once and she sat up, urgently grasping his coat again with her free hand. "Benedict the *will.* All is lost! I have ruined everything, and Aycliffe says there is little hope of your succeeding in a contest with Araminta.''

Benedict did not appear to be unduly concerned. His eyes roved her features, as if he was recalling every item of the lines and planes that made up her face.

''You are more beautiful than I remember,'' he murmured, his eyes alight, ''in spite of reducing yourself to a scarecrow.'' Then he frowned, as if her words had only just reached him. ''The will? Oh, I care nothing for the will. Why should I?''

''Care nothing?'' repeated Theda in a bewildered tone. ''But what will you do? Aycliffe and I are trying for a way to have the will stand. You *must* support us. You cannot allow Araminta to make away with all your inheritance, Benedict. I won't let you!''

Benedict grinned at her. ''My ghost, Araminta does not want the only part of this inheritance in which I have an interest.''

''Have you run mad?'' Theda demanded, gazing at him blankly. ''If she has her way, she will have the house and *all* the money.''

''But she will not have *you*,'' he said in a guttural tone, and, seizing hold of her, he dragged her against him. His eyes searched hers with fierce intensity, and his lips hovered over her own. Huskily, he murmured, ''Did you mean it, Theda, when you spoke those tender words outside this room? Was it the truth?''

The grey of her eyes deepened, and she moved a little to touch his lips with her own. They felt hot and dry and her veins tingled to his fever.

"Well?" he demanded, his hold tightening. "Answer me!"

"You see only one flame," she said softly, smiling. "There is another, deep in my heart...It burns for you."

"Oh, *Theda!*" he uttered on a sigh, and his lips claimed hers.

At once, heat engulfed them both. Theda felt the flame lick at her loins, and the lassitude that had so possessed her was gone. Urgent now, she pressed again the strong body, thrilling to the arms that held her clamped there.

Then, abruptly, she was released, falling back against her pillows with a gasp. Her eyes flew open to see Benedict flinging off his greatcoat and throwing it aside. His coat and waistcoat swiftly followed it and his fingers ripped away the neckcloth about his throat, heedless of the ruin they effected. His shirt hung open as he sat again, and Theda's eyes were riveted to the long column of his neck, the golden glow of his chest below it.

His own eyes gazed down at her, watching the tip of her tongue pass unconsciously over her parted lips. Her gaze came up and met his.

"Benedict," she whispered, in sudden realisation of his intention, her tone half fearful, half alive with longing.

He did not move, but his hand sought hers and he brought the soft fingers to his lips, mouthing them gently, one by one, turning her palm up to press a kiss inside it, passing his tongue lightly over the pink tips, so passive in his grasp.

Theda gasped as the little touches of his mouth sent flickers of heat rippling through her body. All the time, his eyes held hers, watching how his ministrations excited her. At length his other hand stole forward to play with the copper tresses that fell about the pillows. His fingers drew strands across her bosom, lightly caressing the small breasts beneath.

Theda squirmed at the feather touch, and closed her eyes. In seconds, his breath was warm on her cheek, and her eyes flew open as she felt him chest to chest above her.

"Theda," he murmured caressingly, "I *want* you. Will you come to me?"

She hesitated, her parted lips trembling, her eyes locked with his, their grey deepening. "I have n-nothing else to give you, Benedict," she faltered.

"Do you think I care for that?" he said, a smile in his eyes.

"Do you not?"

His hand brushed down the length of her body so that she shivered, then came up to cup her breast beneath the thin cotton of her nightgown. As he squeezed gently, and felt her tremble beneath him, his lips mouthed a kiss on hers, briefly, and came away.

"Will you have me, my witch?" he persisted.

She ached to say yes, but all her instincts rebelled. Why was he doing this? If he meant to take her, why did he not do so? He knew—he *knew*—that she was at his mercy, that she would not, *could* not, resist.

"Do you need my permission?" she countered.

"I have always said you must be willing," he responded, and the smile did not leave his eyes. "*Are* you?"

Again, his fingers teased her, running a path of torturing heat about her thigh, and up over the jutting bone of her hip, close—far too close!—to that part of her where the aching need had its centre. His hand moved, and she hissed in a breath.

"Yes," she uttered involuntarily. "Lord in heaven, *yes*!"

His weight left her. "That's all I wanted to know."

Theda stared at him as he rose from the bed, reaching towards his discarded neckcloth. Her loins seemed to tear in protest, and she groaned aloud. Benedict turned his head and saw the naked want in her eyes. Fire consumed him.

"Hell and damnation!" he swore. "Theda, you *witch!*"

Then he was beside her, laying his length, his arms seizing her to him, and his lips, no longer teasing or gentle, dragging at hers. Theda responded instantly, herself aflame, her own arms gripping his chest, her hands running up and down his strong back, as if she must feel all of him at once.

Benedict's hands tore at her nightgown, and his fingers found her flesh. He let out a groan, and his mouth and tongue pressed more deeply into hers as his hands began to roam her bare skin, which burned, tormented, at his touch.

Unknowing what she did, Theda tugged at his shirt, her own lips fighting to take possession of his mouth. Then her fingers found his bare flesh and a streak of intense heat shot through her. As of instinct, their mouths came apart, only to hiss out their passion.

"God, *Theda!*" he uttered hoarsely, burning his face in the copper tresses that echoed the flaming fire in his loins. "*Burning*...I'm burning in you... witch...*witch.*"

"I'm—yours!" she managed on a gasp. "I love you, Benedict, I *love* you. Take me now!"

He cried out then, in some species of unutterable agony, and she felt him move to cover her, while his hands signalled his purpose to her eager limbs.

She was aware of a blinding flash of pain as he mastered her, and groaned weakly. But his lips were at her mouth, murmuring tenderness.

"My ghost...my witch...my lovely one."

The pain receded in the warmth of his caresses, and then he began to move and she found herself given over wholly to sensation. Every motion sent her senses reeling, deeper and deeper into the furnace they had entered together, until at last, as she soared to a height of such intensity of feeling that she thought she must burst, something exploded in her brain, and she was awash with the dizzying sensation of all-consuming love.

She knew, in that instant, that she belonged to Benedict, to this conqueror of her mind, her heart and her flesh. She was his, irrevocably.

She came to awareness to find Benedict's body heavy on hers, to hear his rasping breath harsh in her ears, and to feel his ragged heartbeat pounding against her own.

They stayed thus a few, pulsing moments. Then

Benedict raised his head from where it rested in the wild disorder of her flaming hair, and his gaze met the misty love in the deep grey of her eyes.

To her intense disappointment, he groaned as one in pain, and dragged himself off her. He swung himself to sit on the edge of the bed, and dropped his head in his hands.

Theda sat up, shocked and mystified, and put a hand to his shoulder. "Benedict, what ails you?"

"The devil take you!" he uttered in distressed tones. "I never meant to do this to you." He turned a ravaged countenance upon her. "Theda, I swear to you, I never meant to take you! Not now. Not *yet.*"

She was hurt and it showed in her eyes. "You said you wanted me."

He reached towards her briefly and cradled her face. "Don't *look* like that, my pale ghost! Of course I wanted you. But I meant only to gain your consent—if I could. Only you looked at me so, and then..." His fingers left her cheek and he clenched his hand, pulling away. "*Confound* you!"

His eyes raked her still half-naked limbs and fell on the sheet beneath her. What he saw there made him groan again. He dragged at the covers and threw them over her.

"Conceal yourself, for God's sake, lest I am tempted again!"

Theda huddled against the bedhead, drawing the covers up and over her breasts, as she watched him tidy his clothes and wrap the wrecked neckcloth carelessly about his throat. As he dragged on his coat, she spoke, tentative, out of the misery that consumed her.

"Benedict, you *had* my consent...I *was* willing."

He turned on her. "Not for *this.* I did not mean your consent to this. I meant for you to marry me!"

Her face dropped. "I *cannot.* You *know* I cannot."

Benedict seized her by the shoulders in an ungentle grip. "I know that you say you cannot. But I know also now that you *love* me. Deny it, if you dare!"

"I don't deny it," Theda said desperately. "I *do* love you. I loved you *long* ago. But it alters nothing."

He shook her. "Don't *say* that! Especially *now.* Dear God, as if I needed this complication! I *knew* how it would be. You will think I want to marry you only for what I have done, and you will refuse me on that score."

"Benedict, *listen* to me!" Theda said, distress turning to anger. "I have *tried* to tell you in the past—at least to make you *see*—I am not fit for marriage, don't you understand?"

His hands left her shoulders. "I understand only that you have a deal of false pride. Oh, I am not a fool! I know there is something in your past of which you will not speak. I can guess its import, I dare say. But you—" his fingers reached across to take her face between his hands, and there was deep compassion in his gaze "—you, dear ghost, don't understand. Do you think I would stand aside and let you suffer, as my mother did? Do you think I could *bear* to let you sink into ignominious disgrace?"

Theda's eyes filled. "Benedict, Benedict, don't! I could better bear disgrace in solitude, don't you see?"

"Yes, the coward's way!" he exclaimed angrily, releasing her. "I thought you had more courage."

"Dear lord, but we are poles apart!" Theda said in frustration. "What is there courageous in dragging my name through the mire? And now you would have me add yours? I think you are mad!"

Benedict beat his fist on the bed and glared at her. "I *am* mad. Mad for *you,* the more fool I! *I can't live without you,* don't you understand?"

"But you need not!" Theda exclaimed, seizing his hands. "Benedict, you *have* me. I am *yours.* Let me be your ghost in truth. When you want me, come to me. I shall go—oh, I don't know, anywhere you wish. Only—"

"Yes, to some out-of-the-way place to hide yourself!" he interrupted, grasping her fingers frenziedly. His eyes were aflame. "Once before you *dared* to think I would so use you. Theda, Theda, I never meant to take you, but at least I took you in *love.* I will not violate the sanctity of that union! You *must* marry me, whatever it costs."

"And bring you to ruin also?" she cried despairingly. "Is that how I am to express my love? Enough that I would be publicly disgraced. Believe me, I *know*—I have reason to know now, for while you were gone I've tried it and am waiting even now for the blow to fall!—that there is *no* future for me in the world I left behind so long ago."

"You are being foolish beyond permission!" he declared angrily, his hands dragging her to him so that his feverish glare burned into her eyes. "What *is* this history of yours that you think it irrecoverable? Who *are* you, Theda?"

"I am your *mistress,* Benedict!" she threw at him.

"That is all I am fit for, and you have taken up that option. It is that or nothing."

Benedict almost threw her from him, and leapt off the bed. "Then it is nothing! For I will have you to wife, or not at all." His eyes blazed at her. "Are you going to tell me your story, or do I demand it of the world at large! For I *will,* if I have to—and marry you in the teeth of them all. Now *tell me!*"

"Oh, go to the devil, as you said you would!" Theda snapped. "Or go and drag the whole affair out of that dreadful Lady Usk."

"Woolacombe's grandmother!" uttered Benedict, his brows snapping together. "By God, if that evil old woman has *dared* to bandy your name—!"

"She will not be the only one," Theda told him furiously.

Unheeding, he picked up his greatcoat and strode towards the door. With his fingers on the handle, he turned his head. "I'm not finished with you yet, Theda, so don't think it. I'll be back for you, and you had better be ready to face a pastor!"

"Never," Theda yelled after him, as he slammed out of the room. Then she flung herself down into her pillows and gave way to tears of frustration and rage.

It was not many minutes before Theda's lamentations were interrupted by the eruption into her bedchamber of Hector, barking and whining, closely followed by Agnes Diggory.

"Oh, be quiet, do, you stupid dog!" scolded the housekeeper, slapping the animal smartly on his nose so that he leapt back down off the bed on to which he had just jumped.

"I'm that sorry, Miss Theda. I tried to stop him, but it were Mr Benedict coming down through the kitchens in such a bang and shouting for his groom that started it."

Theda was too occupied in trying to compose herself and wiping her wet cheeks to notice the oddity of there being a groom in Benedict's train. But she had not spoken before Taggy took in her condition.

"Why, Miss Theda, whatever is the matter?" She set her arms akimbo, and her face flushed up. "If it's Mr Benedict as has upset you, mum—"

"No, Taggy, it's nothing," Theda said huskily, drawing the back of her hand across her cheeks. "At least, it is something, of course, but—"

"And I thought all would be well, if only I was to leave you both to yourselves!" uttered Taggy crossly. "When I see Mr Benedict—"

"Don't, Taggy," Theda begged, stretching out a hand to her. "It is as much my fault as his."

Mrs Diggory shook her head as she took the hand and held it tightly. "Six of one and half a dozen of t'other. Been that way all along with you two, ain't it, Miss Theda?"

Theda sniffed and smiled a little. "I suppose it can't get any worse."

"But it can, Miss Theda," contradicted Taggy worriedly, squeezing her hand. "That's what I come to tell you. That there traitor, Mrs Elswick, had to pick this of all days to come and visit. She's downstairs now, looking ever so knowing, just as you'd expect."

"Oh, no," Theda sighed. "Do you think she guessed?"

''Well, it wouldn't be right to deceive you, Miss Theda,'' Taggy said flatly, ''and she saw Mr Benedict come through, of course, and guessed where he'd come from. Sure as check, she'll tell Miss Ara he was here, and in your chamber.''

''And Araminta will tell the world!'' Theda cried despairingly. ''Lord help me! Can I not take one step without falling on my face?''

''Now don't fret, Miss Theda,'' Mrs Diggory began.

''There is no use in fretting,'' Theda said wearily. ''What does it matter, after all? Already the world may know my story. Anyone who has heard it will declare that this is but of a piece with all the rest!''

There was a silence, while Hector, climbing back on the bed, nuzzled at her free hand. She stroked him absently, and Mrs Diggory got up in a determined way.

''I'd best straighten you out, Miss Theda. Only look at your hair! And the bed looks like a troop of soldiers has been over it.''

Realising what she had said, she flushed bright scarlet.

But Theda let out a gurgle of laughter. ''Not quite as bad as that, Taggy!''

Mrs Diggory took refuge in scolding the dog and dragging him off the bed. Then she suddenly slapped at her apron pocket.

''If all that pother has not made me forget! One of the lads come over from Switham House while Mr Benedict was here. He left this.'' She brought out a sealed billet.

"From Rose?" Theda asked, taking it and breaking the seal.

"She come over while you were ill, Miss Theda," said Taggy, with an apologetic look. "I wouldn't let her trouble you, especially as I could tell she'd no *good* news."

"No, indeed," Theda agreed, running her eyes down the sheet of paper. "For she knows it all. Lord, she had it from Lady Usk! But why so urgent!"

Next instant, she uttered a shriek that made the housekeeper jump.

"Whatever is the matter, Miss Theda?"

"Dear lord in heaven!" A pair of deeply troubled eyes were turned on Mrs Diggory. "Why didn't he tell me?"

"Who, miss?"

"Benedict...He has become...have you ever heard of Lord Dacre, Taggy?"

"Dacre? Ain't that Miss Isabel's family? Or rather, Mr Benedict's uncle?"

"Not *Mr* Benedict, Taggy. He has himself become...Lord Dacre."

"Mercy me!" uttered Mrs Diggory, sitting down plump on the bed, her eyes almost popping from her head.

"He has estates in...Cheshire," went on Theda, talking almost to herself. "*Dacre.* And still he wants to marry me—but he does not know, he *can't* know...Oh, dear lord, Rose will tell him! She says here that of course there can now be no question of marriage, and she is right."

She bit her lip, crumpling the note in her hand, and

into her eyes came a look so desolate that Taggy's heart contracted. In a hushed tone, she spoke.

"What is it, Miss Theda? What does it mean?"

The deep grey eyes turned to her, and a tear traced a lonely path down her pearly cheek. "It means...that I shall have to go away."

"Nothing could exceed my delight, Benedict!" uttered Mrs Alderley, beaming. "If your poor mother had ever dreamed of this!"

"She would not have exhibited such joy as you are doing," said the new Lord Dacre drily. "I imagine she is turning in her grave!"

"Oh, nonsense! You know nothing of women if that is what you believe, my dear. Such a sweet revenge!"

She looked across to where the lawyer stood, quietly detached by one of the windows of her large saloon, gazing out on to the extensive gardens.

"Surely you, Aycliffe, with your wide experience must agree with me?" she appealed to him.

The lawyer turned, smiling. "I think there is more honour among your sex, ma'am, than you give yourselves credit for."

Benedict glanced at him. "Is that a hint to me, man? If you think I will respect her honour to the point of releasing her, you much mistake the matter!"

"I made no such suggestion, my lord," protested Aycliffe. "Believe me, I have the lady's best interests very much at heart."

"If they march with my interests, that is all to the good. If not—"

"What in the world are you two talking of?" interrupted Rose, whose perplexed gaze had been going from one to the other.

"We are talking of Theda," Benedict said at once. "And that is what we came for, in fact."

"Theda? But why have you come to me? I have not seen her for days."

"I know that," snapped his lordship. "She's been lying there in a state of collapse, and not a soul has been next or nigh her!"

Mrs Alderley stiffened. "If that is a reproach to me, you are wide of the mark, Benedict. Taggy turned me away! As she has done everyone else who tried to visit."

"Sensible woman, Taggy," commented Benedict, with a lightning change of face. "But never mind that. Tell me, Rose, what is all this about Lady Usk? Does she know something of Theda's history?"

"Everything!" Rose said comprehensively.

"She told you?"

"I asked her. When there was Theda behaving like a cat on a hot bakestone, what would you have had me do?"

"Well, go on! Tell us what she said."

Rose blinked. "Why should I? What has it to do with you?"

Benedict's eye kindled. "You don't think, as her future husband, that the matter concerns me?"

"Husband!" gasped Mrs Alderley. "Benedict, have you taken leave of your senses? You have no need to marry her *now*. As Lord Dacre, you certainly *cannot* do so."

"I shall be the judge of that," said Lord Dacre icily. "And I don't need you against me as well as Theda herself, I thank you, Rose."

"If Theda will not marry you, then she shows a deal more sense than you!" Rose told him roundly. "Good God, have you *no* sense of what is fitting?" She stopped, arrested by the expression in his face. Uncertainly, she added, "Don't look at me like that, Benedict. Anyone would suppose you meant to murder me!"

"I will, if you continue in that vein," he promised savagely. "What is '*fitting*'? Confound it, who am I to hold up my nose in such a fashion? The son of a woman disgraced by the scandal of divorce, brought back to respectability only by some freak of fate. To hell with what is fitting! Now do you tell me the story you had from Lady Usk, or do I go to the old witch myself?"

Rose eyed him a moment. Then she looked across at the silent lawyer. "What is your role in this, Aycliffe?"

"His interest is in the matter of Aunt Lavinia's will, of course," Benedict told her, answering for him.

"Not entirely," the lawyer said. "Officially, I must learn Miss Kyte's true identity. I am preparing papers for the relinquishment of the claim, but once she signs them she will be literally on the streets and penniless. Unofficially, therefore, I am anxious to assist her—and Lord Dacre, I may add—to come out of this coil in the best possible way."

Mrs Alderley sighed. "Well, I had hoped that she

might still be received. I cannot tell whether or not Lady Usk has spoken out, but I suspect not. I cannot think that Taggy would have been obliged to turn away her admirers otherwise."

"Admirers?" Benedict's steely gaze was upon her, a most ugly light in his eye. "*What* admirers?"

"Why, Taggy told me she had been obliged to deny entrance both to Tiverton and to Finchingfield."

"Tiverton and Finchingfield!" echoed Benedict furiously. "Hell and the devil, I'll cut both their livers out! Calling themselves my friends, too!"

"Benedict, mind your tongue!" Rose snapped, adding crossly, "In any event, how are they to know you have an interest there yourself?"

"They'll know soon enough," Benedict said grimly, making no apology for his lapse. "There is no time to lose, Rose. It only needs for Araminta to get hold of the latest development, and the fat will be in the fire."

Mrs Alderley gazed at him, appalled. "The latest development? You mean you have...?" Understanding flooded her face, mingling with dismay and disapproval. "Really, Benedict, how *could* you?"

He grinned suddenly, unholy amusement in his eyes. "How could I not?" he countered. "I am bewitched, and wholly under her spell!"

"Good God, you will have to marry her now!"

"Well, thank heaven you finally agree with me!" was all his comment.

Aycliffe bit back a laugh. "Come, ma'am. There is no arguing this matter with Lord Dacre, as I have already discovered. Will you not enlighten us as to what you have learned?''

Outnumbered and outgunned, Rose capitulated. The story she had to tell came as no surprise to either gentleman, but Benedict no sooner heard the introduction of the name of Kirtlington than he smote his forehead.

''Dear *God,* of course! Come, Aycliffe, we must be off to Cheshire at once.''

''Cheshire!'' exclaimed Rose, moving to intercept him as he turned for the door. ''But surely you would do better to confront Theda with this and demand the truth from her?''

''Don't be ridiculous, Rose! Don't you know Theda better than that? No, no, believe me, the less she knows of my activities, the better. The only way to handle my witch is to present her with a *fait accompli.* I only pray heaven she may not take it into her head to run away while I am out of reach!''

''Oh, dear, Miss Theda, I wish you will think better of it!'' Taggy said tearfully, as she nevertheless assisted to fold the clothes that had been washed and pressed, ready to pack. Hector, disturbed by the preparations, ran to and fro, whining now and then.

Theda shook her head in a determined way. ''No. Mr Aycliffe will be back today or tomorrow, so his clerks told me. If it had not been for the circumstance of his being away, I should not be here now.''

''And what am I supposed to tell Mr Benedict when he arrives to find you gone?'' demanded Taggy crossly, tucking a nightgown into the battered portmanteau.

"You will have no need to tell him anything. I shall leave a letter."

"Dear knows why he has not been back here these few days!" muttered the housekeeper fretfully.

"He has other calls on his time now, you know," Theda said lightly, to conceal the ache in her heart, for in spite of her intention his absence could not but be painful. "I dare say he has had to return to his estates."

"Estates, indeed! And him with nothing to his name if it weren't for my late mistress!"

"Now, Taggy, you know well it is because of her that he had nothing. For my part, I am very happy for his good fortune."

Taggy sniffed. "All very well if he was inclined to share it, naming no names."

Theda had to smile. "Will nothing convince you that it is I and not he who is trying to escape?"

The housekeeper snorted. "He had ought to have been here, that's all. Certain sure *he'd* have stopped you from going, even if I can't."

A shrieking call from below interrupted them. "Taggy! *Tag-gy!* Where are you?"

The dog immediately began to bark, and made off out of the room. Mrs Diggory froze with her hands in the portmanteau, her eyes fearful.

"It's Miss Ara! Oh, lordy, lordy, she must have heard from that wretched Mrs Elswick! I could strangle that woman, so I could!"

Theda had gone paler than usual, and she grasped

at the bedpost for support. "I had hoped to be gone so that I would not be obliged to face her."

"Stay here!" ordered Taggy. "I'll tell her you're out."

She began to march towards the door, but Theda ran after her and grasped her arm. "No! Allow me some little spark of pride, Taggy. After all, my reputation is in all likelihood blasted in any event. What more have I to fear? If I am already doomed, what have I to lose?" With an air of determination, she straightened her shoulders and put up her chin. "I have borne enough. I will *not* cower away for fear of Araminta Quatt!"

"Bravo, Miss Theda!" applauded the housekeeper. "Time and past someone told her what's what!"

The call came again, angry now. "Tag-gy! Come here at once!" Then was added, "Adam, get this dratted animal away from me!"

Gathering her dignity together, Theda turned and walked slowly out of the bedchamber. She was dressed in one of her old dark, low-waisted gowns for warmth, for she had purchased no winter clothing among the new, but her glorious hair was uncovered and half falling about her shoulders from a careless knot on top of her head. But she bore herself like a queen as she slowly descended the stairs, and knew that Araminta, staring up from below, was disconcerted by the picture she made. She saw old Diggory shuffling off to the back regions, the protesting Hector in tow.

"You want something, Mrs Quatt?" she enquired politely.

''Pah!'' burst from Araminta as she found her tongue. ''Flaunting yourself again, like the low creature you are, I see! Just like Isabel Beckenham, even as that *disgusting* hair marks you. Two of a kind, you and she together. How apt for Benedict's pleasure!''

Theda flinched inside, but nothing showed in her face bar the contempt she felt for this woman. ''What is it you want?''

Araminta's smug, thin smile creased her mouth. ''I'm here to give you notice to leave. The place will be mine before long, and I want you *out.*''

''Indeed? Have you then made a successful contest of the will? I had not heard of it?''

''No, I have not. But I don't need to, Madam Harlot!''

Theda's lips whitened, but she gave no other sign of the distress this label caused her. ''You are very free with your assumptions, and your—*names,* Mrs Quatt. Pray can you substantiate any of this?''

''Don't come your highty-tighty airs and graces over me, you common baggage, you!'' snapped the other woman venomously, coming close and poking her pinched features almost into Theda's face. ''Very well for Benedict to hold his head up high—though *that's* a farce, if ever I heard of one! Viscount Dacre? Pah! Viscount Muckraker, if you like— but *you?* The world knows what you are, and so does he. Taken his pleasure and gone off, has he? Well, it's all I'd expect.'' She laughed jeeringly.

''Have you finished?'' Theda asked quietly.

''By no means! Finished? I've not started. *He* don't want the place any more, nor the money neither, I'll be bound. So it's all *mine,* understand? I'm here to take it, and I want you out. *Now.*''

Theda stood her ground, aware of Taggy hovering on the stairs behind her, the listening ears of the maids above, and Adam Diggory's unseen shadow at the back of the hall. For she knew he had put Hector into the kitchen but remained himself. Her heart was hammering and she felt sick, but she drew a steadying breath and began to speak, as if addressing an importunate stranger, her voice icily calm, and frightening in its intensity.

''You are tardy, madam. We here have known of Lord Dacre's inheritance these three days. However, it is not for me or you to presume upon the gentleman's intentions. Therefore, until Mr Aycliffe informs me that the will has been overturned, I shall remain here. You, Mrs Quatt—'' flinging out a pointing finger and thrusting it into Araminta's chest ''—*you* will leave this house, not I. *At once!*''

The woman was so surprised that she fell back a step. Theda, her voice low to steady it, began to move forward, poking at Mrs Quatt as she was driven, just as she had driven Theda on a previous occasion, backwards, step by step, towards the front door.

''Ever since I entered Merchiston Lodge, Araminta, you have snarled and screeched, and torn your claws like the cat you are. Well, the worm has turned, madam! What I am, what I may be, is none of your concern. But whatever I am, you, madam, are *not* going to browbeat me, or insult me by one—word—more.'' The finger jabbed for emphasis.

By now Araminta was backed up against the door,

stricken to silence, and Theda came close, her deep grey eyes burning with fury in the flaming setting of her hair. Like an avenging witch, she stood over the pinched, sallow face, in which fright had at last replaced venom in the pale eyes.

"Now *go,* and leave me in peace!"

Seizing Araminta's arm, Theda dragged her away from the door. Flinging it wide, she made to thrust the other woman from the house, only to be brought up short by the sight of two gentlemen standing at the other end of the long covered porch. One was the Reverend Saul Quatt. The other was Mr Warren Caswell.

Chapter Twelve

Too angry to take in the significance of the second visitor, Theda pushed Araminta through the door and addressed the vicar, who was staring open-mouthed.

"In a very good hour, sir! Take your wife, if you please, and remove her from my sight."

"Saul!" cried out the lady in a quavering voice. "She raised a hand to me, Saul! *Do* something."

But Mr Quatt only grasped her arm, uttering in an urgent undervoice, "I *told* you not to come, Araminta. You *must* wait for the law. Another time perhaps you will listen to me when I warn you of the dangerous ground you are treading."

"But it is my *right.* This is *my* house."

"As to that," answered her spouse, pushing her inexorably towards the waiting gig, "there may be another way to go to work. Now come home, do!"

Araminta paused with her foot on the step. "What do you mean, Saul?"

"I will explain it to you presently," said the Reverend gentleman, with a harassed glance over his shoulder to where Theda stood glaring at her second visitor. "*Get in!*"

"Don't speak to me in that tone!" protested his wife, but nevertheless responding to the pressure of his hand in her back.

Saul Quatt snapped suddenly. "Araminta, sit *down* and be *quiet!*" he shouted.

Mouth agape, she watched him take his seat beside her and gather up the reins. Then, as the gig began to move, she started to scold. Theda could hear them arguing even as the horse trotted off down the drive. But she had no leisure to enjoy the spectacle of Mrs Quatt's sudden drop from favour. Victorious from her own encounter with the woman, she confronted Mr Caswell with belligerence.

"What do you want?"

"I—er—I had to see you, Theodosia!" he said a little diffidently, but without preamble, his voice low. "We must talk."

All at once Theda became fully alive to the implications of this visit. Was there to be no end? No peace? She sagged wearily. "Oh, lord above! You had better come in."

Turning, she led the way to the library and preceded the visitor into the room. Then she closed the door behind them both, and moved to confront him where he had gone to stand by the desk, clearly nervous.

"It has been a long time, Warren," she said evenly.

He was silent for a moment, looking her over, his eyes clearly appreciative. "You have changed very little," he ventured.

Theda did not smile. "I would I could say the same of you."

Caswell glanced briefly down at his own person and gave a self-conscious laugh. "Yes, I—I have altered, I suppose. Marriage, I dare say."

Wincing inwardly, Theda asked, "Have you children?"

"Two." He glanced away, across the shelves of books, as if he found it hard to meet her gaze. "It is for them—for their sake, really, that I am here."

Theda stiffened. "Pray do not attempt to move me to pity by a tale of innocence and woe, Warren. You will find I am hardened against all that."

His eyes, in their now puffy setting, came back to her, and there was a trace at last of the old look that had warmed her all those years ago.

"I can't believe that," he said, with a pathetic twist of the lips. "You were ever tender-hearted."

"Unlike you!" Theda threw at him before she could stop herself, as an echo of the pain he had inflicted rose again inside her.

"Don't Theodosia! I *had* to do...what I did. I had no choice."

"Why?" she demanded, suddenly angry. "Had you debts, is that it? My fortune was denied you at the last, and *that* was the spur. Was it not, Warren?"

His coarsened features reddened. "I had need of money, it is true. But I *cared* for you, Theodosia. Can you doubt it?"

Theda fell back against the desk, a disbelieving laugh on her lips. "Can I doubt it? Are you out of your senses? You professed to love me, oh, yes." Her voice shook. "With what passionate words did you not wrench my young heart from its bosom? And when my father refused consent, what then? Oh, he knew you better than I, for all my rebellious ravings! I've had time enough to learn that."

"That will do!" cried Caswell, his anger now matching hers. "I did not come here to rake up old scores."

"Did you expect to find me quiescent, then?" Theda raged. The fires of her fury against him, long buried, had risen up, and were not to be contained. "And what old 'scores' have you? Was it I who persuaded you to fly from your home? Was it I who, finding your purse empty, ran from you?"

"You are beside yourself!" he uttered, stepping involuntarily backwards.

"Have I not reason?" she demanded, as the years seemed to roll away, and she felt again the anguish his desertion had inflicted. "You *left* me, Warren. You took my youth, my innocence—everything I had!—and then you flung me aside when you knew I could give you nothing...and you left *me* nothing!"

"I—I did not mean it so," he faltered.

"You did not mean it? Is that all you can *say?*" she flared, coming at him with her hand rising to strike.

"No, Theodosia, no!" he uttered, cowering before her vengeance. "Pray don't! Pray, pray, be calm!"

"Calm!" she almost screamed, ready to smash a blow into his once comely face.

She saw the terror there, and was arrested. This bloated, coarse-featured wreck was not the man she once had thought she loved. What had he to do with the woman she now was? And she *had* chosen her own destiny. Her hand came down and the fire died out of her eyes. She saw the relief that crept into his face, and a deep sigh escaped her.

"All these years," she said in a tired voice, looking him up and down. "All I ever cared for, all I ever hated you for, Warren, was the *lie*."

"It was no...lie," he uttered. "I cared for you."

"Don't compound it!" she flashed. "And that isn't the lie I meant."

"I tell you it was no lie," he said in a desperate tone. "I know it was wrong to—to leave you. But I had no choice. If you will have it, yes, there were debts that did not permit of my marrying a penniless girl. But I thought—I hoped—you would go back."

Theda stared at him. He did not take her meaning. She was surprised to find that she felt only contempt. The anger seemed to have drained away.

"Did you? Then you were wrong."

For the first time, she thought that her life—wretched as it was—had been preferable to marriage with this man. She did not want to look at him, and crossed to stand before the mantel over the fireplace, gazing down into the empty grate.

"What did you come for, Warren?"

He cleared his throat. "To—er—to make reparation. I thought—I wondered—if perhaps you might be in need of..." He paused, as she turned again, her expression so forbidding that he scarcely knew how to continue.

"Go on," she said evenly.

"I have a sum of money put by, which I can give you," he said quickly.

"Unbeknownst to your wife, no doubt," remarked Theda. "And in return? I presume there is a condition attached."

Again, he cleared his throat, and his unquiet gaze moved away from her. "I thought you might care to go abroad. Not France, of course, for we are at war there. But Holland, perhaps. Or Italy?"

Theda fought for control. "I wonder you have not already arranged a packet for me! So I am to be bought off—like a common harpy!"

"No, no," he began in protest.

"Don't waste your breath! Lord above, I thought I had endured the worst of insults already this day! How—*dare*—you?"

"Wait, Theodosia!" he begged anxiously. "I meant no insult. I—I was fearful for my wife, my family. After all, you *had* shown yourself in public. And Lady Usk—God knows *when* the blow might fall!"

"Then doubtless it has not yet fallen. But did it not occur to you," Theda said, her breast heaving with the passion she was only just holding in check, "that I have lately *not* been seen? *Who* do you think is to be the most hurt by such a scandal? *Myself,* Warren. Not you. And you dare to come here and try to make reparation—*reparation,* you call it!—for ruining my life?"

"That will do!" he ejaculated, suddenly losing patience. "You were willing enough at the time. And, if rumour is to be believed, you have readily found consolation elsewhere!''

Theda paled, her eyes dilating. Her voice was a croak. ''What? *What* did you say?''

''You may cease this pretence of virtue,'' he said in a testy voice. ''I know what you are!''

The thought flitted through her mind that Araminta had already done her worst. If the world did not know her history, which was by no means certain, they at least knew of her liaison with Benedict. Dear lord, she *would* have to go abroad! But not at this man's expense. She would die first!

''Whatever I am,'' she said, in a voice of dangerous quiet, ''it is what you made me, Warren Caswell. Long before...anyone else...came on the scene. May you take that knowledge to your grave!''

''I have a right to protect my wife and family,'' he said in a blustering way.

''What do you imagine I will do—go and tell your wife my story?'' Theda gave a bitter laugh. ''Perhaps I should. Why shouldn't she know what manner of man she married?''

''You *dare!*'' roared Caswell, and, starting forward, he seized her shoulder and cried out, *''Bitch!''* as in his turn he raised a hand as if to strike at her.

From the doorway a furious voice stopped him in his tracks. ''Unhand my wife, villain!''

Caswell let Theda go and whirled about as Benedict strode forward into the room.

''Your *wife!*'' he gasped.

''Touch her again with your filthy paws, and I'll ram my fist into your ugly face!'' Benedict promised, his eyes blazing, and his clenched hands threateningly raised.

Caswell backed away, one hand held protectively before him. ''I d-didn't know you had married her, Beckenham—I mean, Dacre.''

''Well, you know now,'' snapped his adversary, his tall person almost entirely concealing Theda's figure behind him where he had moved to protect her. ''And if you know what's good for you, you'll keep your mouth *shut.*''

''I'm not going to talk,'' Warren said hastily, edging towards the door.

''See you don't, or it'll be the worse for you! You don't know her. You've never met her before in your life, do you understand?''

''Oh, I understand. I came here to prevent scandal, Dacre, not to start it. But you may well catch cold at it, anyway, marrying such a woman.''

Benedict took a step forward, his eyes smouldering dangerously. ''One word more—just one—and you'll face my pistol at dawn!''

Caswell blenched, and hurriedly made his exit. Benedict watched him go and then turned to find Theda leaning back against the mantel, white to the lips, one hand at her bosom. He took a hasty pace towards her, and she flung out a hand.

''No, wait! Don't come near me!''

''Not come near you?'' he echoed incredulously, making to move. ''Don't be stupid!''

''I beg you!'' she said desperately.

He relaxed back, his voice dropping to a tender note. ''What is it, my dearest ghost?''

Theda passed a tongue over her dry lips. Her voice shook pitiably, but she forced herself to speak. ''Now you know...you *must* know, or you would not have spoken to him so, the reason I am *not* your wife...and can never be so, Benedict.''

To her astonishment, he smiled. Not the smile of practised charm, but one of real warmth and tenderness. ''Yes, Lady Theodosia Kirtlington, I know all about it.''

Theda gasped. ''Then you *do* know—at least who I am. But you can only have heard—who told you? Was it Rose?''

''Yes she did, but only under duress,'' he answered gently.

''Then, Benedict, you have heard only the *scandalous* tale. The rumour from the lips of Lady Usk. You cannot know the truth.''

''Oh, yes, I do,'' he said grimly. ''*All* the truth.''

Theda's eyes were dark with distress. ''But you cannot. Only Caswell and I know the full sum of it.''

Benedict's gaze was steady. ''And one other.''

She was too overset to guess what he meant. She watched him walk to the door and open it.

''Come in, sir,'' he said to someone outside.

A gentleman stepped slowly through the doorway and stood stock-still, staring at her, a not over-fashionable but well-dressed personage in late middle age, with greying hair cut short in the prevailing mode. He was of medium height, with a spare frame, a little unsteady on his feet, perhaps, and with the sallow complexion of recent illness on features that bore a striking resemblance to the girl before him.

Theda's knees almost buckled under her, and she grasped the mantel for support. Faintly, she uttered, "*Papa?*"

The Earl of Kirtlington found his tongue. "Lord in heaven, but you are the *image* of your mother!"

Theda put trembling fingers to her lips and then stretched them out unconsciously. "I th-thought—they said you were *dead!*"

"Almost," he said smiling. "But I thank God that He spared me for this!"

Next instant, he had crossed the distance between them, and enfolded his daughter in his arms. Theda raised a tear-streaked face to gaze up into the older one above her with loving eyes.

"Oh, Papa! How can you bear even to *speak* to me?"

The Earl's own eyes were moist, but he dug a hand into the pocket of his frock-coat and brought out a handkerchief. As if she were a little girl, he wiped her cheeks, and his voice was not quite steady.

"My darling, *foolish* child! Don't you think I've longed to speak to you, to hear your voice? You thought me dead these few weeks...How much more heavy has been *my* burden, and your poor mother's, do you suppose, not knowing—all these years, Theda!—whether you be alive or dead?"

Her tears overflowed again. "I am sorry...I am *so* sorry," she whispered.

Lord Kirtlington's hand caressed the bright copper head, gentling it against his shoulder. "Don't, my sweet! It is myself and your mama who have cause for repentance. Well do I know that we drove you into flight. I knew your ways, that streak of obstinacy that would make you always run counter, even as an infant. We went the wrong way to work with you, and were amply punished for our mistake.''

''Papa, *Papa!*'' Theda cried out, raising her face once again. ''Pray don't speak so...You will break my *heart.*''

Her father pressed a kiss to her forehead, and smiled, releasing her at last. ''Hearts are not so easily broken. And—'' with a grateful glance at Benedict, who was standing by, mute, moved as he had not expected to be by this reunion he had brought about ''—thanks to this intelligent and resourceful young man, it is over now.''

Theda could not forbear a smile as she turned her head to look at Benedict. ''Resourceful, yes,'' she agreed.

Benedict's eyes narrowed, but his lips twitched. ''Careful, Theda!''

She laughed. ''I shall desist, since I am again in your debt.'' Her eyes came back to her father's face and she drew a breath. ''And you are truly recovered? I can't describe to you the agony of being told—and then having no means by which to find out...Well, no more of that! How is Mama?'' Her eyes clouded. ''Do you think she will ever forgive me?''

''She did so long ago. Indeed, she was hot with me for my part in the business, and rang a fine peal over my head!''

Theda smiled. ''Poor Mama! I know what it is to be cursed with that temper.''

''You redheads!'' sighed Lord Kirtlington, shaking

his head, and caressing her cheek with a gentle finger. "But she is, thank God, in high bloom, and yearning for a sight of you. She did not even *try* to prevent my journey, although she has been a perfect tyrant these many weeks, making me keep my bed! She bade me tell you that she loves you very dearly, and has never ceased to miss you."

"Oh, dear lord!" Theda murmured, her eyes misting over. "That is a worse reproach to me than any that she ever uttered." She bit her lip. "You were right, both of you, on all counts, Papa. Caswell was unworthy, just as you said, and untrue, as dear Mama would have it. And I was too stubborn to see it."

"You were only a child, my dear," sighed the Earl. "You could not be expected to foresee how he would turn out."

"Did you see him? Outside just now, I mean?" Theda asked. "He is perfectly gross!"

Kirtlington laughed. "I have been aware of it for some little while. You forget. We move in the same circles. Not," he added, his voice hardening, "that I should dream of addressing the young scoundrel! The last time I did so was when he reappeared in town, *without* you."

"*What?*" ejaculated Benedict. "Do you say he dared to show his face after what he did?"

"As bold as brass!" the Earl confirmed, his eye kindling. "Having contracted, if you please, an engagement to the woman who is now his wife."

"Devil take him! I wish I *had* landed him a facer!"

"Did you then accost him, Papa?" Theda asked, intervening swiftly.

"Certainly I did. He informed me that you had run away. I was furious that he should leave you destitute upon the world. Though I am forced to admit that his searches, like mine, would probably have been futile."

"You searched for me?" Theda said wonderingly.

"High and low. For months. I advertised. God knows what I did not do! Except call in the Bow Street Runners, although your mama would even have had me do that, she was so distraught." He reached out to take one of her hands and hold it between both his own. "My child, why did you not come back to your home?"

For the first time in their interview, a trace of her old defiance came back. "I *could* not. You see, Papa, I did not run away. After you found us, and Warren told you we were already—he had already..." Her voice died. She drew a breath and began again. "*Then,* when you disinherited me on the spot—oh, I don't blame you for that, don't think it!—when you said we might reap the just rewards of our flight and marry as paupers, he...he left me flat."

"Scoundrel!" burst from Lord Kirtlington.

Behind him, Benedict's breath hissed, bringing Theda's head round to see his face a mask of livid fury. She put out a hand to him at once.

"*No,* Benedict! It is too late now for revenge. Pray leave it! For *my* sake."

He strode forward to grasp the hand she held out to him. It clutched his tightly, and he drew it to his lips.

"Let him not cross my path, that's all!" he said

curtly. Then he looked at the Earl. "I understand her, sir, if you do not. She would not return to you because you believed her to be a fallen woman, and nothing she could say would convince you otherwise." He kept her fingers closely imprisoned, but he did not look at her. "I tell you now, sir, that the villain *lied.*"

"Benedict!" Theda gasped, shocked.

Lord Kirtlington eyed his prospective son-in-law with interest. "Did he so?"

"He did so, sir," Benedict said staunchly. "You have my word on it. If it had not been so, if I had found that—" grinding his teeth with menace "—well, suffice it that he may yet live his natural life out!"

"I understand you, I believe," said the Earl, an unmistakable twinkle in his eye. "I have to thank you, Dacre, for your honesty in all this matter." He looked at Theda. "He has told me all your story, or as much as he knows. He even brought a lawyer to support him. In fact, he had no need of anything more than a lock of hair he showed me."

At that, Theda's eyes came round to Benedict's and he grinned, his expression rueful. "The one you gave me on account, remember?"

"I remember," she said, flashing him a look that spoke volumes.

The two gentlemen exchanged glances. But it was the Earl who said gently, "Theda, my child. Don't let that fiery temper of yours betray you now!"

She bit her lip, but the words escaped her anyhow. "I take it you have between you concerted your schemes for my future?"

"Well, Dacre came to find me for the purpose of asking my permission to address you," said Kirtlington.

"*And* to find out if you *were* his daughter," Benedict put in quickly.

"Trying to force my hand!" Theda said crossly, dragging her fingers from his grasp.

"On the contrary," came a new voice from the doorway, and Mr Aycliffe walked into the room. He bowed. "Forgive me, Lady Theodosia, but I could not help but overhear something of what has transpired in this room."

"Lord!" she exclaimed. "You, too? Is this a conspiracy?"

Her father intervened once more. "You may rest easy, Theda. I myself will see Lady Usk. I know her all too well. When she hears what I have to say to her, there will be no question of her opening her lips on this subject. Once you are wed, and known once more as my daughter, the rest will soon be forgotten."

"Papa, this is all very well, but—"

"Lady Theodosia," interrupted Aycliffe, "I think you should know that his lordship—Lord Dacre, I mean—went to find your father not only to discover your identity for the purpose of saving your reputation, if he could. It was also because he knew that you were to become again destitute."

"The will!" Theda said at once, utterly ignoring his words. "Have you the papers I must sign? I have been waiting only for that so that I might go."

"I knew it!" Benedict snapped. "You are going nowhere, my good girl!"

As Theda turned on him, Aycliffe hastily intervened. "Your pardon, my lord. Lady Theodosia, you mistake. Mr Beckenham—I mean, Lord Dacre—wanted you to have the security of your home so that you might have a *choice* about your future."

"I thank you, Mr Aycliffe," Theda said drily, "but I know him a little better than that!"

"So I should hope!" came instantly from Benedict, as he grasped her hands again. His eyes on hers, he spoke over his shoulder. "I think, sir, that it would be better if you—and Aycliffe also—would be so good as to leave us to settle matters to our mutual satisfaction."

"Mutual!" echoed Theda crossly, not even noticing as her father and the lawyer left them together and closed the library door. "How *could* you tell my father—say *that?*"

Benedict dropped her hands, but seized her bodily, snatching her to him, and holding her trapped so that she could not move.

"I said it because it was true. You are mine—and *only* mine. I knew it at once when we lost ourselves in our *mutual* passion. And if I had needed proof, it was there to be seen after. Do you think I will *ever* let you go, now that I've claimed you?"

Her heart was rioting madly, and her limbs were going weak, but a gleam entered her eye.

"You might let me go just a little...I know you call me a ghost, but flesh and blood must breathe!"

Laughing, he loosened his hold enough so that she could pull her arms free. Then he dragged her close again and bent his head to kiss her. Theda's arms crept up about his neck, and her lips met his.

When they came apart, she said wonderingly. "It is all still there. You have only to *touch* me."

He smiled. "Did you imagine one drink would slake so raging a thirst? It will take a lifetime!" He let her go, but retained hold of her fingers as his face became serious. "Theda, there is no other future for us, you must see that. Aside from the rest, after what I have said to Caswell—that you *are* my wife—we should make it good. Especially as your reputation is blasted already in the village. And *that* is to my account."

"Don't, Benedict! I am ready to face all that. I told you so," Theda said, a trifle tremulous again. "I would do anything I could for you, save—"

"Save that which I *want* from you," he finished. "And you would have run from me to escape it, confound you!"

Tears sparkled on her lashes. "I was almost packed."

"You would not have got far!" he said grimly. "I would have come after you, and unlike your father I'd have *found* you, had I to go to the ends of the earth!"

"You want me that much?" Theda whispered.

"I *love* you that much!" he corrected.

There was wonder and doubt in her eyes. "You love *me?* Not...not my hair? Oh, Benedict, I have learned from Rose about your mother, and I see that my hair is the key, but—"

"*No,*" he burst out. "No, Theda! The flame was

there between us *before.* When I saw your hair—" touching it lovingly, fingering the fiery strands "—it was perhaps the trigger that sprang the flame. But when I was at Dacre, in spite of all the painful memories—Theda, it was *your* face that haunted me, not my mother's! I knew then that I *loved* you, more than anything in the world, more than life itself!"

Theda bit her lip, her heart turning to liquid in her bosom. She touched her fingers to his lips.

"I would like to die now," she said shakily, "that this moment might last forever."

"Fool!" he uttered lovingly, kissing the fingers and taking them again within his own. "We *have* forever." Then he dropped her hand, and swept her back into his arms, nestling his face in the glowing tresses about her head. "Oh, my ghost! My beloved, beautiful witch, *will* you marry me? Not to save your reputation, nor to satisfy society or your father, or even me—but only because you love me and I you?" He drew back his head so that he might look into her eyes, misty with unshed tears. "Theda, will you?"

Her lips trembled on a smile. "And my father called *me* obstinate!"

Benedict shook her. "Will—you—*yield?*"

"I thought I had," she uttered on a shaky laugh. "Well, Lady Lavinia told me to make something of you. I suppose I had better try!"

"Witch!" he told her, his eyes alight.

Then his lips found hers again and it was some time before either said anything at all.

"Where shall we go?" Theda asked him at length.

"To Cheshire? You guessed as soon as you heard the name of Kirtlington, I dare say?"

Benedict nodded. "Immediately, though I took little notice of it when I was in Cheshire, I admit. All I could think about while I was taking up that extraordinary inheritance was you." He was playing with her hair again, curling strands about his finger. "I realised then, you see, that, of all my ambitions, *you* were the one I could never *bear* to lose! I had to rack my brains for ways to force you to wed me. When I learned your probable identity, and knew I had Kirtlington for my neighbour—"

"Yes, I know the rest, you scheming wretch!" she said, mock-stern. "But shall we live there?" Her eyes clouded. "The pity of it is that Araminta will get the Lodge after all. And I expended so much energy making it beautiful for you!"

He cupped her face, his eyes tender. "For me?"

"Of course. I never had any intention of remaining here, though I have grown to love it." She sighed. "I wish it were not to be lost to you."

Benedict grinned. "You shall have it for a bride gift."

"Are you serious?"

"Dearest ghost, did you imagine I would let it go to that hag of a cousin of mine? All I have ever known of love has been here in this house. My mother, Sir John—and now *you.* How could I give it up, even for the splendid trappings that have fallen to my lot? You see, since I was last here, Aycliffe's clerks have been in negotiation with Quatt."

"You mean to purchase it? But Araminta will never allow him to sell it."

"She will have no choice," Benedict said austerely. "You forget that, as her husband, it is he and not she who will take possession of the money."

"Ah, I thought there was some cogent incentive for you to seek out my father!" interposed Theda with a twinkle. "You think he will reinstate my lost inheritance, I dare say?"

Benedict grinned. "I was ever a gambler, remember?" He kissed her again as she gurgled. "But in all seriousness, we understand from the clerks that Quatt is dissatisfied with his reception here—as well he might be!—and has the intention of taking up a post as archdeacon somewhere in Worcestershire, where he was living before. I gather that since he is to become a man of substance the world has become his oyster."

"You mean that Araminta will no longer be living here?" cried Theda joyfully. "What a merciful release! And we shall have this house! Oh, Benedict!"

His lips brushed hers. "I don't know why you should be surprised. This is all your spells, you witch! You have been casting them from that very first night when the gods sent you to haunt me!"

Theda laughed. "Perhaps it is Lady Lavinia pulling strings."

"In hell? You are jesting!"

"For shame, Benedict! I, for one, shall certainly pray for Saul Quatt!"

Benedict came away and grasped her hand, pulling

her towards the door. ''Speaking of Quatt, I must tell Aycliffe to go and fetch him at once.''

''Here? For what purpose?'' demanded Theda, amazed.

He grinned, turning at the door to seize her once more in his arms. ''A sufficient one. And while the messenger is on his errand, you may array yourself suitably. Did you buy something new, as I instructed?''

''Yes, but under protest,'' Theda said, a fleeting vision of herself in the peach gown passing through her mind, together with a swift question as to how Benedict would think she looked in it. ''But what for! Why must I change my dress? Why is Quatt to come here?''

''Why else but to marry us, my lovely one? I have a special licence in my pocket, you see.''

''Have you, indeed?'' Theda said politely, the gleam back in her eye. ''You had no doubt of carrying the day, I collect?''

''None at all,'' he said, laughing. ''I had—and *have*—every intention of sharing a bed tonight...and every night from here on.'' He kissed her again, adding softly, ''A *marriage* bed, my lady, with my beloved wife.''

* * * * *